Also by Whitney Dineen

D1521918

The Mimi Chronicles

The Reinvention of Mimi Finnegan
Mimi Plus Two
Kindred Spirits

She Sins at Midnight
Going Up?

Non-Fiction Humor

Motherhood, Martyrdom & Costco Runs

Conspiracy Thriller

See No More

Middle Reader Fiction

Wilhelmina and the Willamette Wig Factory
Who the Heck is Harvey Stingle?

Children's Books

The Friendship Bench

You're So Vain

Whitney Dineen

Made in the United States.

September, 2021

ISBN: 9798460249992

Ebook Edition ASIN: B08XTMM1RG

https://whitneydineen.com/newsletter/
33 Partners Publishing

Dedicated to all the Cinderellas waiting for their happily-ever-afters.

Chapter One

Sharon

Sharon pours herself another cup of coffee before sitting down at the dining room table. "I'm going to help Lu, if it's the last thing I do. And she's gonna like it. I'm going to make that daughter of mine realize that giving up on love isn't the way to go," Sharon tells her sister Tooty while flinging her arms out dramatically and knocking her coffee mug onto the floor. As it shatters, she thinks, great, just another mess to clean up—a perfect metaphor for her offspring's life.

"It *might* be the last thing you do because I'm pretty sure Lu will run you over with her car if you interfere in her life anymore," Tooty replies.

"Anymore? You make it sound like I'm a busybody," she grumbles while bending down to pick up the more prominent shards.

"You know I love you, hon, but you've been on Lu's back nonstop about her wanting to have a baby on her own."

"Having a baby is hard work. You know that as well as I do."

"Not all of us are as lucky as you, sis. Phillipe is the perfect husband and father. What if Lu winds up with someone like my

1

first husband, Chuck?" Before Sharon can answer, Tooty adds with a shudder, "She's better off on her own than procreating with a jackass."

"Your point is well taken." Sharon dumps the pieces of pottery into the garbage can. "But that doesn't mean I'm going to give up trying to help her find someone. Everything about Lu's life is my business and I'm not going to stop until I know she's going to be happy."

"She'd better buckle up then. Poor girl."

Waving her hand dismissively, trying not to break any more dishes, Sharon says, "Please. She's going to thank me when I'm through with her and you know it."

Lutéce

Dating in Los Angeles is about as much fun as duct taping your ankles together right before going for a swim in the Pacific. Don't let the mermaids fool you, it's work. Hard work. I've let my friends set me up; I've let my co-workers give it a go; I even let my mom's neighbor talk me into meeting her nephew—thanks for the tacos, Brad, but they weren't good enough to listen to you talk about your workout for two hours.

My unfortunate dating history notwithstanding, I've decided to give love one more chance before heading back to my fertility doctor for a second round of in vitro fertilization. I prefer not to dwell on that first, unsuccessful attempt.

Brushing through my auburn hair, I realize that I really do want a partner to share my life and children with. Either that or all the hormones that have been racing through my body have forced me around the bend of Sane Town right into Crazy Place.

Unfortunately, as far as I can tell, single men in LA have one of two problems. They're either players who are always looking for the next best thing, or they've recently discovered it's okay to come out of the closet and embrace their love of men.

Like my last boyfriend, Daniel. I cyberstalked him after our breakup and discovered his new boyfriend was a bald South African bodybuilder with a Fu Manchu and multiple tattoos. In other words, nothing like me, which confirms that Daniel was only with me to further his pipe dream of becoming a singer. He wasn't a country music fan so he was probably hoping Romaine would give him a leg up.

If that isn't traumatic enough, sixty-year-old men with receding hairlines, halitosis, and pot bellies somehow think they're entitled to date twenty-year-old bikini models. It's beyond gross.

While putting on my new dangly earrings with the feathers and crystals, my phone rings. "Hey, Liza, what's up? I'm getting ready for my date." Liza and I have been friends since we were in grade school. She's currently married and raising her three delightful children in the Valley with her gorgeous cameraman husband. Barf.

"Don't despair if tonight's encounter isn't the one," she announces brightly. "Dillion just met a great guy on the set of *Evil Geniuses*. He sounds pretty amazing." My friend is downright giddy with excitement. How she can still be optimistic about my love life after what she's watched me go through is anyone's guess.

Although, I suppose I should be happy that one of us is optimistic.

"Ah, so what you're saying is that Dillion's gay, too?" I can't help but tease her. Liza's husband is as gay as I am twenty. I'm thirty-six.

Ignoring me, she says, "His name is Beau and he's never been married, nor does he have any children. He just moved here from the Midwest and when Dillion told him about you, he was super excited to meet you."

"Did Dillion tell him how old I am? Because you know that always makes them turn tail and run." Men seem to think that single women in their thirties are only after one thing—their Y chromosome. I'm not judging because in my case that's one hundred percent accurate. My biological clock is ticking like a time bomb.

The trick is not letting them know that before the first date.

"Thank Dillion for his concern, but if tonight doesn't go well, I'm washing my hands of the whole dating thing. I'll just go back to the fertility doctor and hook up with some nice anonymous sperm and start my family without any more drama."

"Oh, Lu. You are the prettiest, smartest, most talented woman I know. It's unfathomable to me that you aren't already hitched with a half-dozen kids at your feet."

When we were kids, Liza and I used to talk about how much fun it would be if we both had big families that could grow up together. "Now, I could only have two, three tops. I'm too old for more."

"Who's tonight's lucky guy?" She thankfully changes the subject before my watering eyes can turn into full blown tears and ruin my eye makeup. She is the kindest, most loyal friend.

"His name is Benedict, and he's a restaurant supply guy. I met him on JDate."

"Don't you have to be Jewish to use JDate?"

"No." I finish putting on my lipstick before telling her, "You only have to be open to dating a Jew. I've decided a man of faith might be less superficial and more interested in a woman my age than, you know, every other man in LA."

"I'm sure Benedict is lovely. I can't wait to meet him." Liza's optimism is exhausting. While I'm truly grateful for it, it often feels like she's standing behind me cheering while I try to climb Mount Everest stark naked. In other words, it's hopeless.

Although, at least with dating, I won't lose any fingers or toes to hypothermia.

"I'm off," I tell my friend. "Give the kids a kiss for me."

"Are we still on for brunch on Sunday?" I've been going over to Liza's for brunch nearly every week for the last ten years.

"You bet," I tell her. "I'll bring the fruit salad and champagne. Now, I really do have to go."

"Love you, Lu. You've got this."

Slipping my phone into my purse, I give myself one last look in the entryway mirror. Ben's profile says he's five-ten, which I know means five-eight. As I'm five-ten, I'm wearing flats so as not to make him uncomfortable.

While driving over Laurel Canyon Boulevard to meet my date at Chow's—the latest West Side hotspot—I think about how online dating is really performed in code. Men lie about their height, their weight, and their net worth. Women lie about their age, their desire to start a family (men don't want to hear the word "baby" come up until they've been married for five years), and how many boyfriends they've had.

Men want a young woman with minimal baggage and no obvious desire to procreate. Women want a guy who isn't always looking for a better option. I almost turn my car around in the next driveway.

Instead, I flip on the sound system to distract myself from thoughts of bailing on tonight. My favorite Spotify playlist blasts vintage Enya through the speakers, causing my throat to fill with so much emotion I feel like I've just swallowed a bowling ball.

I love Enya and her ethereal melodies about memories from past lives where she was a princess and love spanned multiple incarnations. Thank God for playlists. I've already burned through five Shepherd Moons CDs.

By the time I pull up to the valet at Chow's, I'm full-on bawling—damn these hormone shots! *Oh, Enya, I long for the love you sing of!* I can't have always been the social pariah I am in this lifetime. Someone had to have loved me somewhere down the line.

"Ma'am, I'm going to need you to step out of the car." *Am I being arrested?*

I look up and am jolted back to the present by a surfer-looking dude in a valet uniform. With a sigh worthy of a Disney Princess, I put my car in park and get out. Then I take my ticket and make my way to the front door.

Weaving through what can only be described as a throng of fashionable people—the extremes Angelinos will go to be seen at the latest, hippest, coolest place is legendary—I finally make my way inside and up to the hostesses stand. "Hi there, I'm meeting Benedict Solomon."

The *Baywatch* babe wannabe looks up from her reservation book and excitedly declares, "Are you Bennie's mom?" I'm either totally delusional about how old I look, or this girl is a cow.

"His grandmother, actually," I tell her with a smirk. Then I raise my left eyebrow with my most intense I'm-gonna-shiv-you-in-a-dark-alley-if-you-don't-take-me-to-my-date-right-now look. She takes the hint and leads the way.

Bennie is waiting at a table by the window. From a distance, he looks a lot younger than his JDate profile pic. A lot younger. Like twelve.

The hostess says, "Bennie, your grandmother is here. Remember, order whatever you want, and Jocko will comp the bill."

Staring at my date, I announce, "I think there's been a mistake."

He jumps to his feet and comes around the table to pull my chair out. Whistling under his breath, he says, "No mistake. You're hot."

"That's very nice of you to say, but who are you?"

Bending at the waist, he replies, "Benedict Solomon at your service."

"What I mean is, you can't possibly be the guy I've been corresponding with online. That guy is in his forties."

"Oh, yeah, that guy is my dad. They won't let me get my own profile until I turn eighteen."

"Which will be in what, six years?" I cannot believe this. This is a new all-time low, even for me.

"Four," he says very seriously. "I had my bar mitzvah last year, so in the eyes of God, I'm already a man."

OMG. "Ben," I say, sounding like a schoolmarm, or you know, his mother, "I'm thirty-six years old."

"Perfect. You could teach me all kinds of things."

"I could teach you how to tie your shoes, but I'm guessing you already know how to do that." At least I hope he does. I resist the urge to glance down to see if he has Velcro sneakers on. This kid can't be for real.

"I want you to teach me the ways of love." His eyes are glazed over with possibilities.

"I'd go to jail if I did that," I tell him plainly. I don't have the heart to tell him that what he's suggesting is an abomination.

"It would be our secret." He waggles his eyebrows in such a way I can't help the bark of laughter that erupts out of me. "Ben, why aren't you dating girls your own age? You're obviously a young man of great refinement." Lies.

His shoulders slump, causing him to look like a lost little boy. "I want to date girls my age, but they're not interested. They like guys like Robby Stein, whose palms don't start to sweat at the very thought of kissing them. Robby has already kissed a bunch of girls. I haven't kissed any."

"I didn't have my first kiss until I was sixteen," I tell him while opening my menu. It looks like I've decided to have dinner with this kid. In a totally platonic big sisterly way, of course.

"Really? But you're a total Veronica."

"I wasn't when I was a teenager. We all go through an awkward stage, but we all grow out of it. You will, too, Ben."

"You don't know what it's like," he says, sounding defeated. "I go to school with all these kids whose parents are agents, directors, and lawyers. My dad does well but nothing compared to the other kids' parents."

"What about your mom?" I ask, wondering if his dad really has a JDate profile.

"She died when I was four."

"I'm very sorry for your loss," I tell him honestly, before losing my mind and asking, "So, is your dad single?"

"Kind of. He's been dating his yoga instructor for a few months. I don't think he's serious about her though." Putting his napkin in his lap, he adds, "If you really aren't into me, I suppose I could fix you up with him."

Even *I* haven't fallen so low as to let a strange kid set me up with his dad. "Thanks, but no. Why don't we just enjoy our supper and then part ways?"

"You're gonna eat with me?" He sounds excited enough that I'm genuinely flattered. He may only be fourteen, but so far, I like him more than I've liked my last three dates combined.

"Only if we go Dutch," I tell him.

"But my dad really is in restaurant supplies, and he's friends with the owner here. I don't have to pay."

"I'll leave the tip then. How does that sound?"

Ben reaches his hand across the table to shake mine. "Deal. Now, being that we're not on a date or anything, what do you want to talk about?"

"Why don't I tell you what fourteen-year-old girls are really looking for in a boyfriend? There might be something I can teach you after all."

I spend the next two hours on the best date I can remember having. On my drive home I'm once again overwhelmed by my desire to be a mom. I decide to call the IVF doc and set up another appointment—stat.

I don't know if the next treatment will take or not, but I do know one thing: I'm tired of waiting for other people to make my dreams come true. If I've learned anything from my perpetually single status, it's that when you try to control the outcome of a relationship, you will fail one hundred percent of the time.

From this moment forward, I'm going to let go and allow my future to unfold as it will. Surely if it worked for Enya, it can work for me.

Chapter Two

Queen Charlotte

"It's time for those sons of ours to settle down already," Charlotte tells her husband Alfred over breakfast.

"You have to trust that it will happen when it's supposed to. Look at us. If I'd domesticated when my mother ordered me to, I would have married Chantelle Auclair. Instead, I waited and met you."

"Don't change the subject," Charlotte tells him before taking a bite of her omelet.

"All I'm saying, darling, is that just because we desire for something to happen doesn't mean it will be the best thing for our children. We must let them live their own lives and trust that things will turn out the way they're meant to."

"There has to be something I can do," Charlotte says, ignoring her husband's well-intentioned advice.

"You're not listening to me at all, are you?"

Looking up from her plate, the queen's eyes meet Alfred's across the expanse of the dining table. "I heard you."

"But you're not going to let things go, are you?" he wants to know.

"Alfred, I'm a mother. Mothers do more than love their children. They guide them and help solve their problems."

"Whether they like it or not, huh?"

"Absolutely."

Alistair

"It seems there's more than one lady after you tonight, Al. You up for a bit of fun?" Grady, my friend and captain of the royal yacht we're on, asks me.

"I've been ordered to stay away from gossip, Grady," I tell him while raising my champagne glass in a mock salute toward the beautiful evening sky. "Of course, there's no way I can do that when it follows me like a row of ducklings traipsing after their mother…"

"Hallie Fox has been eyeing you like you're an all-you-can-eat buffet. She's something else, isn't she?" He leans against the railing with a conspiratorial grin on his face.

"She's fine. But I assure you, I'm not interested in having a hoard of American reporters following my love life. Dating an actress from the States would double the size of the target the press has already painted on my back. It's bad enough they've been circling around my brother ever since they caught wind that he's dating one of their own."

"I seem to recall you mentioning your future sister-in-law has a rather remarkable sister. Will she be joining the festivities this week?"

I don't know the answer to his question, so I simply say, "As you know, I'm on a dating break."

"You've been on a break for the last couple of years. Are you really going to let She-Who-Shall-Remain-Nameless continue to mess with your head?"

"First of all," I tell him, "you're the only one who believes me when I say I'm not involved with anyone—the press is relentless, and my family seems determined to believe them over me. Secondly, I'm tired of meeting women who are enamored by my title. I just want to find a nice girl and have a nice life. Is that too much to ask?"

"In your case, yes." Taking off his cap, he runs his fingers through his dark hair while saying, "You are who you are."

"How deep," I reply with a sardonic drawl.

"Why do you keep throwing parties if you aren't interested in socializing?" he asks.

"I suppose I enjoy living up to my reputation. What would my mother have to complain about if not for her incessant disappointment in me?" I really wish my family would believe I'm not the playboy I've been portrayed to be. They knew me before Ellery, so they should know better.

"Your mother would love to know you're nothing like you pretend to be. If I had to guess, I'd say you like annoying her."

"Everyone needs a hobby. But the truth is, I do enjoy being social. I have several friends aboard who couldn't give a fig that I'm the second in line to the throne. I like spending time with them."

"Come on then,"—Grady pushes himself off the railing—"let's go mingle."

I follow my friend to the other side of the boat where Hallie Fox immediately slithers to my side and worms her way under my arm. She looks up at me like a hungry snake looks at a fat mouse. "Is there someplace we can go to be private?" Pressing her body against mine, she adds, "But first, let's get a picture together."

Ah, there it is, proof she's trying to link us together. I stretch out my other arm and grab the first person within reach. The black pants and white shirt aren't de rigueur for one of my evening cruises, which leads me to believe she's a waitress. She looks shocked to be manhandled in such a fashion, so I lean down and whisper in her ear, "Can I borrow you for a quick photo?"

Being photographed with two women is always safer than one. It makes it harder for anyone to sell a tale of love to the press. Of course, it also makes me look like a total player, but if that's the price I have to pay, sobeit.

The waitress nods her head once as her face glazes over with what? Adoration? Admiration? Infatuation? Flashes of light immediately fill the air, confirming that Hallie had several people at the ready to photograph us together. As Grady's crew is supposed to confiscate all phones and cameras before boarding, I can only assume these devices were smuggled on. I wonder which newspapers will be printing them tomorrow.

The actress pulls me in the direction of the roped off area we rarely let guests go beyond. "Let's play spin the bottle, Alistair." I've never heard of that game, but if her tone is anything to go on, it must be akin to strip poker, which I have played.

"As appealing as that sounds," I respond while trying to put some distance between us, "I have an interview with a French newspaper below deck." Of course, I'm lying, but she doesn't know that.

"Oh, I can come too! I bet they'd love to have a chance to interview us together."

I send a wild-eyed look of panic at Grady, who makes it his duty to always stay close by. He hurries to my side and offers Hallie a half bow. "Miss Fox, I'd be delighted to give you a private tour of the bridge. I'll even let you steer the boat for a while if you'd like."

I make my escape to the salon while she considers his offer. Kicking off my shoes, I settle onto the sofa and pick up a remote for the sound system. My mother's all-time favorite easy listening music surrounds me, and for the first time ever, I don't immediately turn it off. Instead, I listen while Enya waxes poetic about eternal love and marble halls.

The song is so eerily enticing, I can't help but wonder if such love really exists.

Chapter Three

Sharon

Sharon: Hey, Sugar, I need you to run by my house and make sure the gardener is watering my roses.

LuLuBug: Uh, no.

Sharon: I can't let my Lady Di's wither on the vine!

LuLuBug: Why don't you call Miguel? Why do I need to go?

Sharon: Because the last time your father and I were both away, he started slacking on our maintenance and I came home to wilted bushes. I've been working too hard on my roses to have them bite the big one now.

LuLuBug: Why don't you get a new gardener?

Sharon: Easier said than done. I'm on three waiting lists, and unless one of their existing customers croaks, I'm not moving up the list any time soon.

LuLuBug: Why don't you have a neighbor check?

Sharon: The last time I did that, Stephanie Edwards invited her friends to come with her. They spent half an hour peeking through our windows. I have it on video.

LuLuBug: Sorry, Mom. I'm not driving forty minutes to your house to make sure your gardener is doing his job.

Sharon: I gave you life …

LuLuBug: And I thank you for it. As a tribute to your generous gift, I don't plan on wasting my time with busy work. I do love you though.

Sharon: Well, poop, be that way. But just so you know, I'll get my revenge when you have kids and find out what ungrateful snots they can be.

Lutéce

As soon as I caffeinate, I go onto the internet and click the link to the Westside Fertility Clinic website. While pleasant enough, my date with young Benedict has convinced me that no normal men will ever be interested in me. The upside is, Bennie is going to look me up in four years when our "forbidden love" is legal. I don't know whether to be amused or excited. But for now, it's time to move on.

I've added Ben to the top of my list of ridiculous dating encounters. He's right up there with such stellar specimens as the guy who cut my steak for me before offering to pre-chew it and spit it into my mouth baby-bird style, and the one who gave me a two-hour lecture on do-it-yourself grouting. This list is proof that a real live father for my kids is more trouble than he's worth.

My top choice for the next attempt at IVF comes from a stuntman named Chad. He claims to have a degree in biology and no known allergies. I know most of these profiles are probably made up, but what if this one is true? What if Chad's swimmers are both daring and smart *and* they don't have trouble gobbling up shellfish and peanut butter—not together— like they're mother's milk? I'm not sure this is an opportunity I can pass up.

All I need is a credit card and some gumption. Luckily, I've got both in spades.

In my bleaker moments, I imagine myself starring in a sitcom based on my dating adventures. It's called Lu's Sad Life, and the theme song is inexplicably sung to the tune of "Elmo's World."

Do, do, do, do
Do, do, do, do
Lu's sad life

Lu goes on dates,
They never work,
Thaaaaaaaaat's Lu's sad life!

Clearly, I'm not the musical genius in my family. That title goes to my brother, Romaine, who's the lead singer of the rock band Turnip Garden; my aunt Tooty, who's won as many Country Music Awards as Dolly Parton; and my mom, Sharon, who writes all of Tooty's songs. While I play classical piano decently well, I have no real creative forces at work inside me.

When my phone pings, I pick it up to see if the person messaging is worth pulling myself away from Chad's profile. It's not. It's my sister, Claire, which causes me to put the phone back on the coffee table and ask myself, "Is five foot six too short for my future offspring's baby daddy?"

I'm a bit of a height snob. Not that Chad and I will ever have to appear in public together, but still, I want my kids to have the vertical advantage. The ability to see over crowds is a huge boon and has kept more than one panic attack at bay for me.

Ping.

Pest: Lu, are you there?

The last time I tried in vitro I used Stanford sperm—as in, the guy claimed to have an engineering degree from there. Chad graduated from UCLA, which makes him smart but hopefully not pretentious. I don't need any Stanford sperm looking down their nose at my Pomona College eggs. I've secretly decided that's the reason my first in vitro attempt didn't take.

Ping.

Pest: Lu, I really need to talk to you. Please answer me.

After college, I became a music therapist for kids with behavioral and learning problems. Music forces them to focus on something that gives them a tangible reward for their effort. While working hard at school gets them good grades, it often takes weeks or months before their reward is seen in the form of a good report card. Music offers the almost immediate gratification of hearing the results of their efforts. It also helps them focus.

Ping.

Pest: Lu, I'm not kidding. This is BIG news. So big I can't bring myself to tell Mom yet.

If I had to guess, my little sister has either gotten engaged or pregnant, or both. Those are the only things I imagine she'd be reticent to share with Hurricane Sharon. Even though our mother is enormously busy in her own life, she's chomping at the bit to add the title of grandmother to her résumé. I don't know if she does this with Claire, but she asks me weekly about my parenthood plans before reminding me that my baby might be born with two heads if I use a sperm donor. Her opinion is seriously affecting how much time I spend with her.

Me: What do you want, Claire? I'm in the middle of picking out my baby daddy. I decided to try a new guy.

Pest: You're there! I'm going to call you now.

Yay. *Not.*

I let the phone ring six times before I answer. "What?"

"Oh, thank God! I thought maybe your battery went dead or something." My sister's tone is borderline hysterical.

"Are you okay?"

"Yes … no … I don't know."

"Have you been in an accident?" I ask, hoping I haven't just entered a game of twenty questions. When we were kids, Claire never let the game end at twenty. It often went to forty or more.

Yawn. I don't have time for this. Chad's frozen fellas are waiting for me.

"Geoffrey proposed!" [Insert eardrum-puncturing scream here.] Geoffrey is my sister's boyfriend who also happens to be third in line to the throne of some European country named Malquar. I can't find a normal man between thirty and fifty who knows what dental floss is, and my sister moves to Oregon and snags herself a real live prince. I'm tempted to hang up on her.

"Lu, are you still there?"

"Yeah, I'm here. Did you say yes?"

"Of course, I said yes. Geoffrey is perfect for me."

"Well then, congratulations, I guess." I sound like I've been sucking on sour grapes—which I totally have—but I can't help it. A wave of self-pity washes over me like a tsunami. "Why haven't you told Mom?" I ask after taking a deep breath to help ensure my voice doesn't crack.

"Because she'll be off and running making wedding plans. I want to catch my breath for a hot second before I have to field twenty phone calls a day."

Claire doesn't have to worry about Mom asking her to water her plants. Claire is going to be a princess, while I'm relegated to gardener status. I didn't think I could get more depressed than I already was. I was wrong.

"When is the palace going to make the official announcement?" I don't know how things work in Malquar, but both rom-coms and the Brits would have you believe all news gets filtered through official royal channels.

"We're going to tell everyone later in the week in Malquar. I want you all to be there for it."

"You want me to drop everything in my life and fly across the world to hear you announce what you just told me on the phone." *Really, Claire? Does the whole world revolve around you?*

"I want you to be with me to celebrate my exciting news. You're my sister and I love you. Also, I'm hoping you'll be my maid of honor." She does sound hopeful too, if not a bit scared that I'll say no.

I can't blame her. I've made no bones about what a disappointing social life I've had. How many people have had their last three boyfriends in a row cheat on them, the most recent with another man? I'm cursed.

"While I would love to help you celebrate the news of your engagement, my schedule is pretty full right now."

"I thought you were on a six-month sabbatical." She sounds hurt.

"I am, but I'm using that time to get pregnant." My doctor recommends I stay as calm and placid as possible, so my body will get on board with my desire to procreate. *Do you hear that body, relax already!*

"Lu, please," Claire begs. "Tara can't come because the lodge needs her in the kitchen while Geoffrey is away." My sister's intended is a chef as well as a prince. *Hurry, call Hallmark, I smell a movie deal.* "Please, please, please, please, please."

After letting her plea hang in the air for several beats, I unleash my sarcasm and relent, "Only if you say please." Who knows? Maybe I can use the time to check out some European sperm banks. I wonder if my kids would have dual citizenship.

"You're the best, thank you! Can you fly up tomorrow? That way you can take the private plane with Geoffrey and me. Mom and Dad are in Tennessee with Tooty, so I'll tell them the news tomorrow after I book them on a commercial flight."

"What? We're not going to stop and pick them up?" I don't think about the repercussions of such a question until the words are out of my mouth.

"It never occurred to me that we could do that. But now that you mention it, I'll ask Geoffrey."

Oh, crap. All I need is an eight-hour flight listening to my mom and aunt yammer on about how thrilled they are for Claire, all the while sending me covert glances of concern over my single status. Why didn't I keep my big mouth shut? "If I've got to be there tomorrow, I'd better get going," I tell her.

"I love you, Lu. I can't wait to see you."

"Thanks Pest, I love you too." And I really do. I just have no idea how I'm going to suffer through a royal engagement party with my whole family present. While I won't be the center of their attention, I won't be far off. Claire's good news will cause them to pity me, and that's never been my favorite thing.

I need to call Liza and cancel brunch. After that, maybe I should call my doctor. I wonder if she'll prescribe me some kind of tranquilizer over the phone.

Malquar, here I come.

Chapter Four

The Queen

The newspaper is on the nightstand where it always is. Queen Charlotte of Malquar sips her preferred strawberry blossom tea in preparation to peruse the daily news. It helps to keep her blood pressure even. That is, until she sees that photograph and headline. No amount of tea will help this.

The Spare is at it Again!

Alistair George Henry Bere Hale, Prince of Malquar, poses on the royal yacht with two new friends. Most readers will probably recognize Hallie Fox (on his left) as the star of the American television program *Fox Hunters.* But what of the beauty on his right?

Guests of the prince's latest excursion inform us she's none other than one of the catering staff hired to serve at the event.

We've seen it before, and we presume we'll see it again: Prince Alistair is an equal opportunity playboy. While that must give the everyday gal hope—who doesn't dream of becoming a princess?—we're sure it's a cause of despair in the monarchy.

King Alfred and Queen Charlotte are generally all smiles when asked about their offspring, but we can't help speculating they must be ready for the wayward prince to settle down and take his royal responsibilities more seriously.

Tossing the paper aside, Charlotte picks up the bell on her tray and rings it. When her maid comes in, she says, "Please get me Prince Alistair immediately."

Alistair

There are several things I enjoy about my life. The food is world-class. I quite like the travel—our planet is such an interesting place. The housing is decent. I have my own cottage (six bedrooms, seven baths—so not a cottage really, but that's what we call it) on the royal grounds. I mostly adore living near my family. Lastly, it's nice not having to worry about my future security.

That being said, the scrutiny of the press is unbearable. I can't throw a party without the country speculating on my supposed debauchery. I love women, but the last time I looked, that wasn't a crime. I'm single, and therefore allowed to date, even though I haven't been. The articles they run about me are one hundred percent fiction.

According to my mother, I'm making a spectacle of myself and should treat the whole "looking for my future duchess" thing more seriously. The last time I was in a relationship, the woman had her sights set higher than me, so forgive me if I don't give the impression that I'm looking for a wife. I'm not.

I wonder what the queen expects me to do, send out invitations and interview for the position? I don't think that's how it's done. It's sure as heck not how I plan on doing it, anyway.

The knock on my front door is followed by it being opened with such force, I wonder if the wall it slams into is still intact. Putting my coffee cup down on the kitchen counter, I head toward the entry.

"If it isn't the heir," I say when I spot my older brother, Andrew, charging in my direction. He hates when I call him that.

I can practically see the steam coming out of his ears. *Mission accomplished.* "Why can't you throw parties here?" He gestures wildly with his hands as though spokesmodeling my living room for me.

"Drew," I reply calmly, "I do have gatherings here, but I occasionally like to be let out of prison and take a ride on the boat. Is that a crime?"

"It should be," he mutters. "Because every time you get out, as you call it, I wind up being held to an even higher level of decorum. 'Thank God you aren't like your brother,'" he mimics our mother's voice—poorly— before adding, "And then she starts in on me about why it's taking me so long to find a wife."

"If you'd just do that already," I tell him, "she'd get off my back and have something else to focus on." I lead the way into the living room before dropping down onto the sofa.

Hot on my heels, Andrew declares, "About that … Geoffrey and Claire are coming home this week to officially announce their engagement."

Clapping my hands together sharply, I reply, "Wonderful! Mum will have her royal wedding to plan which means the two of us will be off her radar for the foreseeable future."

"You'd think." My brother sits on the chair across from me. "The truth of it is, it's about to get a lot worse for us. Our mother will be fielding questions about why the third in line is marrying before the heir or the spare. The heat is on, brother. And with that heat comes Mum's scrutiny that we do not appear in the news carrying on with two women at once."

"I'm not carrying on with *either* woman. I was just being friendly." I don't bother to tell him that I was trying to evade the clutches of a Hollywood starlet. He's the target of enough social climbing women, I'm not certain he wouldn't be sympathetic.

"While that may be, to anyone who saw the picture in today's news, it appears you were on your way to an orgy. That crap has to stop, Al."

"I have never been the orgy type," I tell him, trying to redeem some of the fraying image my family has of me. "I'm not dating Hallie Fox *or* the waitress. I'm not dating anyone."

"That's not what the papers are selling," he says in an almost warning tone.

"Because truth doesn't sell papers. You know that better than anyone. I can't help what people say about me, Drew. The press loves sensationalism. With the exception of Chéri, who just married her longtime girlfriend, our sisters are as traditional as they come. Geoffrey has lived abroad since college, so they never got much dirt on him, and you're about as exciting as dry toast. That leaves me to fulfill their slot for 'wild, partying, bad-boy royal.' It's not a spot I've earned, trust me. It was appointed by default."

"Good, then it won't be hard for you to behave while Claire and her family are here."

"Her family?" I met Claire's mother and aunt before when they were at the palace for a private royal concert. Our father has a real thing for American country music. But I didn't meet Claire or her sister for the first time until Chéri's surprise wedding, which took place at the lodge in Oregon where Geoffrey and Claire work. It's the sister who's currently piqued my interest.

Andrew seems to be aware of this and says, "Keep it in your pants, party boy. Lutéce Choate is not an option for you."

"Why, because she's prickly as a pear? You'd think that would be exactly the kind of woman who would please our mother." I cross my arms across my chest in a belligerent fashion. *Is there no satisfying these people?*

"She's not an option because her sister is marrying our brother. What if you two got together and it didn't work out? Can you imagine the upset that would cause for future events?"

"What if it *did* work?" I reply heatedly. As I've mentioned, I'm not really looking for something serious, but I do love to rile my brother.

It's my second favorite pastime.

Drew snorts. "What are the chances of that happening? I'm not just giving you a hard time, either. From what I remember, Lutéce isn't exactly a warm and welcoming person."

"I thought her snippiness was her most endearing trait." She isn't the kind of woman who would be interested in me for my title. She made that abundantly clear in Oregon. If she ever did desire something more, it would be as my equal, not subordinate.

That may be her most attractive quality.

"You're just looking for a challenge. And while I might normally be on board with that, you may not involve yourself on a personal level with Claire's sister. That's a direct quote from Mother."

"Mmmmm." The one thing I hate more than empty adoration is being told that I can't do something, especially by my parents. The petulant teen inside me comes roaring out every time.

That's not to say I'll embark on anything more than flirtation with Miss Choate. If memory serves, she *was* a bit of a handful. In fact, she treated me like I was a particularly virulent strain of mold she'd found growing in her basement.

"When do they arrive?" I ask.

"Tomorrow. The dinner announcing their engagement is on Saturday evening, so don't make other plans," Drew says.

"As it's already Wednesday, I think it's fair to say my social calendar is otherwise engaged."

"Alistair …" my brother says in a warning tone.

"Fine, I'll cancel. I don't suppose Mother wants me to bring a date?"

Shaking his head, my brother replies, "Family only."

"Whoever will I bend to my wicked ways then?" I reply with a mischievous grin. "Unless Mum has hired some attractive servers, that is," I say with a wink.

"Come alone, and that's an order." Andrew gets up and strolls toward my front door before calling back, "Seriously, Alistair, do not mess this up." Slam.

How insulting. I'm known throughout Europe as the "Party

Prince," a moniker that I have always hoped meant that I was the fun one. But now I'm starting to wonder if it's not the compliment I've always thought it to be.

My brain immediately zooms back to thoughts of Lutéce. Talk about stuck up and bristly, she'd be the perfect royal. Alas, I've been warned to stay away from her.

It's a good thing I don't always do as I'm told.

Chapter Five

Sharon

Leaning over their shared armrest, Sharon asks her sister, "Why don't you get one of these things?"

Without looking up from her book, Tooty replies, "If you mean a private airplane, hon, these things cost millions."

"And?"

"I've got better ways to spend my money."

"Are you still hoping to find the perfect land to open your theme park?"

"Nah, Tootyville is a thing of the past. I've been thinking about starting a summer camp for underprivileged kids. You know, a place where they can get away and learn to dream of a brighter future."

"Tooty Jackson, I love that idea! You need to talk to Lu. That kind of thing is right up her alley."

Tooty looks across the jet at her niece who's sitting on a loveseat by herself. "I think Lu has enough on her mind right now, don't you?"

"She does look like a hot corn kernel about to pop, doesn't she? I wish she'd realize we were all on her side already."

Lutéce

If I had a dollar for every time my mother gave me "the look"—the one that says, "Poor Lu, why can't you just live the life I planned for you?"—I'd be flying to Malquar on my own jet.

Not only did I pack up my bags at the spur of the moment to support my little sister's happy ending, but I've subjected myself to endless glances of disappointment from my mother. They started the moment she boarded the plane.

Looking up from my laptop, I stare right back at her. "Is there something on your mind, Mother?" I ask, making it perfectly clear that the question is rhetorical. I don't want to hear the answer.

Instead of grasping the nuance of my mood and leaving me alone, she stands up and walks over to me. "Now that you mention it, why do you want to have a stranger's baby again?"

Geoffrey overhears this and his eyes pop open with interest. He looks uncomfortable as my sister explains, "Lu wants to have a baby, but she's not in a relationship right now."

He smiles at her lovingly before saying, "I can't wait to start our own family."

I'm tempted to get up and kiss Prince Geoffrey right there. That one statement causes my mom to shift her focus from me to them. "Are you trying?" she asks boldly.

"We thought we'd get married first," Claire says. "You okay with that?"

Our mother shrugs nonchalantly. "I suppose."

Geoffrey adds, "My parents are pretty strict on protocol. As in, babies don't come before the wedding. It used to be that if they came less than nine months after the wedding, they were called premature. It's harder to sell that now that everyone wants to know how much the baby weighed."

Mom goes back across the aisle to sit with Tooty, and my dad takes her place. "How's my girl?" he asks. Dad has always been the calm in our storm. He doesn't ride the highs and lows of emotion like he's a trapeze artist hanging onto a greased bar a hundred feet off the ground the way the rest of us do. Instead, he instills tranquility wherever he is.

"I wish Mom would leave me alone," I tell him honestly.

"Believe it or not, Lutéce, your mother loves you. She only does what she does because she wants you to be as happy as she is."

"I'd be a whole heck of a lot happier if she didn't always think she knew what was best for me."

He takes my hand and gives it a squeeze. "She does it out of concern. She just needs to say her piece is all."

"I don't know how you've lived with her for forty years," I say unkindly.

"Your mother is the love of my life, Lu. She brings sunshine wherever she goes." He turns and gives her a look of adoration that causes my heart to physically ache. What I wouldn't give to be on the other end of a stare like that by a man who loves me.

Dad has always been very vocal about how much he adores Mom. It's sweet and nauseating at the same time. It also feeds my mother's unrealistic pipe dream that we are all destined for the same outcome she's had. Sharon Choate is an optimist, and while I was once like that, life has beaten me down in the last several years.

Changing the topic, I announce, "I bet you're getting excited about walking Claire down the aisle."

His smile is radiant. "A father wants nothing more than to know that some lucky person loves his daughter as much as he does. Honey," he starts to say. My eyes tear up at that one word alone—damn these hormone injections. "I don't know how I know this, but I do. Somewhere out there is the man who will love and cherish you above all else. Don't give up hope, okay?"

I want to believe that he has an inner line to some higher source, but my well of hope has been sucked dry. I've even started to wonder if I should pack up and move to a normal place. I'm not sure where that might be—maybe Iowa or Oklahoma or something. The only problem is that most people my age in those locations are probably already settled down and raising their families.

Unconsciously, I release a sigh of yearning for taco Tuesday, pizza Friday, family bowling nights, and camping trips. I have this deep-rooted pie-in-the-sky dream that if I ever do meet Mr. Right, he won't already have a family. It's not that I couldn't love someone else's children—I certainly could—I just selfishly want to have my own kids that I don't have to share with someone else. I've also seen enough movies to know that I never want to be on the receiving end of some kid yelling, "You're not my mother!"

The last man I dated with kids used to reprimand me if I asked his four-year-old monster twins not to kick me. It was ultimately the reason we stopped seeing each other.

The flight attendant comes by and offers us a lunch menu. "We will be serving in a half hour if you'd like to make a selection," she says with a hint of a French accent.

"Thank you." Dad takes the menus and hands one to me. "Oh, chateaubriand—I know what I'm getting. How about you?"

My stomach is heavy with dread at the thought of the week ahead. "I'll probably just have a salad."

"Have I told you how excited I am that you're planning to make me a grandfather?"

I look up, surprised. "You are? I thought you and Mom were both of a mind that I should wait until I find the man I want to marry." I say the last bit like I'm referring to a unicorn or other mythological creature.

"I'd love for you to share the journey of parenthood with your soulmate, but that doesn't mean I don't support you if you choose another path. Any baby of yours will be one hundred percent welcomed and adored by me *and* your mother."

I scoot over so I can rest my head on his shoulder. "I love you, Dad."

"I love you too, honey. So, so much."

In that moment I feel like I'm a little girl all over again. Even though I'm from a generation that believes you don't need a partner to fulfill you, I've lived alone for long enough to know that I really want to share my life.

Call me old-fashioned, but I was raised on the fairy tale ending, and I can't stop myself from hoping mine is still out there somewhere. But first I have to get through the next week in Malquar.

God help me.

Chapter Six

The Queen

"I don't care if you have other plans, Alistair," Queen Charlotte tells her middle son. "We're all going to the airport to greet Claire and Geoffrey. The press will be there, and your father and I don't need them speculating on which inappropriate woman is keeping you from performing your royal duties."

"Tell them I'm reading to orphans. Surely that will be enough to get them to focus on Geoffrey," Alistair responds grumpily.

Giving her son a look of pure disbelief, the queen says, "Reading to orphans? That's the best you can do?"

"Your lack of faith in me is truly heartbreaking, Mother. Do you know that?"

"Darling, I have more faith in you than you have in yourself, which is why I have such high expectations of you. You can do so much better than you've been doing, and it's high time you meet your potential."

"Fine, I'll cancel with the orphans and go to the airport with you. Although, I have no idea how that will aid in my reaching your lofty aspirations."

"Make sure to wear a suit jacket," his mother tells him.

Alistair grumbles as he walks off. "Yes, Mother. Whatever you say, Mother."

Alistair

"I'm sorry, Sister Hennepin, I need to cancel today's reading session. Our family has a reception to attend," I tell the nun who's in charge of the orphanage.

"The children will be disappointed," she replies sternly. "Will we see you next week?"

"How about if I come tomorrow afternoon instead?"

"That would be fine. That way the little ones can still serve you the scones they made this morning."

"I'll plan on taking my mid-afternoon meal with you then."

As I put my phone back into my pocket, I once again wonder why I've never told my parents I'm more than the person who writes the checks to keep the lights on at Shepherd's Home. They know I'm their patron, but they have no idea how much time I spend with the children.

I suppose the truth of the matter is that I like having something in my life that's just mine. I don't want my time with the kids viewed as charity work. Reading to them, tossing a ball with them, and helping them with their artwork fulfills me in a way that playing polo and attending social events never could.

Also, maybe it's because when I do tell them, they don't believe me.

My mind drifts as I walk across the palace grounds to Fernmore Cottage. The next several days are going to be chockablock full of events celebrating Geoffrey's upcoming nuptials. I'm assuming now that my brother has chosen his bride, he will be returning to Malquar full time. Even though he was expected home on his thirtieth birthday, our father relaxed his rule at Chéri and Brigitte's wedding.

That was when our whole family met Claire for the first time. It was obvious to a blind man that my brother was falling in love with her even then. Hence, his reprieve to rejoin royal life at the prescribed time.

Some people will do anything to shirk their royal responsibilities, even fall in love.

While we were all once expected to choose our mates from Malquar society, our little sister married a French woman, and now Geoffrey is marrying an American. It appears the king and queen are modernizing their thinking and opening the borders for us to find our future mates. All of us with the exception of Andrew, that is. As the future king, he's expected to marry a woman from our country.

As I pass my sister Aubrey's cottage, I spot her out front filling a basket with freshly-cut roses. "Do you want to drive to the airport with me?" I call out to her.

"Sounds good. I'll just put these in water, and then I'll meet you over at your place." There are four cottages that share the same five-hectare grounds. We've created our own little royal village.

Chéri and Brigitte live in Paris with their daughter, Estelle. Our sister, Sophie, was engaged to Baron Harquart, but she called off her wedding when she discovered her intended planned to keep his mistress once they were wed. While I in no way support extramarital activities, who in the world tells their fiancée they don't intend on being faithful once the vows are said? *Is this the Middle Ages?*

Aubrey, or Bree as she's known to the family, lives next door to me and seems to be having as much trouble as I am finding the person she wants to spend her life with. Which just goes to show that jumping through our mother's hoops and living according to her rules isn't necessarily the key to happiness.

I have just enough time to shower and get dressed before Bree walks through my front door. "What is it with you people just strolling in here like this is your house?"

Wearing a fetching dark green dress, my sister raises an eyebrow and replies, "You expect me to knock on your door? What are you, a prince or something? If you're so precious, use your lock."

That gets a laugh out of me. None of us lock our homes. We're so secure on the grounds that the only people who can even get to us have to pass through security at the front gate. Once they do that, they need to obtain another pass from the palace to enter our little cottage community.

"Are we caravanning, or can we just drive over on our own?" I ask Bree.

"As long as we're all there by three, we can make our own way over." As we head toward my entry hall, she asks, "Has Mother started giving you a hard time about getting married?"

"No more than usual. Her main objective seems to be that I cease having fun immediately. She's determined to believe everything she reads in the papers," I grumble before asking, "Is she giving you a hard time?"

"Not even a little bit. Which worries me, actually."

Opening the passenger side of my vintage Aston Martin DB5—just call me James Bond—I ask incredulously, "You're worried the queen isn't pushing you toward the altar? Are you unwell?"

My sister inhales deeply before forcing her breath out in a rush. Once I'm behind the wheel, she answers, "I'm concerned that she doesn't think I'm marriageable."

"What are you talking about? You're as marriageable as the rest of us."

"Yet I never get asked out by anyone other than royal suck-ups. And, FYI, I'm not in the market for one of those," she says dejectedly.

"Bree," I tell her in no uncertain terms, "you never go out where any normal men can meet you. How do you expect to find one to date?"

Taking the twists and turns of the Coast Highway with more speed than needed, my sister clutches the door handle like it's her lifeline. "Short of signing up for a dating app, I'm at a loss. Do you have any ideas?"

"Do what I do," I tell her. "Throw parties. Let your guests invite a plus one. Maybe the non-royal worshipping man of your dreams will show up."

My sister snorts. "If I threw a party and invited my regular group of friends, I can assure you it would be another boring tea party."

Reaching out, I gently touch her arm. "You should come to my next party. I promise you a much more enlightened kind of event."

"Mum would lay an egg if I showed up in the papers at one of your events."

"But you'd meet a slew of new and exciting people. Dare I suggest, some of them don't even care about our royal status?"

After some hemming and hawing, which once again has me wondering at the image my family has of me, she concedes, "Okay. But so help me, Alistair, this better not hurt my reputation."

"Ye of little faith. You'll still be you, just *you* surrounded by different people."

While she stews on that, my mind works to conjure an image of what my life could be like if I settled down. I used to think that domesticating was an unpleasant thought, but I've done a lot of living in my thirty-two years, and I'm getting bored with the same old-same old.

Also, spending so much time with the kids at the orphanage has gotten me thinking about having a family of my own.

Now all I need to do is find their mother.

Chapter Seven

Sharon

Sharon: *We just landed in Malquar! I wish you were here.*

Romaine: *I do too, Mom, but I have concerts every other night this week. There's no way I could get there.*

Sharon: *You're coming to the wedding though, right?*

Romaine: *As long as I have enough notice.*

Sharon: *I'm sure you'll have at least a year.*

Romaine: *Then I'll be there.*

Sharon: *Now that Claire is getting married, dear, don't you think it's time that you settle down as well?*

Romaine: *I've gotta go rehearse, Mom.*

Sharon: *I mean it, Romaine. You need to quit sowing your wild oats and act your age.*

Romaine: *Goodbye, Mother.*

Lutéce

My mom pulls out a compact and refreshes her lipstick before saying, "We're finally back in Malquar, Tooty." Then she smiles at Dad and adds, "You're going to love it here, hon."

"Maybe you and Dad should look at houses while you're here," I suggest hopefully. My life would be so much easier if they moved far away from me.

"You can't get away from me that easily, Lu. I'm sure Geoffrey and Claire will have plenty of room for us when we come and visit. Isn't that right, Geoffrey?"

"Absolutely. In fact, I'm looking forward to showing you all our future home. My sister Aubrey has overseen getting it ready for us to move into, but I'm sure Claire will want to have some say. Maybe you can help, Sharon."

"I would love that!"

Hurray! In addition to adding her two cents to all the wedding plans, Mom can keep herself busy decorating Claire's new home. That means I might be able to unclench a little while I'm here. After my last attempt at IVF, my doctor suggested I take a long vacation and do my best to relax. Not that a family trip is any way to do that—especially with my family—but you never know.

After the pilot comes over the intercom to welcome us to Malquar, we all stand to deplane. Mixed emotions flood my thoughts as the strains of music from a live band start to fill the atmosphere around us.

"They're playing the Malquarian anthem," Geoffrey explains. "I didn't come home for my thirtieth birthday, as per my parents' plan, so I can only assume there might be a bit of a circus out there."

Stepping back into the cabin, I bend down to look out the window. Yup, there it is, the circus. There must be a fifty-piece band playing on one side of a red carpet. The other side is full of reporters and photographers.

The image of an old ringmaster, full-on with a red coat, tails, and black top hat, pops into my head. He's holding a bullhorn to his mouth, and I can practically hear him shout, "Will everyone please turn their attention to the center ring. Our prince has returned home with his bride and her illustrious family of *yodelers*!" Tooty and Mom love to yodel as a means of decompressing. It's enough to make your ears bleed if you're not a fan of the genre.

And sometimes, even if you are a fan.

I return to our little exit line and watch while Geoffrey and Claire disembark. They stop and wave as the crowd cheers wildly. Crap, I should have brought some better clothes to change into. The jogging suit I'm currently wearing was chosen for comfort, not to meet the press.

As if reading my mind, my mom turns around and looks me up and down before saying, "Oh dear, maybe you should stay on the plane until the crowd disbands." *Ouch.*

Ignoring her, I run my fingers through my auburn hair and pinch my cheeks to bring some color to them. By the time it's my turn to get off, most of the press is on the tarmac, crowding around my sister and her intended. The rest seem to be vying for Tooty's attention.

I scan the masses, feeling oddly separated from my body. It's like I'm watching a scene in a movie. I'm about to step down onto the stairs when my gaze locks with a pair of dark chocolate brown eyes, penetrating eyes that cause me to stop dead in my tracks and gasp audibly.

"Settle down, Lu," I chastise myself silently for such an absurd reaction to Geoffrey's brother. Alistair was nothing but a flirtatious annoyance at his sister's wedding, and I'm not looking forward to more of the same. Yet, even as I try to convince myself of this, my heart beats in double time and perspiration starts to form on my palms.

Great. Not only am I dressed like a college kid returning home for break, but I'm nervously sweating. Which is super fun, as what I'm guessing is the entire national press corps is out there ready to film the scene for posterity.

Before my foot hits the tarmac, all eyes are drawn to the King of Malquar as he announces, "We are so happy to have our son back home where he belongs." The crowd erupts as Geoffrey opens his arm to pull my sister to his side. "I would like to introduce you all to Geoffrey's lady friend, Claire…" The engagement won't be made public until after the official dinner.

His announcement renders me invisible, and even though I prefer that, it still kind of smarts. I could probably walk back up the stairs into the airplane and watch as my whole family drives away without knowing that I'm missing. I realize how immature that sounds, but still, a person likes to be noticed.

When the king introduces Tooty to the crowd, I feel a presence brush up against my arm. *Personal space, people, it's a thing.* I instinctively shoot my elbows out like a clucking chicken to send a hint. When the nudge is returned, I turn my head and find myself staring into Alistair's eyes. "Welcome to Malquar," he practically purrs.

"Yes… well… thank you." Really, what else is there to say? For as annoying as the man is, he is also downright gorgeous. I've always been a fan of tall, dark, and handsome. Add a squared jaw, masses of dark wavy hair, and soulful brown eyes, and I'm toast.

"Would you like to get out of here?" he asks flirtatiously.

"With you? I'd sooner lie down and roll all the way back to California. I'm perfectly aware the Atlantic Ocean lies between us." I arch my eyebrow as though challenging him.

Releasing a soft chuckle, he grins broadly. "You could make a faster escape if you came with me."

The idea suddenly has merit. Crap. "Your parents will let you leave this dog and pony show early?" I demand.

"Watch this," he whispers close to my ear, resulting in giant goose bumps erupting all over my skin. My gaze follows him as he approaches his mother. He leans down and says something to her which results in her turning around and looking at me with concern.

When Alistair returns, he says, "Mother is sorry you're feeling poorly and is happy for me to take you home ahead of all the pomp and ceremony."

A bubble of laughter bursts out of me before I can stop it. "You told her I was sick?"

Shrugging nonchalantly, he offers, "It was that or suffer through another thirty minutes of torture. Which do you prefer?"

"Which car is yours?"

Taking my arm in his, Alistair leads me to a jaw-droppingly

elegant silver sports car that I know for a fact is the same kind James Bond drove in *Goldfinger*. I'm a huge Bond fan.

Before I can get in, Alistair's sister, Bree, comes running toward us. "Are you leaving me here?" she demands.

"Poor Lutéce has a horrible headache," Alistair tells her. He further lies, "Mum asked me to take her back to the palace."

Turning her attention to me, her voice softens. "I'm sorry you're unwell."

"You can crowd into the backseat if you want," Alistair suggests.

Bree rolls her eyes in response before walking away. She stops after a few steps, turns around, and in a warning tone, says, "Remember what mother said, Al."

I have no idea what she's referring to, but Alistair practically snorts, "She says so much, it's hard to keep it all straight." Then he opens the car door for me.

Once I'm situated, I watch as he gets behind the wheel. Against my better judgment, a ripple of something like anticipation rolls through me. Dear God, it's the hormones again.

I should not have gotten into this car with this man.

Chapter Eight

The Queen

"Where is Alistair going?" King Alfred whispers into his wife's ear.

"Claire's sister was feeling poorly. He's taking her back to the palace to rest." The look in her husband's eyes inspires her to add, "Don't worry, I've already warned him away from her."

The king smiles down at his wife. "I'm not worried about Alistair. Of all our children, I was the most like him during my youth."

"I remember," the queen replies with a note of censure. "The papers were full of your many conquests when I was growing up."

"Are you jealous?" he asks with a twinkle in his eye.

"Hardly, as I'm the one you married." She adds, "But if you're not worried about Alistair, why the look of concern?"

"Something feels off about Claire's sister."

"She wasn't exactly a ball of fun at Chéri's wedding. I think she might just have a sour disposition."

"I don't think it's that," the king replies. "I think she's been hurt and has put up a defensive shield."

The queen laughs. "If this royal thing doesn't work out for you, you could become a psychic or a therapist." She squeezes his arm and whispers, "Front and center, dear, the cameras are catching our little chat and I'm guessing the reporters are starting to speculate."

The royal couple focuses their attention back on the press as they ask Tooty Jackson a myriad of questions.

Even though the queen outwardly looks interested in the proceedings, her mind is elsewhere. *Would Alistair really take Lutéce back to the palace for unselfish reasons? Or does he have ulterior motives?*

Alistair

"So, you've never been to Malquar before?" I ask Claire's sister as we drive the coast road back toward the palace.

Shaking her head, my beautiful passenger answers, "No." That's it, one word.

"What do you think of our little country?" I'm going to get her to converse with me if it's the last thing I do. We've spent twenty minutes in virtual silence and it's starting to grate on me.

"I can't really say. I haven't seen much of it yet."

In response, I veer sharply to the right and take the exit I'd practically already passed. "What are you doing?" Lutéce demands sharply.

"I'm going to show you one of the highlights of Malquar," I tell her.

"I'd prefer that you just take me back to your parents' place and let me get settled." Her words sound like a threat. Too bad for her I don't respond well to threats.

"First, I'm going to show you our white sand beaches."

"I can see them from here," she replies petulantly. Call me crazy, but I enjoy getting a reaction out of this woman, even if it is an angry one.

Ignoring her, I find a parking place in one of the public lots. Being that it's September, the weather has started to cool and many of the hardcore sun worshippers are elsewhere.

As I open the car door to get out, my passenger announces, "I'll stay here."

"The whole point of being here is to show you around," I tell her. "Plus, it will help destress you. There's nothing like walking through the sand with the Atlantic washing over your toes to calm your soul."

For some reason, that seems to do the trick because she opens her own car door and gets out.

I take off my sport coat before rolling up my shirtsleeves and pant legs. Then I take off my shoes. "You might want to do the same," I suggest.

Lutéce responds as though I just asked her to strip naked and perform a lap dance for me. "I'm fine," she says tightly. Oh boy, she really is a thrill ride of fun.

Calm permeates my body as I lead the way toward the water. I point to a large rock on the left and declare, "That's where we used to play King of the Mount when we were kids. The objective of the game was to be the first one on top."

"Interesting."

She doesn't sound the least bit interested, so I add, "Geoffrey pushed me off once and I landed on my head and needed eight stitches."

"That explains a lot." For as beautiful as she is, I'm starting to think Lutéce Choate is nasty to the core.

"I was six," I up the ante.

"I'm sorry that happened to you." Finally, some sympathy. "Romaine knocked me off my bike when we were young. I landed headfirst into a tree."

"Did it leave a scar?"

She points to her temple where there's a faint white line visible on her porcelain-smooth skin.

In return I show her the four-inch-wide ridge at my hairline. "It makes me look pretty dashing, don't you think?" I shrug my eyebrows up and down like a comedian.

Instead of agreeing about my roguish good looks, Lutéce stops abruptly and announces, "I'm here for my sister's engagement party. I'm not looking for romance."

So much for being nice to the woman. "Well, it's a good thing I haven't taken you into my arms to ravish you then, isn't it?" I feel the need to add, "As part of the hosting family, I assure you, I'm only doing my duty by showing you around. Think of me as your tour guide."

My words seem to take her off guard because she stammers, "I …I … I'm sorry. It's just that when we were in Oregon, you were rather flirtatious."

"It's part of my charm," I tell her. "I'm like that with everyone." I'm really not, but there's no point in being vulnerable around this sharp-tongued she-devil. I already have enough people thinking the worst of me.

Instead of continuing this line of conversation, I tell her all about our little island country and entertain her with stories about the pirates who used to land here and hide out in our cove when they were being pursued by the British navy. Before I know it, thirty minutes pass.

While my companion initially seems interested, she still only manages a grand total of eight words the whole time. "Interesting, I see," and finally, "Can we leave now?" Any attraction I ever felt for her dries up like a puddle in the desert. I don't care how beautiful she is, she has the personality of dirt. Mean dirt, at that.

Ignoring her, I turn my attention to the water. Then I perform the same ritual I have ever since I was small. I run toward the incoming tide and let the water crash against my calves. I feel it pull the tension out of me as it returns to the sea.

I stand there for three more encounters before turning around. Lutéce is already halfway back to the parking lot.

It's no wonder she isn't married or otherwise engaged. That woman is an ice queen. I don't say anything else to her after getting back to the car. I just drive us to the palace surrounded by unsettling quiet. I vow not to be the one to initiate conversation. Let her see what it's like.

Once we pull through the palace gates, one of the footmen opens her door. Unrolling my window, I say, "Stephen, this is Claire Choate's sister. Can you please take her to her room?"

I don't wait for his response. Instead, I put my car back into gear and pull out onto the road that leads to my cottage.

While I may not be interested in a woman who fawns all over me because of my royal standing, I certainly won't subject myself to one who's made it clear she can't stand me.

Chapter Nine

Sharon

"I can see why you love it here," Phillipe Choate tells his wife as their car winds around the coastal highway.

"It's the perfect place for us all to unwind, especially Lu."

"She'd relax more if you'd quit talking to her about her plans to become pregnant."

"I'm her *mother,* Phillipe. I can't just sit back and watch her do something I think she'll regret later."

"Lu is a smart girl, just like her mom." He leans into his wife and adds, "We've raised her well. As such, it's time to step back and let her make her own decisions."

"That, my dear, is easier said than done."

"Maybe so, but you have enough on your plate with Claire and her upcoming wedding. Focus on that and let Lu find her own way."

Sharon lays her head on her husband's shoulder and sighs. "Our baby is getting married, Phillipe. How can that be when I still feel like a bride myself?"

Lutéce

I can't believe Alistair dropped me off without saying a word. That man has two speeds: fast and flirtatious, and alarmingly rude. As the footman, Stephen, leads me through the stunning halls of Hale Castle, I make a vow to ignore Geoffrey's brother for the remainder of my time here. Which, according to my calculations, is roughly four days and ten hours. But who's counting?

I've been assigned a beautiful, silvery blue bedroom suite that overlooks a rose garden. Talk about feeling like a princess. I can't unpack without my suitcases, so I decide to lie down on the silk duvet and close my eyes.

The trip has taken its toll on me, and my heart is pounding so loudly, I can hear it inside my head. Ever since I started on this journey to have a baby, my anxiety has shot through the roof. While I'm physically driven to have a child, I have no idea how I'm going to handle it on my own. How will I manage long nights with a hungry or cranky baby and still have enough energy to go to work the next morning?

Sometimes I wake up in a cold sweat, worrying that I'm doing the wrong thing.

I must have fallen asleep because the next thing I know, the mattress compresses next to me. "Honey, you'd better get up if you want to change for supper."

My eyes open slowly, and my mom comes into focus. "I'm so tired," I moan.

"We all are. But you know as well as I do, we need to stay awake so we can be semi-functional while we're here. It's the only way to minimize the jet lag."

YOU'RE SO VAIN

"You look nice," I tell her when I notice the long, navy gown she's wearing. We were warned ahead of time that all evening meals would be formal affairs. Needless to say, I had to fit in a last-minute shopping trip.

My mom smiles at the compliment before saying, "I have a bath running for you. I'll unpack your clothes and make sure your dress is ready by the time you get out."

As crazy as my mom makes me, I truly do appreciate her at times. Right now is one of those times. Standing up, I drag myself across the room toward the sound of running water.

The bathroom is practically the size of my whole bedroom at home. There's a large, round, sunken tub right in the middle of the room that is surrounded by a sheer silky curtain. With all the marble surfaces and the crystal chandelier hanging above, I feel like I've been transported to the pages of a fairy tale.

After taking off my travel clothes, I step into the steaming hot water and lie back, letting the heat surround me. Replaying my time with Alistair, I realize I might have been a bit rude to him. But even so, the man gives as good as he gets.

Between the soothing warmth surrounding me and my jet lag, I'm about to fall asleep again when my mom comes in. "I hung up the buttercup yellow gown for you. I bet it's a real stunner with your hair color."

"The lady at Saks Fifth Avenue certainly thought so. Either that or she was busy calculating her commission on my purchases and would have said baby poop green was a lovely shade on me, too."

"You're going to look beautiful," she says in that dreamy way moms do when their kids are all dressed up.

"How was the rest of the press conference?" I ask.

"Boring. You know how they are. Did you have a nice time with Alistair after sneaking out early?" She busies herself pulling the makeup out of my toiletry bag like she's trying to make the question seem casual. But I know my mom well enough to know she's really asking if a romance is starting to bloom.

"The man is nothing but a lothario, and before you get it into your head that he and I might be right for each other, don't. I've had my fair share of relationships with men who have wandering eyes; I'm not in the market for another."

"Darling, I would never push you toward a handsome prince. What kind of monster do you take me for?"

I can't contain the laughter that bursts out of me. My mother is the worst actress on the planet. "Good," I tell her. "I'll find my own prince, if that's even in the cards."

"Well, hurry up and get out of the tub. You only have twenty minutes before we're expected downstairs."

After she leaves, I wash my face and shave my legs. Then I get out and apply my makeup while wrapped in the most sumptuous towel I've ever rubbed over my body. Seriously, it's like velvet. I'm tempted to take it to bed with me tonight to snuggle.

I wonder if they'd notice if I sneak it in my suitcase when I leave.

Once I'm all made up and dressed, I twist my hair into a French knot before pulling out a few strategic tendrils to frame my face. Standing back, I take in the whole look in the full-length mirror hanging on my bedroom wall.

Good God, I'm flipping gorgeous! Seriously, I might have to wear this gown to Whole Foods and see if I can meet some fine fellow thumping melons in produce. Like a punch in the heart, I once again wonder if I'm doing the right thing trying to have a baby without giving that little person an opportunity for a father.

When I hear a knock at my door, I give myself one last look in the mirror and force a smile on my face. I tell my reflection, "You are finally away from your daily grind, Lu. All you have to do is ignore Alistair and you'll have a great time."

Although, I'm not sure ignoring him is an option. The man fills a room like hot lava, moving slowly but with intent. Oh, my God, what am I even talking about? I'm waxing poetic about lava and Alistair.

What I need is a good night's sleep. After that, I'm sure I can handle whatever the man throws my way. I'm almost sure, anyway.

Chapter Ten

The Queen

Queen Charlotte stands at the head of the table and gently taps her glass to draw everyone's attention. "We are so pleased to have you all here as we celebrate our children. I just know the merging of our two families will bring so much joy. I will now turn the floor over to my son, Geoffrey."

Geoffrey stands while giving Claire a loving glance. He raises his glass to her before addressing the rest of us. "Claire has recently done me the greatest honor by agreeing to become my wife. Please join me in toasting to my lovely fiancée."

As the room hums with sounds of celebration, the king smiles down the length of the table. He stands and raises his own glass. "Welcome to the family, Claire!"

"Thank you all." She blushes prettily like a modern-day Cinderella.

The queen turns her attention to her older sons and they both shift around like they're sitting on hot bricks. "May Andrew and Alistair be so lucky in their choice of brides."

Lutéce Choate scoffs so loudly, the entire assemblage stops what they're doing to look at her. "Sorry, must be something in my throat," she says as her skin turns a color nearly as red as her hair.

The queen's eyes meet Sharon's. Both mothers appear intrigued by Lutéce's outburst. They share an unspoken thought that they need to keep an eye on their other children.

What are the chances that Alistair and Lutéce might find romance together? After all, aren't protests often the first indication of affection?

Alistair

"It's too bad your brother Romaine couldn't make it," I tell Claire, hoping to restart the conversation after her sister's outburst. Lutéce needs a muzzle. "I know Chéri and Brigitte are sorry not to be here. Little Estelle is giving them a run for their money, and they're exhausted."

"I imagine they need sleep more than travel," Claire replies. "As for Romaine, his band is on tour right now, and there was no way he could get away."

"It must be exciting to have a rock star in the family." I'm making stupid small talk now, but I'm doing it to keep from calling Lutéce out for her ridiculously bad manners.

"It's probably about as exciting as having a future king as a brother," my future sister-in-law says.

"Ah, well, then you have my sympathies." I like Claire, and I think she's going to fit right in with my family. Unlike her sister, she's got a sense of humor and doesn't appear to be afraid to use it.

Speaking of Claire's sister, I make a concerted effort not to look at her during the meal. Unfortunately, not looking at her doesn't mean I'm not thinking about her. My thoughts aren't exactly pure, either. The animal side of me wants to pull her into my arms and teach her a lesson about poking the bear.

Shifting uncomfortably in my seat, I hear my dad say, "Tooty, I don't suppose we could talk you into singing for us while you're here?"

"I don't suppose you could stop me, Alfred," my dad's favorite country music star answers. Then she smiles at Sharon and adds, "What do you say we try out that new number we've been working on?"

"'Yodeling Rodeo'?" she asks. "I don't know, Toot, we've been struggling with that one riff a bit."

"That's why we should get some feedback from friends. We'll practice it tomorrow before letting them hear it."

While my dad enthusiastically declares his interest in hearing a new Tooty Jackson song, my eyes finally travel around the table until they rest on Lutéce. She catches me watching her and attempts a stare down in retribution. Poor girl doesn't realize that you don't grow up with as many siblings as I have without learning how to win such a childish game.

I slowly count to twenty, expecting her gaze to veer away by the time I hit ten. When it doesn't, a pleasant warmth starts to flow through my veins. She might be annoying and rude, but Lutéce Choate is a strong woman with a backbone of steel. I can't help but be impressed.

"Alistair. Alistair? Alistair!" I finally come out of my trance—and lose the contest—as my mother calls my name.

"Mother, what can I do for you?" I ask, hoping I sound more relaxed than I feel.

"I was going to suggest you show the ladies the rose garden. You know how pretty it is along the lighted path at night."

Before I can reply, my brother Andrew interjects, "Why don't I do the honors, Mother?"

"That would be lovely, darling," our mom says.

"I'm afraid I'm bushed," Sharon announces.

"I need a good night's sleep, too," Tooty adds. "I'm sure my nieces would enjoy a tour, though."

"I was going to show Claire the orangery," Geoffrey says, causing both Andrew and me to smile. "Showing a girl the orangery" has always been code for making out in the greenhouse.

Andrew clears his throat. "It looks like it's just me and you strolling through the rose garden, Lutéce. Are you game?"

I expect her to call him all kinds of evil names for suggesting such a thing, but that's not what happens. Claire's sister smiles in the most warm and engaging manner. "That sounds lovely, Andrew. I'm sure I would enjoy that." I practically see red. How dare she want to spend time with him after being the queen of rudeness to me?

"Call me Drew," my brother purrs with the intent of a predatory cat.

"Call me Lu," she replies.

"You can call me Al," I interject, hoping to encourage the end of what is starting to sound like budding romantic interest between my brother and Lutéce.

"Al," my brother says, "I know you cancelled plans this evening to join us for dinner. Maybe you can still fit in part of your night." He has the audacity to wink, suggesting my plans were of an amorous nature. Which they were not. I was meeting some friends to play darts.

I'm about to defend myself when Lu's gaze turns to me. She looks … what's the word? Shocked? Angry? Jealous? Hmm, maybe I can make this work for me.

"I'm sure my *friend* is otherwise engaged by now." I add, "There's nothing I'd rather do than accompany my brother and our guest for a walk."

"I think maybe I should call it an early night after all," Lu decides, clearly not wanting me along.

"Don't be ridiculous," my mother says. "A nice stroll through the gardens with my boys will ensure a wonderful night's sleep."

Lu's mom pipes in with, "Just think, Lutéce, you can enjoy the company of two handsome princes. It's not every girl that gets so lucky."

Lu looks like she might start spitting bullets, but I don't care. I specifically told Drew at Chéri's wedding that I had my eye on the elder Miss Choate. Even though I've recently decided I'm not interested, he doesn't know that. The brother code demands he not poach on my territory, which is something I know we both agree on.

Before I can say anything else, Bree says, "How about if I show you the garden, Lu? That way you won't have to listen to my two bonehead brothers fight over you."

"I'll join you," Sophie adds. She's been uncharacteristically quiet through the entire meal. Although the truth is, she's been that way for the last few months since her engagement ended.

Lu pushes her chair back. "I think a stroll through the garden with the ladies is just what I need." They all stand and walk away like my brother and I don't even exist.

I glare at Andrew, but he refuses to make eye contact with me. What just happened here? I know I'd decided to ignore Lutéce for the rest of her visit, but I'm suddenly determined to do no such thing.

I'm not going to let her spurn me in favor of the heir. "Andrew," I address him, "would you like to join me for a walk of our own?" I'm sure my tone suggests I'm about to give him a piece of my mind, which is my plan.

"Thank you, no," he answers. "I think I'll call it a night."

As everyone gets up to leave the table, I think about joining my sisters and Lu in the garden. I can't help but wonder why I'm so interested in a woman who clearly wants nothing to do with me. But darn if I can help it, I am.

Chapter Eleven

Sharon

"Lu was the belle of the ball," Sharon tells her sister on their way up to their rooms.

"Sharon …" She hears the warning from her husband who's walking several steps behind them.

"Phillipe, you need to leave this to me and Tooty." Before he can reply, she adds, "I'm not saying Lu has to marry either of them; I'm just hoping she'll discover all men aren't scoundrels."

"Men from LA are a rare breed of trouble," Tooty interjects.

"Your son is a man from LA," Phillipe reminds his wife.

"Exactly! I've practically given up hope on Romaine. That boy has been engaged twice and it didn't stick either time. I've resigned myself that any grandchildren he gives me will be from groupies." Her body convulses in a shiver that makes clear her distaste at the idea.

"We'll love *all* of our grandchildren equally," he replies.

"Of course, we will. I just want our kids to have the opportunity to co-parent with someone *they* love. I'm not saying Lu needs to marry one of the princes, but it would be nice for her to realize there are good men in the world."

"You won't push her toward Andrew or Alistair then? Do I have your word?"

"Please, hon." Sharon stops and waits for her husband to reach her side. Putting her arm around his waist, she tells him, "I'm here to celebrate Claire and Geoffrey. That's all."

Tooty stops at her door. "Y'all have a good night."

As Sharon and Phillipe pass, Sharon gives her sister a wink that clearly states, "You see how it's done?"

Tooty flashes her a thumbs up. The sisters learned long ago how to let a man think he got his way without technically giving it to him.

Lutéce

"Men are such babies," Bree announces as the women reach the entry to the rose garden.

"I can't remember a time our brothers fought over a woman," Sophie adds.

"They weren't exactly fighting over me," Lu says.

A few steps down the dimly lit path, Bree stops and sits on an ornately carved bench. "Oh, they were fighting, all right, which is odd as they normally have very different taste in women."

"Except for…" Sophie starts to say, but Bree makes a motion for her to stop talking.

There appears to be a story there. One they aren't going to share. "What kind of women do your brothers tend to go for?" I ask as I sit down on the bench.

"Andrew has been instructed that his wife has to be the perfect future queen," Sophie answers. "Therefore, he tends toward love interests who are, well, shall we say, tightly wound."

"Like you," Bree tells her sister.

"It's true," Sophie agrees, not sounding the least bit offended. "I've always tried to live up to the whole 'royal expectation' thing and what has it gotten me? A stuck-up fiancé who tells me he doesn't plan to be faithful once we are married."

"What?" I know this isn't my business, but Sophie opened the door.

"I thought I'd done well by falling in love with someone from the aristocracy. Turns out, I'm the only one who felt that way. My intended was more interested in marrying one of the king's daughters than marrying *me*."

"It's dreadfully hard out there," Bree agrees dejectedly.

"I know what you two are going through," I tell them. "I can't seem to find a decent man to date either. They're either using me to get close to my famous family, or they're just settling for me until someone better comes along." I totally forget to ask what kind of woman Alistair normally dates.

We sit quietly for several moments, when Sophie decides, "There have to be good men out there somewhere."

"Obviously there are. I mean, look at Geoffrey, he's near perfect," I offer. "The problem seems to be finding more of these perfect men." I sigh like I'm competing in an Olympic sighing event.

I'd totally be a gold medal contender.

"I've recently heard about some parties where there might be male guests who aren't users," Bree says.

"I don't want to meet my future husband at some nightclub." Sophie's face scrunches up in distaste.

"I'd be game," I volunteer. "I haven't had any luck in the United States. Maybe the man of my dreams is right here in Malquar." Alistair's image pops into my head and I have to force it out. I didn't mean him.

That would be ludicrous.

"Well, if he is, you're probably not going to meet him in the next few days. You ought to stay on for a while," Bree says.

"I wasn't looking for an invitation." I explain, "It's just that I've recently been thinking about leaving LA."

"Well, if you're thinking about leaving anyway, you should stay with us. You can continue on in the palace with Sophie and our parents, but I'd love it if you'd bunk with me in my cottage."

"Is it big enough?" I ask, wondering if I'm really considering her offer while picturing us both crowded into a one-room quaint cabin like something out of *Little House on the Prairie*.

"Five bedrooms, four baths. I think we'll both fit," Bree says.

Huh, what if I did stay? I would be doing exactly what my doctor suggested I do before trying my second attempt at in vitro. I'd be getting away and hopefully relaxing. "I'll think about it," I tell her.

"You could help us plan the bridal shower. We were contemplating having a tea party right here in the rose garden," Sophie says before adding, "I'm so sick of tea parties I could spit."

"Soph," Bree tells her sister, "you need to come to at least one real party with me, where the only tea served is the kind from Long Island. We've got to break you out of your funk."

"If I stay, I'll go too," I tell her like my presence would be a draw.

Sophie exhales loudly. "Fine, but only if both of you go. I

can't see us getting in trouble if we all have each other's back."

"Good." Bree claps her hands together. "I don't know when the next party will be, but I'll keep you both posted."

"I'm still not sure I'm going to stay on," I remind them. I wasn't even looking forward to coming here for the engagement party. How can I seriously be thinking about prolonging my visit?

"Oh, you're staying," Bree tells me. "Sophie and I need you, and as future family, it's your duty to help us." Luckily, her tone is teasing, or I might think she's as pushy as Alistair.

"What's Claire and Geoffrey's wedding going to be like?" I change the subject. "I've never been to a royal wedding."

"You've seen them on television though, haven't you?" Sophie asks.

"I saw Prince Harry and Meghan Markle's wedding." I hope to God Claire's won't be like that. I'd probably break out in hives having to stand up in front of so many people.

Much to my chagrin, Sophie says, "Well, then, you know what it's going to be like. Five hundred of our closest family and friends witnessing the exchange of vows in the cathedral. Three hundred of those will be invited for a sit-down supper, and then the bride and groom's closest one hundred will enjoy some less-formal fun."

"That sounds like a very long day." My blood runs as cold as a glacial stream at the very thought.

"Very long," Bree agrees. "Because the whole time the guests are celebrating Geoffrey and Claire, they'll be speculating how long it will be until the next royal wedding."

"They'll also be pitying me," Sophie says with a hitch in her throat. "Which I can assure you will be excruciating, unless I can find a suitable date to take as my plus-one."

It's more than a little disconcerting that neither of the princesses sitting next to me has been able to find their mate.

If they can't do it with all they have going for them, what chance do I have?

Chapter Twelve

Queen Charlotte

"Did you see how our boys practically came to blows over which one of them would accompany Lutéce for a walk in the garden?"

"Darling," King Alfred snuggles closer to his wife in bed, "I don't think either of our sons are interested in Claire's sister. You're seeing something you wish was there."

"What?" Charlotte pushes against her husband's chest. "Of course, they were interested. Although, I don't think Andrew should pursue anything. He needs to marry a Malquarian woman."

"Charlotte, you have weddings on the brain. Leave the boys alone and focus on Geoffrey and Claire. Andrew and Alistair will be tamed in due time."

While her husband nibbles a pathway down her neck, the queen distractedly replies, "We'll see. But just so you know, if I spot a potential romance, I'm not going to take a backseat."

"Any romance that may brew will have nothing to do with you, and I assure you that your interest will cause more trouble than good. Now, get over here, woman, and remind me of one of the many reasons I love you so much."

Queen Charlotte crawls into her husband's arms and for the time, anyway, forgets about the possibility of any connection between one of her sons and Lutéce Choate.

Alistair

After Lutéce went off with my sisters last night, I reminded myself that I should not get involved with her. Yet, when I woke up this morning, an image of her immediately popped into my mind. Apparently, I can't tolerate having a woman dislike me. What a baby.

What I need right now is a good ego boost and the best place to get that is at Shepherd's Home. Orphanages are no longer common institutions in Malquar, what with an uprise in foster care, but we still have two. One of them is in a small town in the countryside and the other is right here in our capital city. Both are very well-funded and have high adoption rates, especially amongst the younger children.

After grabbing a quick breakfast, I head over to the one place that brings me more contentment than any other I've known. Shepherd's Home is in a large, two-hundred-year-old facility that used to be a nunnery. The stone abbey currently houses forty-two children between the ages of two months and sixteen years.

All five feet of Sister Hennepin greets me at the door. "Prince Alistair, we're delighted you were able to fit us into your busy schedule." On the surface that may sound like a nice greeting, but I've known this nun since I was a child. She's censuring me for missing my assigned time with the children yesterday.

"Between you and me," I lean in to tell her like I'm about to divulge my deepest, darkest secret, "my brother Geoffrey got engaged, and I needed to be present yesterday to show my support."

"Hmm," Sister Hennepin responds with a deadpan expression on her face.

"My family met my future sister-in-law's family at the airport. It was on television." Sister Hennepin was my math tutor when I was a young boy. Our shared history makes it particularly uncomfortable when she's disappointed in me. The good news is, that discomfort led to my getting excellent marks in school.

"You know I don't watch television," she says curtly. "But regardless of *why* you didn't come yesterday, the children are very excited to see you today. They're in the parlor."

Without waiting for my response, she heads down the entryway hall like she's leading a military coup. As soon as she opens the double doors to the comfortably-equipped living room—large, overstuffed sofas and reading chairs abound—I'm surrounded by children.

The oldest hang toward the back of the crowd while the youngest throw themselves into my arms, eager for outside attention.

"You didn't come yesterday," eight-year-old Millicent admonishes with her hands on her hips, an obvious sign of her displeasure.

"I'm sorry about that," I tell her. "I had official royal duties that I could not get out of."

"Be that as it may, my lemon curd does not taste its best on the second day. So, if you don't like it, you only have yourself to blame." She sounds like a mini–Sister Hennepin, which makes sense as the nun is the only parental figure she's had since her parents died four years ago.

"I take full responsibility."

I ruffle a few heads and accept hugs from the smaller children who haven't learned all the protocols yet. I'd hug them all, but Sister Hennepin is a real stickler for formalities. While she doesn't seem to hold my royal standing in any regard, she makes sure the children do.

"I've been practicing my stickball, and I can hit the bugger farther than the abbey gate!" Curtis, a red-headed, freckle-faced ten-year-old proudly announces.

"You can hit *what?*" Sister Hennepin demands. She's so forbidding, I feel myself shrink in the face of her displeasure.

"The ball, Sister," Curtis tells her as he scurries to the back of the room out of her line of sight.

"I thought I'd read to you all today," I announce to my young friends. "How does that sound?"

"I want to sing!" four-year-old Charity exclaims while dancing around the perimeter of the room. "I want to sing the yodel songs you taught us the last time you were here."

The yodel songs, as she calls them, are none other than my father's favorite Tooty Jackson songs. I briefly wonder if I can entice the lady herself to come to the orphanage and perform for the children. I'm guessing there won't be time with the many official events that surround the engagement, but it's worth thinking about.

"No yodeling today," Sister Hennepin announces. "No reading, either." She aims her last comment in my direction.

"Today, we're going to learn how to serve a proper tea. The older girls and boys will do the honors, while the younger children and the prince act as guests." She claps her hands together as everyone hurries to get into position.

While the older children leave the room, ostensibly in pursuit of our refreshments, the younger ones scurry to find chairs to sit on. The only two left standing are me and little Beatrice, who I think is five, but I don't quite remember. She's a very quiet little girl who doesn't make enough noise to stand out in a crowd.

"It looks like it's just you and me, Miss Beatrice," I tell her. Then I bow and offer her my hand. "What do you say we find ourselves a spot?" Her face turns red as she slips her tiny hand into mine. She doesn't say a word.

Sister Hennepin long ago decreed that the large, comfortable reclining chair next to the fireplace was to be reserved for me. As such, I walk right over to it. After sitting down, I offer Beatrice the choice spot on my lap.

I spend the next two hours with the children of Shepherd's Home. The tea is excellent, the service, nearly spot-on—with the small exception of having a bowl of lemon curd dropped on my shoe— and the company is unparalleled.

I regale my audience with stories of royal teas and catastrophes that took place when my siblings and I were learning the ins and outs of proper etiquette.

"Tell us about the dances!" Millicent demands. She's once again on her feet looking fierce.

"Are you referring to the balls, Miss Millicent?" I ask, knowing full well that she is. Millicent is a renowned lover of fairy tales, and there is nothing so appealing to her as a royal ball.

"Yes!" She starts to sway to the pretend music in her head. As she leaps over one of the smaller children who's laying on the floor, she says, "Tell us about the beautiful princesses and their beautiful dresses."

With Beatrice sound asleep against my shoulder, I begin, "Once upon a time, there was a woman with hair the color of the setting sun." The girls sigh in unison as several of the boys groan.

"Is there a prince in this story?" someone shouts.

"As a matter of fact," I tell her, "there is. And his name is Alistair." Giggles ensue.

"Is this a story about you?" Millicent wants to know. But before I can answer, she demands, "What's the name of the beautiful girl?"

"Her name is Lutéce, but this isn't your typical fairy tale with a happy ending," I warn.

"Why not?" Curtis demands.

"Because …" I let the tension build before telling them, "Lutéce doesn't like the prince."

"What?" another of my rapt audience demands. "The beautiful lady always loves the prince. That's how the story is supposed to go."

"Unfortunately for Prince Alistair, that isn't the case." I spend the next half-hour painting Lutéce Choate in the most unflattering light. I speak of her surly disposition; I call her haughty and self-absorbed. I might even mention that her feet are so big, she has to wear potato sacks instead of shoes.

"But is she beautiful?" one of the boys demands.

"Aside from her monstrous feet, yes," I answer. "But even a

beautiful woman can be considered plain if she isn't nice."

"Alistair," Sister Hennepin intervenes.

"Yes, Sister?"

"I hope this lady you speak of is not real. It would be highly improper for you to say such a thing about a *real* lady."

"I thought you said you didn't watch television," I reply.

"I lied." She lifts one eyebrow so high it's nearly absorbed by her hairline.

"Isn't lying a sin?" I ask, hoping to distract her.

"Not if a nun does it." Now it's my turn to raise an eyebrow.

I look back at the children and wrap up my story. "The moral is that nice people are automatically prettier than mean people."

"But what happens with Lutéce? Does she ever fall in love with the prince? Do her feet ever shrink?" Millicent wants to know.

"That, my dear girl, is a tale for another day. All I can say is that unless Lutéce decides to be nice, the prince isn't going to want anything to do with her." Now it's my turn to lie.

It would seem that the more cantankerous Miss Choate is, the more I'm intrigued by her.

Chapter Thirteen

Sharon

"Why in the world would Lu go off with Geoffrey's sisters when his brothers were so eager to spend time with her?" Sharon demands after stopping to smell a large orange rose during a walk in the rose garden.

"Maybe because she isn't interested in either of the princes in a romantic sense," her husband responds with a hint of warning in his voice.

"Don't be ridiculous, Phillipe. Andrew and Alistair are every bit as charming and attractive as Geoffrey. Can you imagine what it would be like to have both of our daughters married to princes?"

Taking a seat on a stone bench next to a small fountain, Phillipe pulls his wife down onto his lap. "The next thing you're going to suggest is that we set Romaine up with one of Geoffrey's sisters."

"I never thought of that. What a wonderful idea!" Sharon exclaims.

"I was joking, dearest. I think you need to leave Lu and Romaine alone and focus your attention on the wedding at hand."

Shaking her head, his wife says, "That's not going to happen. Lu wants a baby and I want that child's father to be a part of her life. She deserves to have her dreams come true."

"Life doesn't always have a storybook ending," her husband says. "Which doesn't mean Lu can't still have a very happy life."

Ignoring his comment, Sharon says, "Won't it be fun to spend time here once Claire and Geoffrey are married?"

"Spending time with you is fun anywhere." Phillipe kisses his wife on the cheek before slapping her on the butt. "Now, let's get you back inside, or you're going to be late for your meeting with the queen."

Lutéce

We've been offered all sorts of entertainment today—tours, horseback riding, and cricket, to name a few—but I've opted to spend the day alone walking around the capital city. It's no London or Paris, but it's still delightful. According to the sign welcoming you when you enter the town square, only twenty-five thousand people call it home.

Walking into the first bakery I pass, I buy myself a hot chocolate and a croissant. Then I sit at an outdoor table to enjoy my treat when I hear a telltale ping. Pulling my phone out of my purse, I see a message from my mother.

> *Busybody: Lu, where are you? Claire and I are meeting with Queen Charlotte in the drawing room. I thought you were going to join us.*
>
> *Me: I decided to walk into town and check out the*

local hot spots.

Busybody: What local hot spots? Are you at a bar or something?

Me: Strip club. You wouldn't believe all the hot Malquarian men shaking their man business up on the stage.

Busybody: …

Busybody: …

Busybody: …

Me: Relax, I'm just kidding. I'm having a cup of hot chocolate and a pastry while watching old ladies feed pigeons by a fountain.

Busybody: How boring. You'd have a much better time here at the palace. I'm sure that Andrew or Alistair would be happy to show you around.

Me: Turning my phone off now, Mom.

Busybody: …

And click. Phone off. It's not hard to imagine me as one of these old gals someday, wandering off to a fountain to feed pigeons. It's sad and sweet at the same time. I'm about to join them and give the birds part of my croissant when I see something across the square that causes my heart to swell.

A man is twirling his little girl around and around under a large shade tree. The ancient stones of the courtyard are dappled with sunlight breaking through the overhead covering. The whole scene is remarkably captivating, and I can't seem to look away.

I can't hear what they're saying, but the little girl throws her head back and laughs when her father gives her one last spin before bowing down in front of her. I used to dance with my dad just like that.

The little girl curtsies before walking into the medieval-looking building next to them. The man turns around and heads in my direction. He's practically upon me before I realize I know him. It's Alistair.

I hurry to lower my eyes, hoping he doesn't recognize me, but I'm not fast enough. He lifts his hand and waves in a tentative fashion like he doesn't know whether his greeting will be well-received. "Lutéce, good morning."

"Alistair." I can't think of anything else to say. Was that Alistair's daughter? If so, where is her mother? Is he still involved with her?

"Are you enjoying our little town?" he asks.

"I've just gotten here, but so far, I can highly recommend the hot chocolate." Like he needs my recommendation.

"Yes, Julia makes wonderful chocolate. Would you like some company, or are my sisters joining you?" He lifts his eyebrow in a supercilious way.

This man is so arrogant and full of himself, I want to knock him down a peg. "I'm alone, by choice." Put that in your pipe, Alistair. I don't want you here.

"Well then," he pulls out the chair across the table from me and sits down, "I'll join you."

I jump to my feet and say, "I was just finishing up."

"Lutéce, sit down." His tone is forceful.

I don't want to sit down, and I'm sure as heck not going to do it because he commanded me to. But when he quietly adds, "please," my knees weaken, and I sort of collapse back onto my chair. "I'm not your enemy," he says.

"I never said you were." I sound bratty, even to my own ears.

"Yes, but you treat me like a wad of chewing gum on the bottom of your shoe, and I can't figure out why."

"You mean because I'm not falling down at your feet in awe that you're a prince?" Heat-infused anger burns my cheeks.

"I don't know what I've done that has caused you to dislike me so much. I certainly don't require that you worship me, but as your future brother-in-law, one might think there would be some familial kindness in you somewhere."

"You're not my future brother-in-law, Geoffrey is."

"But Geoffrey is my brother, so that must make us …" He picks a piece off the corner of my croissant and puts it into his mouth.

I'm totally captivated as I watch the morsel pass his full lips and land on his tongue. "That makes us nothing," I assure him while trying to force myself out of my trance.

"Would you feel better if I told you that I have no romantic interest in you? I just want to be friendly and get to know you in the vein of a distant relation." Oddly, that doesn't make me feel better.

"You're very flirtatious for someone who claims to only have friendly intentions." I sound like a Victorian maiden on the verge of having the vapors.

"I'm a friendly man, Lutéce. I'm also a fairly bright one. I promise to take your lack of interest to heart. But just because you aren't interested in a wild, passionate affair doesn't mean that we can't be cordial. Wouldn't you agree?"

My brain jumps straight to an image of having a wild, passionate affair with Alistair. My mouth goes as dry as the Sahara. "I… I… that is to say… I…" I have no idea what to say.

"Why don't you let me show you around a bit. I promise I won't do or say anything the least bit untoward." A wave of something like disappointment washes over me.

Well, damn, now what do I do? If I say no, I'll look petulant and prissy, not that I should care. "I suppose that would be okay," I finally manage.

"Why don't we start with the fountain?" He stands and offers me his hand. I take it, but only as a support while I get on my feet, then I drop it like a hot potato.

As we walk across the cobble stones, Alistair announces, "This fountain was built over two hundred years ago by King Charles. It was to honor his great love of birds."

Said fountain resembles a giant three-tiered bird bath with stone birds perched all around the perimeter. "It's very nice," I somehow utter without my throat closing on me. Alistair is standing so close our shoulders are touching, and I'm left once again trying to exorcize the image of a passionate affair with the man.

"I used to come here with my siblings, and we'd take our shoes off and wade in the water. Do you want to try it?"

"Is that even allowed?"

He winks at me while kicking off his loafers. When he bends down to roll up his pant legs, I look around, expecting a police officer to blow a whistle. After his mission is accomplished,

Alistair stands up and walks barefoot the few feet to the fountain, then he gets in. "Come on!" he calls out.

I want to, I really do, but I don't want him to think it means anything. As though reading my mind, he adds, "It will just be two future non-relations cooling their toes. Nothing more."

Kicking off my flats and leaving them next to his shoes, I tentatively join him. One toe in confirms the water is icy cold and very refreshing. But when my foot hits the bottom, it nearly slides out from under me due to all the coins that have been tossed in the water. "What are the coins used for?" I ask as he reaches out to help steady me.

With his hands around my waist, he says, "The sisters at the abbey collect them once a year and use them to purchase Christmas presents for those in need."

"That's lovely," I say, pulling away from him and almost falling again. "I think I'll just sit on the edge."

His eyes twinkle in a way that causes my stomach to react in something I call the roller coaster effect. "It takes great skill and technique to run in a fountain full of coins." He takes one slow step, steadies himself, then slowly picks up speed until he's full on splashing around in a circle. The whole scene looks as ridiculous as it does enticing. I can't help the laughter that bursts out of me.

"Hey now, you there, shoo!" the old lady calls out. "You're scaring the birds away."

Alistair stops running and replies, "I'm terribly sorry, madam."

"You should be. All you kids think about is your own fun, but you never stop to consider the birds." Her arms are crossed in front of her like a genie about to nod her head and make him disappear. I wonder if she knows who he is.

"My family has a great love of birds," he tells her.

"Your ancestors did, but you lot have been scaring these poor creatures away since you were wee ones." *Ah, so she does know him.* I like how she doesn't treat him with deference.

Alistair bows his head. "You have my most humble apology."

"Psh, I don't need your pretty manners. I need you to get out of that fountain and quit disturbing my friends."

As he follows her orders, I cannot help but tease, "I don't think she's a fan of yours."

He winks before answering, "You should get her phone number. The two of you could have hours of fun sharing your many reasons for disliking me."

And while the truth is that I want to dislike Alistair very much, I can't help but find him charming at the same time.

No good can come from this.

Chapter Fourteen

Queen Charlotte

"Andrew and Alistair both seem to enjoy Lutéce's company," the queen says while passing her guest a tray of bite-size tarts.

"I was telling my husband the same thing just last night." The corners of Sharon's mouth turn up in a smile before she adds, "He told me to mind my own business."

"Alfred told me the same thing. What do you say we ignore them?" Queen Charlotte pours a cup of tea and hands it across the small coffee table.

"I never take bad advice. Do you have a strategy in mind?"

Stirring a spoonful of sugar into her cup, the queen answers, "As Andrew is the future king, he should really marry a woman from our country. For that reason alone, I suggest we set our sights on Alistair."

"I don't think Lutéce likes him very much." Then with a laugh, Sharon declares, "Which actually makes him perfect for her."

"How so?"

"Lu has a long history of claiming to dislike men she's really drawn to. It goes back to Tommy Langham in the eighth grade.

She spent all year claiming he was the stupidest, vainest boy in the whole school. Then Tommy asked her friend to their promotion dance and Lu spent the whole summer crying over it."

"If what you're saying is true, then I think it's safe to assume Lutéce is more drawn to Alistair than Andrew," the queen replies.

"Now, all we have to do is figure out how to get her to admit that what she's feeling is attraction and not annoyance. Any ideas?"

With her eyes shining brightly, Charlotte declares, "Oh, I have ideas."

Alistair

After getting kicked out of the fountain, I sit down on a bench next to Lutéce to let my feet dry before putting my shoes back on. "That same old gal has been feeding the birds here for as long as I can remember."

"Ah, so this wasn't your first rodeo with her, huh?"

"I've never heard that saying before, but I'm hoping I'm not the bull in your scenario." I love American colloquialisms. Even though they rarely make sense, they're always colorful. My favorite is when they say something is a piece of cake. As there's often no cake involved, I finally had to break down and do an internet search to discover its true meaning.

"What I meant is that she's obviously kicked you out of the fountain before."

"Ah, yes, several times. I've never seen her here with another

86

person. I wonder if she regards the birds as her family."

"How sad." Lutéce's brow furrows.

"Not if you like birds," I tell her.

"I meant, how sad that she doesn't have anyone else."

"Again, not if she actually enjoys birds more than people." I seem to be missing her point.

We both sit quietly for several moments, when my companion finally says, "I sometimes worry about winding up alone." She seems to regret the comment immediately because she jumps to her feet. "I think I'll head back to the palace now."

"Nonsense," I say while putting my loafers back on. "You've never been to Malquar before, and there are several sites you should see."

"I don't want to take up all of your time," she says, clearly hoping I'll let her go.

"I have nothing on my schedule for the rest of the day."

"Other than visiting your daughter, you mean." *What is she talking about?*

"What daughter?"

"The little girl you were dancing with across the courtyard." She points in the direction of the abbey.

"That wasn't my daughter, that was Millicent." Does Lutéce think I've fathered children outside of wedlock? What kind of cad does she take me for?

"Who is Millicent?"

"She's one of the orphans at Shepherd's Home. I'm their sponsor."

"You sponsor an orphanage?" She sounds genuinely surprised, which once again offends.

"Why is that such a hard thing for you to believe?"

"It just doesn't fit my impression of you is all," she says bluntly. Too bluntly.

"What *is* your impression of me, Lutéce?" I demand.

"You're rather arrogant."

"Don't hold back," I snap. "You've met me twice, and in that vast amount of time, arrogant is the only adjective you've come up with?"

"No. I also think you're overly flirtatious and stuck-up."

Why am I bothering spending time with this woman? "First of all, arrogant and stuck-up are the same thing. As far as overly flirtatious, I can see why you don't have a man in your life."

"What a horrible thing to say."

"Why? Men are generally flirtatious with women they find attractive. If you think that's a bad quality, then clearly you're not interested in men." A light turns on in my brain and I chuckle. "Why didn't I see it before? You're not interested in men at all are you?" Before she can answer, I decide, "You're a lesbian."

"I'm not a lesbian." She rolls her eyes like that's outside the realm of possibility. "Just because a woman doesn't fall at your feet doesn't mean she's gay."

"I've got nothing against gay people, which you must clearly know as you were at my sister's wedding to her wife."

"I'm *not* a lesbian, you ass!" she yells loudly enough that the old ladies are now staring at us and not at the pigeons pecking at their feet.

"Whatever you need to tell yourself." In truth, I believe her, but I'm still smarting from her blatant disregard. It's not like I'm a hardened criminal who has done something atrocious like put pineapple on pizza.

"I'm going to get going." Lutéce turns on her heel and walks away.

"Fine!" I yell after her. "I don't want to spend any more time with you, either." I sound like a child in a full pout, but I can't help it. This woman brings out the absolute worst in me.

My tantrum has drawn more than the old ladies' attention. Three university-age girls who are sitting at a nearby table jump up and practically sprint in my direction. One of them asks, "Are you Prince Alistair?"

Before I can answer, another wants to know, "Can I get your autograph?"

"I would be delighted to give you my autograph," I tell them. Then, horror of horrors, I call out, "Did you hear that, Lutéce? These beautiful young ladies don't seem to dislike me. They want my autograph!" Even as I yell this, I realize how juvenile I sound.

Lutéce doesn't look back. She just walks away like I'm nothing more than a pesky fly. A smart man would take the hint and give up trying to prove his worth to an unappreciative audience.

Unfortunately, my mind seems to have gone on holiday.

Chapter Fifteen

Sharon

"Which dress are you wearing to the ball tonight, sugar?" Sharon asks her daughter after walking into her room without knocking.

"I'm not going," Lutéce replies hotly.

"Of course, you're going. Tonight is Claire and Geoffrey's official engagement announcement."

"No one is going to care whether or not I'm there."

"Claire will care," Sharon says as she walks to the wardrobe and opens the ornate doors. Pulling out a long, whispery, pink gown, she says, "This is beautiful! You have to wear this."

"Mother, I don't want to go. I have a headache." Lutéce makes a show of rubbing her temples.

"Liar, liar, pants on fire," Sharon says. "We came all this way to support your sister, and that's exactly what we're going to do. Now, you'd better get moving, you only have an hour." With that, she storms out of the room, leaving her daughter to get ready.

Hurrying down the hall, Sharon runs into Charlotte. "Lutéce is threatening not to come down for the ball."

The queen claps her hands together. "How wonderful!"

"How is that wonderful?"

"I just got a call from Alistair. He claims he's not up to coming tonight, either."

"How is that good news?" Sharon asks.

"If they're both refusing to show up, something must have happened between them today to make them mad." She adds, "I know for certain that Alistair was in town today, and you said Lutéce was as well. They must have run into each other."

Shaking her head, Sharon says, "What if they really don't like each other?"

"Nonsense," the queen replies. "My maternal instinct says that there's something there. We just need to keep throwing them into each other's path. Trust me."

"Oh, I trust you. I'm just afraid my daughter is beyond help. The girl is thirty-six years old, and the closest she's ever come to an altar is standing up for her girlfriends."

"Don't you worry about a thing, Sharon. I told you I have a plan and tonight we officially launch phase one."

Lutéce

I am not going to raise my children on fairy tales where the heroine needs saving. And I will not have my daughter dreaming of growing up to marry a prince—not when there are princes like Alistair out there.

The man is an egomaniac. Who brags about someone wanting their autograph? Who cares?

Fine, I care. I can't get the image of him dancing with that little girl out of my head. An orphan? My right ovary does a triple

91

back flip. I mentally try to tell myself that it's just the hormone injections making me hyper-responsive to Mr. Tall, Dark, and Charismatic.

Make that Prince Tall, Dark, and Charismatic. And there goes my left ovary.

I turn on my curling iron to add some loose waves to my hair before putting on my dress. I know I said I wasn't going tonight, but I'm secretly looking forward to seeing Alistair again, if for no other reason than to ignore him. That man needs to be brought down a peg or two, and I want to be the one to do that.

The next knock on my door is from Alistair's sister, Aubrey. She looks stunning in her Grecian-style burgundy dress. It makes me wish I'd been more daring in my color choice and style, but there's nothing I can do about that now.

"You look gorgeous!" Bree announces before pushing her way into my room.

"Thank you. You look quite beautiful yourself."

"I wanted to warn you that tonight is going to be a bit wild."

"How so?" I am not in the mood for anything wild.

"Most people we know haven't seen Geoffrey in several years, and now he's coming home with an American fiancée. That's going to create quite a fuss. Then there's the fact that your aunt is Tooty Jackson. Finally, these affairs are always packed with women, young and old, always making a big to-do over Andrew and Alistair."

"It sounds like a nightmare," I tell her honestly before asking, "Don't the men always make a big deal over you and Sophie?"

"Men by their nature feel like they have the upper hand, so while my sister and I rarely have a free dance, our partners still seem to act like they're God's gift to womankind."

Taking one last look in the mirror, I give my suddenly-pallid cheeks a quick pinch, and say, "We might as well get it over with then."

Walking through the palace halls at night feels like floating through a dream. I'm not sure my feet are even touching the ground as we head toward our destination. A small crowd of family members are gathered by a set of double doors up ahead. "Why is everyone standing around?" I ask.

"We're in line to be presented," Bree tells me.

"I thought that was a Hollywood thing."

"I wish. The ritual gets old, but it's been performed since the dawn of time, so of course, we still do it."

As we approach, Andrew bows his head and greets us. "Lutéce, Bree, you both look lovely tonight."

He looks pretty darn good himself. I love the sight of men in formal wear. "Thank you," I tell him. "You look quite dashing yourself." I feel like I've landed in a Jane Austen movie. I wonder if I'm expected to curtsy or something.

"Who are you walking in with?" Bree asks her brother.

He nods his head toward a man standing by the door with a clipboard. "According to Jenkins, I'm escorting you, sister."

Bree says, "Jenkins will stand by the door and announce us in pairs. The order is according to royal status, so they'll probably start with you. They always finish with the king and queen."

Great, I'm the least-important person here. That never gets old. "Who am I walking in with?"

Neither Andrew nor Bree knows. "Let's go check," Bree says. Jenkins is so stiff I'm willing to bet his underwear is starched.

"Jenkins, this is Lutéce Choate," she says before asking, "Can you tell us who she's being escorted by?"

He consults his chart. "I have her going in with her parents."

Seriously? Am I five? "I'd prefer to walk in by myself," I tell him.

"Madam," Jenkins's tone oozes condescension, "I don't make the list. I just carry out my orders." He turns away dismissively.

"Maybe you can walk in with Alistair," Bree suggests. "Although, he's second in line, so I'm not sure that would be allowed, either."

"I'd rather lick the floor after the dogs come in," I grumble under my breath.

Bree shoots me a startled side-eye which makes me think I said that too loudly. Then, speak of the devil, Alistair joins us. "Bree," he says, his chiseled face full of warmth. When he looks at me, his expression goes dead. "Miss Choate." The small military bow he adds makes it seem like this is our first meeting. Also, that he can't stand the sight of me.

Darn, I probably should have curtsied to Prince Andrew.

"*Prince* Alistair," I reply, putting the emphasis on the title he's so proud of.

"Alistair, Lutéce is scheduled to walk in with her parents. Is there any chance you could escort her?" Bree suggests.

"I'm sure Miss Choate would rather make her entrance sliding down a greased banister than at my side." He inclines his head once again and walks away. Ouch. While his statement is one hundred percent accurate, no one likes to be dismissed so summarily.

"Did I miss something?" Bree asks. "Last night at supper I

could have sworn Alistair was taken with you."

"Your brother is taken with himself. I don't think there's room for anyone else." I shouldn't be saying mean things about him to her, but I can't seem to help myself.

"You've got him all wrong. Alistair is the fun one out of the bunch of us. He's always surrounded by a bevy of friends and admirers."

"I'm sure." Sarcasm positively oozes out of me. He's probably surrounded by sycophant social climbers. No wonder he's so annoyed that I don't bow down and worship at his feet.

Jenkins starts to mill about getting us lined up. As previously stated, the least important are first.

I stand first in front of the double doors with my parents behind me. My mom says, "Isn't this fun? Tooty and I got announced the last time we were here when she performed for the court. I wish we did this at home."

"Could you imagine?" I ask in horror.

"You look beautiful tonight, hon. That pink really sets off the red highlights in your hair. You're going to be quite a hit."

Before I can tell her how uninterested I am in such an outcome, Jenkins and another liveried palace worker open the doors. I'm practically pushed through and barely have time to take in the scene below. I didn't realize I'd have to walk down such a long staircase with hundreds of pairs of eyes staring at me. I should have worn flats. I briefly wonder if anyone would notice if I kicked my shoes off.

"Miss Lutéce Choate and her parents, Phillipe and Sharon Choate," Jenkins practically yells.

I'm supposed to walk down first with my parents behind me.

An inner litany starts in my head. "Do not do a nosedive, Lu. Take it one step at a time. Do not fall. Do not slip ..." As I put a foot on the first step, I try not to think about how lightheaded I feel.

I hear my mom encourage, "Let's go, Lu. You've got this."

I do not have this. I want to run screaming in the opposite direction of this whole ordeal. I'm full on deer-in-the-headlights immobile when I feel a presence at my side. It's my dad. "I've got you, honey. Just follow my lead." I'm so grateful for him right now I could cry. Imagining how that would add to the first impression I will make causes me to almost laugh. Dear God, I'm becoming hysterical.

I'm so focused on not falling over that I don't hear the rest of the party being introduced behind me. By the time my dad leads me to an empty space at the edge of the ballroom, the king and queen are the only ones left.

"Their Royal Highnesses King Alfred and Queen Charlotte," Jenkins booms even louder than he did for the rest of us. Either that or the room is much quieter in deference to their sovereigns. Regardless, I'm so relieved to be out of the spotlight I could cheer.

That is, until I hear a man behind me say, "I'd tell you how beautiful you look tonight, if I weren't so sure it would go to your head."

Chapter Sixteen

Queen Charlotte

"So, what's your plan?" Sharon asks the queen after being introduced to the royal's inner circle—a process that takes a good hour.

"I'm going to throw them together as often as possible."

"No offense, but that doesn't sound like much of a plan," Sharon replies.

"That's just the first part." The queen winks before saying, "But it starts now." She signals her butler, Jenkins, who approaches the band leader. The current waltz ends prematurely.

"Ladies and gentlemen," Jenkins announces, "the next dance is for the royal family and their guests of honor only. If you will please leave the dance floor." The crowd forms a circle around their hosts.

King Alfred approaches Sharon with a bow as Phillipe and the queen pair off. Tooty is escorted by Andrew; and Geoffrey and Claire are matched. As Sophie and Aubrey don't have official escorts, they stand to the side.

By the time the violins start the first strains of Chopin's "Minute Waltz," the only ones who haven't shown up are Alistair and Lutéce.

Alistair

"I don't suppose you would do me the honor of dancing with me?" I practically purr in Lutéce's ear. More than anything I want to stick to my plan to ignore her, but she pulls me in like we're connected by an invisible string.

"I'd rather not," she says, her tone every bit as harsh as expected.

Slipping my arm under hers, I practically drag her alongside me. "Unfortunately for you, this dance is a royal mandate, and I have to partner with someone from our party."

"Alistair …" Lutéce hisses. "I'm not going to dance with you."

I feel the eyes of everyone on us as we pass. "You'd rather make a scene?" I tighten my grip slightly, so she can't easily pull away.

As we approach a break in the crowd, I hear her panicky declaration, "I don't know how to waltz."

Turning her so she's in my arms, I lean down and whisper, "Just follow my lead."

"No."

"You really do want to make a scene, don't you?" I ask.

"No, but I will if you try to force me to dance with you. I'm not very good at it, and I don't appreciate your being so high-handed."

I lean closer to her and inhale a hint of jasmine lingering around her neck. "Close your eyes and let yourself go." Feeling her body tense in my arms, I command, "Release your fears,

Lutéce. I have you." And just like that, she practically melts for me.

How can this feisty, hot-headed woman feel so right in my arms? When I'm with her, I want to kiss her and/or spank her. Right now, I want to devour her. As she opens her eyes, it feels like she's looking into my soul. "It's a count of three," I tell her. "Just keep looking at me, and I'll carry you through."

Once our feet start moving— one, two, three, one, two, three—we float in an effortless confluence. I have never felt this drawn to a woman before, and as much as I want to stay away from her, I don't think I can.

"You're very beautiful," I tell her before I can stop myself.

"Aren't you afraid your compliment will go to my head?" she asks playfully.

"Terribly. But I find I'm hard-pressed to keep my opinion to myself."

"Why do you suppose that is?" She smiles almost wickedly. Are we flirting here? Because I think we're flirting.

"Maybe it's your exotic Americanness."

She laughs out loud in response. "I've never heard of Americans described as exotic before."

"Oh, but you are. You all seem to be so outgoing and sure of yourselves. Most of Europe is in awe of your ability to command the attention of a room just by walking into it."

"Now I know you're teasing. Americans may appear brash, Alistair, but we're simply enthusiastic."

"Perhaps you're correct. You have certainly taken to the waltz with great enthusiasm." I pull her closer into my embrace.

"I'm scared spitless, and the only reason I haven't fallen over is because you're holding me up."

With those words, I pull her toward me until our bodies are practically touching. Relishing the feel of her in my arms, I try to ignore the tap on my shoulder. Unfortunately, protocol dictates that we change partners at least once during the royal waltz.

Andrew steps between Lutéce and me while I reluctantly turn toward her aunt Tooty. "You and Lu sure do look good together," the country music star tells me.

"Your niece is very lovely."

"It's surprising she doesn't have a boyfriend, isn't it?"

"Not really. As pretty as she is, she has a sharp tongue. I'm not sure most men could handle that." No sense in beating around the bush.

"It's a defense mechanism," she says. "Lu has dated some real losers and she's afraid to let anyone else in."

"What was wrong with them?" I fight to keep control of the dance as Tooty seems to want to lead. She's seriously strong-arming me around the dance floor.

"They've been a bunch of cheaters. The last one took off with another man."

"Oh, dear." What else can I say? Being cheated on with another woman would be bad enough, but another man? That must be a real ego buster.

"Dating in Los Angeles is hard enough when you're not part of a famous family. That town is full of users who are always looking for a leg up in the business. It can make a girl bitter. I think that's what's happened to Lu."

Well, that information certainly gives me something to think about. Could Lutéce be nicer than I've been led to believe? If so, how do I get her to show her true colors?

After the waltz ends, the lady in question does her best to steer clear of my attention. If I come within ten meters of her, she bolts to the other side of the ballroom.

I decide not to take offense and consider a new strategy. Maybe chasing after Lutéce isn't the way to go. According to her aunt, she's leery of men who pursue her. Perhaps the way to attract her interest is to ignore her, regaling others with my attention and charm.

I feel her eyes on me repeatedly throughout the rest of the night, but I don't so much as offer her a smile. It isn't until the last dance is announced that I seek her out again.

Lutéce is standing with her back toward me while she's talking to my sisters. She practically jumps out of her skin when I lean in and whisper into her ear, "I hope you've saved the last dance for me."

"I … well … no … that is to say …" I love that I can make her so flustered. Before she can further trip over her words, I take her hand and lead her back onto the dance floor where the band has begun to play "Save the Last Dance for Me," a song made popular in the United States in the middle of the last century.

"I didn't say I would dance with you," she says once I spin her around and pull her into my arms.

"You didn't say that you wouldn't, either," I retort.

"Are you really so vain that you think every woman on the planet wants you?" God, I want to kiss her right now and give that mouth of hers something to do other than hurl insults at me.

"I just wanted to dance with the most beautiful lady in the room," I tell her simply. Then I stop moving to the music, but I don't release her. "If the most beautiful lady in the room doesn't want to dance with me, all she has to do is say so."

"I'm not the most beautiful woman here." She's staring right at my throat.

"That, my dear Lutéce, is a matter of opinion. And in *my* opinion, you're positively gorgeous. Not only that, but you're the only one I want to dance with."

"That's a load of crap. You've been dancing with other women all night long." I revel in her jealousy.

"I didn't think you wanted to dance with me," I challenge.

"Then why are we standing here like this?" She gestures without removing her hand from mine.

"Because …"—I lean down so the warmth of my breath can gently caress her neck—"I couldn't resist you any longer."

Her body trembles in my arms as she says, "Please don't toy with me, Alistair."

"I wouldn't dream of it," I tell her honestly.

But instead of continuing our dance together, she pulls out of my grasp and announces, "I'm going to bed."

I watch as she walks away from me and can't help but wonder what the undamaged version of Lutéce Choate is like. I should forget about her and continue my moratorium on relationships.

And I would do that if I weren't so compelled to find out who the lady really is.

Chapter Seventeen

Sharon

"Lu has been acting as jumpy as a bedbug on fresh tar," Sharon tells her sister after finishing what she's decided is the best breakfast of her life. A buffet of delights was the only thing waiting for them when they arrived in the dining room. They've discovered that breakfast is an eat-at-your-own-convenience meal, and both sisters enjoy more than their fill.

"She's out of her element, is all," Tooty says after wiping her mouth on her napkin.

"I think she's afraid of the attraction she feels for Prince Alistair. That man is giving her a run for her money."

"How do you figure she's attracted to him? As far as I can tell, she runs in the opposite direction every time he's around." Tooty pushes her chair away from the dining room table.

"*That's* how I can tell," Sharon replies, standing up. "Lu is practically a professional at running from her feelings."

"You might be right, but what good can come of a flirtation between the two of them? Lu lives across the world from Alistair."

"Everything is working out for Claire and Geoffrey, isn't it?"

Sharon retaliates as they make their way out of the dining room.

"Well, sure, but they work together so they had a chance to really get to know each other. Their situation is totally different."

"The queen told me that her daughters invited Lu to stay on after this week. If she accepts, then they'll have a chance to get to know each other better."

"Why would she accept?" Tooty demands.

"Because I'm going to make the thought of going home sound so horrible that staying here will seem like her best option."

A small smile starts at the corners of Tooty's mouth before turning into a full-blown grin. "How are you going to do that?"

"Watch this," Sharon answers when she spots her daughter heading in their direction.

Lutéce

"Is there any breakfast left?" I ask my mother and aunt as I hurry toward the dining room.

"We were just going in to find out," my mom answers.

"No, you weren't. You were just walking out."

My mom totally ignores my comment and grabs a hold of my arm. "Lu, I have the best news!" Prickles of fear pop up all over my body, and I release an involuntary shiver. The last time she had the "best" news, she had decided to learn how to fly a jet. I really don't need anything else to worry about right now.

"What's your good news?" I ask, even though I'm afraid to hear it.

"I've decided that as soon as we get home, I'm going to move into your house with you." Her smile is so big, she looks like the

Cheshire cat from *Alice in Wonderland*. It's creepy.

Tooty releases a short bark of laughter before announcing, "I think I'll go lie down for a bit."

As my aunt walks away, I demand, "Why in the world would you move in with me?" There's no hiding my horror at the idea of cohabiting with my mother. I've been there, done that, and have no intention of repeating the experience. Ever.

"I want to take care of you. I can make you healthy meals to prepare your body for pregnancy. I can make sure that you get out every day for a long walk to calm your mind, and I can help you turn your spare room into a nursery." She nods her head once with the conviction of a drill sergeant.

"Yeah, no." Her hurt expression has me adding, "What I mean is, no. No." I'm shaking my head so vigorously I'm getting seasick.

"You need your mother, and I'm not about to desert you in your time of need."

Taking a plate off the sideboard, I begin to fill it with everything in sight. I'd weigh five hundred pounds if I lived here. "You don't even think I should get pregnant," I remind her. *I wonder if it would look too gluttonous if I put three chocolate croissants on my plate.*

"Not the way you're planning to. But you've made up your mind, so I've decided to support you fully."

"What about Dad?" I want to know. "He's not going to be thrilled if you leave your house to move in with me."

"Your father travels so much for work, he won't even know I'm gone," she says brightly.

"No, Mom. Just, no. You cannot move in with me."

Ignoring me, she says, "I was thinking a nice sage green in the nursery. That can be either feminine or masculine, depending on the accessories we choose. Oh, and we should really start looking for gliders. I just loved the one I had when I was nursing you kids."

"I'm not opposed to going shopping with you once or twice," I tell her, "But there is no need for you to move in with me."

"I'm still going to do it. A girl needs her mother at a time like this, and I will not abandon you, Lu. I will be by your side, night and day, until you safely deliver my grandchild." Suddenly I'm not hungry at all.

I don't doubt for a minute she's going to do exactly as she's threatened. I can keep telling her until I'm blue in the face that she's not welcome, but I know my mother and I know she'll totally disregard my wishes.

Before I can further try to disabuse her of the absurd notion that I need her constant companionship, Sophie walks into the dining room. She looks every ounce like the princess in her elegant cashmere dress and low heels. I look like a peasant in my yoga pants and hoodie.

"Good morning," she greets us. "I hope you both slept well." She picks up her own plate to fill.

"I slept wonderfully!" my mom answers like she was just offered a free kitten. I simply jab a forkful of eggs into my mouth.

"Lu, I'm meeting Bree over at her house after breakfast if you'd like to join me. We were going to start discussing the bridal shower," Sophie announces.

"Yeah, sure. That would be nice." Mud wrestling an elephant would be nice too, if it got me away from my mother.

"Lu," my mom says while patting my hand, "I think you'd better have yourself a little nap first. You need to take care of your body."

"I'm fine, Mom."

"No, dear, as your caretaker, I really think it would be best for you to have a rest." OMG, she's treating me like an invalid.

"I don't need a caretaker, Mom." Take the hint already, woman.

"You do, which is why I'm moving in with you, no matter what you say. A mother knows when she's needed. You'll find that out soon enough."

"Yes, well, I'm not going home at the same time you are." I haven't really thought this through, but anything would be better than having Hurricane Sharon move into my bungalow with me.

"Have you decided to take me and Bree up on our offer and stay on?" Sophie asks excitedly.

"Yes, I have," I say. Even as I'm agreeing to this, I can't help but think about Alistair. Being around that man will not be good for my nerves.

"But *I* can't stay on!" my mom exclaims. "I need to get home and make sure my Lady Di's are thriving."

"Oh, I love those roses," Sophie says. "They're so fragrant."

"I'll be fine here without you, Mom. Don't worry."

"I suppose ..." She sounds unsure that I can stay alive without her.

"I'll have Sophie and Bree here if I need anything," I assure her.

"We'll take excellent care of Lu," Sophie adds. "In fact, if she ever needs a mother, I'm sure mine will step right in and lend a hand."

"I guess …" My mom doesn't sound convinced. She leans toward me and asks, "What about that thing you were planning to do?" She's referring to my IVF appointment, but I'm not about to bring that up.

"I'll reschedule it for when I'm home," I say.

"So, you're putting it off?" Why do I suddenly feel like I've just stepped into a trap?

"For now."

"Well then, I suppose if you're putting it off, you won't need me. But as soon as you come home, I'm moving in."

If I know my mom at all, and I do, I know she has every intention of making good on her threat. That can only mean one thing. I cannot hurry back to LA.

In fact, Malquar may have just become my new home.

Chapter Eighteen

Queen Charlotte

"I've just talked to Lu, and she's decided to stay in Malquar for a while," Sharon tells the queen.

"How wonderful!" Charlotte claps her hands together excitedly. "How did you do it?"

"I threatened to move in with her when we got home."

Impressed, the queen replies, "You're devious and brilliant at the same time. But of course, as mothers, we have to be."

"You would have done the same thing," Sharon says.

"I don't even let my kids move off the property." Charlotte offers her friend a conspiratorial wink.

"What about Geoffrey?"

"Yes, but he's coming home with his bride. That makes his time away an investment in the future."

"You know, if both of my daughters wind up in Malquar, I might have to consider moving here myself."

"We'd love to have you!" Charlotte says sincerely. "But first we have to get them both here."

"I'm afraid Lu is going to be a bit of a project."

"Sharon, my friend," –the queen pats her hand—"I'm

nothing if not proficient at projects. To quote one of the songs you wrote for Tooty, 'Buckle up buttercup, we're about to have some fun.'"

Alistair

How can I be out of milk for my coffee? It would be one thing if I was the one to keep the refrigerator stocked, but I'm not. Bree and I share a housekeeper who takes care of that domestic task—as well as most others.

I pick up my phone to send my sister a text.

> Me: I'm out of milk.
>
> Bree: Really? I have three gallons in my fridge.
>
> Me: I think perhaps Marguerite gave you all the milk.
>
> Bree: Do you have any yogurt? I seem to be out of that.
>
> Me: Let me look …
>
> Me: I have ten cups of it. What do you say we make a trade?
>
> Bree: Come on over.

I don't bother to brush my hair or change clothes as I'm just walking next door. There is zero chance that anyone will photograph me and make the image look like a walk of shame, or more truthfully, make it look like I've just put another notch in my bedpost. I do grab a robe, though. It's a cool day, and I'm currently bare chested as I only just rolled out of bed.

As I stroll across my lawn toward my sister's house, I can't help but think about last night. I normally loathe formal balls, but last night was different. Lutéce was there and even though we barely spent any time together, I was still completely captivated by her.

I don't bother knocking on Bree's door. I just walk in carrying my sack of bartering goods. "Good morning!" I call out.

"In here, Al," she yells back.

I follow her voice into her living room and stop dead in my tracks when I see the object of my musings sitting on her sofa. Lutéce looks adorable in her soft-looking sweater and yoga pants. "Bree, Lutéce …" I nod my head in greeting.

"What kind of yogurt do you have?" my sister asks.

"It's all honey."

"Marguerite must have gotten our food mixed up. She put two jars of smoked almonds in my pantry."

"Those are definitely mine," I tell her, all the while staring right at her guest. "What are you lovely ladies up to today?"

"We're starting to plan Claire's bridal shower. I don't suppose you want in on that?" I know she's teasing, and I would normally run in the other direction, but I think I'll make an exception.

"Do you have any coffee?" I ask.

"There's a pot of French roast brewing in the kitchen," she says.

"Then sure, I'll join you for a bit." I smile directly at Lutéce, who looks appalled at the very idea.

"I'm sure we'd only bore you," the American says.

"You don't know me very well," I retaliate. "I love a good party, and probably throw more than all of my siblings combined."

She looks perturbed as she responds, "I'm sure you do."

"In fact," I ignore her tone, "I had a wonderful get together on the family boat last week. You ladies might consider using it as your venue."

Bree looks confused before saying, "We always have teas at the palace."

"Who says you have to have a tea?" I ask.

"But that's what we always do," my sister maintains.

"Bree, you've got to step out of your box occasionally. Why don't I take you out later this afternoon? I'm sure I'll have a million wonderful ideas about how you can make Claire's shower stand out above all of the other boring ones you've gone to."

"I don't think I can make it," Lutéce announces rather loudly.

"Really, why?" Bree wants to know.

"I have to … I should … I need to …" she stammers.

"Quit trying to get out of it, Lu." I use her nickname for the first time. "You'd be missing out on the experience of a lifetime."

"Going out onto a boat with you is the experience of a lifetime?" Sarcasm radiates out of her.

"The boat is exceptional," Bree answers before I can reply. "It was built eighty years ago for our great-grandparents."

"Oh, well …"

"It's settled, then. I'll pick you both up here at six. We'll have supper aboard," I announce, before walking in the direction of my sister's kitchen. I can't help the smile that overcomes me. Lu—I decide to use the abbreviated version of her name from now on—definitely does not like that I'll be with them. I have no idea why she's so determined to hate me, but I'm not going to let it bother me.

After putting my sister's yogurt into her refrigerator, I fill a coffee cup and grab the muffin basket sitting on the counter. Then I return to the parlor.

As I near the doorway, I overhear Lu say, "I really don't think I should go tonight."

"You don't get seasick, do you?"

I hug the corner of the wall so I can eavesdrop without being seen. "No," Lu says. "It's just that your brother is an awful flirt, and I'm not interested in him in that way."

"Alistair?" Bree laughs. "He flirts with everyone. You can't take it personally." Well, *that* seems like a rather mean thing to say about me. I don't flirt with everyone. I'm cordial and charming, not flirtatious.

"So, you don't think it means anything?" Is it my imagination, or does Lu sound upset by that realization?

"Don't get me wrong, I'm sure Alistair would be quite amenable to an affair, but I can assure you, he isn't looking for a wife. He'll probably never marry." *Why in the world does she think that?*

"Well, I sure as heck don't want to marry him. I don't want to have an affair with him either," Lu's voice cracks.

"Then, what's the problem? Let's go and enjoy a fun dinner cruise at sunset. I promise you'll have the time of your life."

I forgive my sister for all the aspersions she's cast upon my character when Lu finally agrees, "I guess I'll go."

"Wonderful!" my sister says. "If Alistair becomes too much of a pest, just ignore him and know that it means nothing." How is it that my family doesn't know me any better than this? I continue to be quite shocked by their misconception of who I am.

I walk into the room, determined to say nothing that can be misconstrued as overly friendly. "What should I order for dinner? Shall we go casual or elegant?"

"Let's have American hamburgers," Bree answers. "Not only do I adore them, but that will make Lu feel right at home. What do you say, Lu?"

"That's fine," she practically whispers.

"In that case, I'll let you get on with your morning. I have some things to take care of before this evening. Ladies," I say, offering a small bow before retrieving my milk and heading back to my place.

"I'll bring the dessert," my sister calls out as I leave the room.

I'm determined to change my strategy around Lu tonight. I will not comment on her beauty, I will not whisper sweet nothings into her ear. I will be nothing but ambivalently kind. My God, you'd think the way Lu and my sister talk, that charm is a thing of the past—that gallantry is a bad thing.

From this moment on, I decide I will treat Lu like she's nothing more than another sister. I will ignore any attraction I feel for her. If I do that, she'll have no reason to dislike me.

As vain as it sounds, I ask myself how such an occurrence could even be possible.

Chapter Nineteen

Sharon

"I really need to get going," Bree tells her mother and the queen. "Alistair is taking Lutéce and me out on the boat tonight."

"Really, why?" Charlotte's head pops up in interest.

Putting her teacup down, Bree tells them, "We're thinking about hosting Claire's bridal shower at sea. What do you think of that?"

"What a great idea. Is it just the three of you going?" Sharon wants to know.

"My sister Sophie wanted to come too, but she has another engagement. It was all decided rather last minute."

"What time are you departing?" Charlotte asks.

"Alistair is meeting us at my cottage at six. Would you both like to join us?"

"Oh no, dear. You young people don't need us around," her mother responds before saying, "Plus, Tooty is going to sing for us tonight, and I certainly don't want to miss that."

"Okay then." Bree stands and gives her mother a kiss on the cheek. "I'll see you both tomorrow."

"Have fun tonight," Sharon says before winking at the queen.

As soon as her daughter leaves, Charlotte announces, "This is perfect, don't you think?"

"It's certainly an opportunity for them to spend time together. Although, I don't know how much good that will do with Bree there," Sharon replies.

Charlotte doesn't comment. She just picks up the telephone and makes a call. "Grady, this is Queen Charlotte," she says into the receiver. "I need a favor …"

Lutéce

I cannot believe I got sucked into going on an evening cruise with Alistair tonight. I should have just said that I wasn't feeling well and needed to turn in early. *Why didn't I say that?* At least Bree will be there to act as a buffer.

As it will probably be cool on the ocean at night, I put on a pair of jeans and a cozy pink sweater instead of something more formal. I mean, we're eating burgers. It's not like I'll be underdressed.

I decide to walk over to Bree's cottage from the palace to get a little exercise. I love hiking the canyons back in LA. It's the best way to pretend I'm not living in a perpetually traffic-jammed city.

Fall in Malquar is enchanting. The leaves on the trees are starting to change color and the air is so crisp and clean I doubt they ever have smog alerts like we get at home. I don't know how long I'll stay here—I have over five months left on my sabbatical— but I do know I'll enjoy the break from the hustle and bustle of regular life.

By the time I reach Bree's house, it's five fifty-five. I'm about to knock on her door when I see Alistair crossing the lawn. The hair at the base of my neck bristles. "Hello," he calls out.

"Hello," I reply with the most monotone and uninterested inflection I can manage.

"Is my sister ready?" he asks.

"Don't know. I haven't knocked yet." *Don't look at him, don't look at him, don't look at him*, I chant in my head. Then I look at him, and heaven help me, he looks good. He's wearing jeans too, and a gray sweater that appears to have been knit right on him. I don't have to use much imagination to know how toned his body is underneath. As much as I tell myself I'm not interested, I can't help the waves of attraction I feel.

"Well then, let's knock." He jolts me out of my daze as he pounds on the door.

Bree walks out of her house carrying a picnic basket. "Wait until you see what we're having for dessert," she says.

"Chocolate cake and raspberries," Alistair guesses.

"No," she answers with a shake of her head.

"Panne Cotta and peaches," he tries again.

"No. And I'm not going to tell you so quit guessing.

"Maple crème brûlée with a candied bacon garnish …"

"Alistair, stop it," Bree laughs. "I'm not going to tell you."

I can't help but smile at their exchange. It's clear the royals are a tight-knit family. I have a momentary pang of regret that I don't spend more time with my own siblings. But Romaine is always on the road, and Claire lives in Oregon, so it's not like we have an opportunity for impromptu get-togethers.

"Which car are we taking?" Bree asks her brother.

"I thought you could drive," he says. "We'll be a lot more comfortable in your SUV than in my car."

Bree leads the way to her driveway. "Pile in," she says before getting behind the wheel. Alistair opens the passenger door for me. My stomach clenches as I walk by him and inhale the spicy scent of his aftershave. It smells of oranges and cloves which is my favorite combination. It's all I can do not to lean in to him.

When we arrive at our destination a few short minutes later, my mouth hangs open like an unhinged door. "That's the yacht? It looks like a small cruise ship."

"It has ten bedrooms and twelve bathrooms," she tells me. She says a lot of other things but I'm not listening.

"I should have worn something nicer," I decide.

"Why?" Alistair asks as he gets out of the car and opens my door once again. "I assure you the boat doesn't care what you have on."

I expect a naughty shrug of his eyebrows to accompany his statement but there's no such thing. Instead, he picks up his sister's picnic basket and leads the way to the dock. Following behind him, I can't help but wish he was just an ordinary guy and, you know, he lived in LA. Against my better judgment, I decide that I'd rethink my opinion of him if that were the case. But he doesn't live in LA, and he's so far away from an ordinary guy it isn't even funny.

But at least I know he wouldn't be interested in me for my family connections.

As we near the boat, Alistair raises his hand and waves. "Grady, my friend, are we good to go?"

A tall, strikingly handsome man in a captain's uniform

answers, "Yes, sir, we are."

"You don't have to act formal in front of Lutéce," Alistair tells him before introducing us. "Lu, this is my good friend Grady. Grady, this is Lutéce Choate. Her sister is engaged to Geoffrey."

The captain nods his head. "Welcome aboard, Miss Choate." Then he turns to Bree and adds, "Your Highness, I have a message for you from your mother."

"What is it, Grady?" Bree is much more formal with the captain than her brother is.

"She asked me to give it to you in private."

"Why?" Bree demands. But before Grady can answer, she concedes, "Fine, I'll meet you on the starboard deck in five minutes. I need to take my basket to the kitchen."

Grady raises his hand to another crew member and tells him, "Please take the princess's basket to the galley."

Bree doesn't seem to be pleased about relinquishing her dessert. She snaps, "That was rather high-handed, Grady."

He looks at her with an expression akin to indifference. "Just doing my job, ma'am. The queen was most insistent that I give you her message before we disembark."

"Fine, lead the way to wherever you're going to tell me this mysterious message." Bree trails behind the captain rather haughtily.

When they're out of earshot, I say, "I don't think your sister likes the captain very much."

"They have quite a history," Alistair replies.

"Really?" This sounds like an interesting story.

"Grady's dad used to be my father's secretary before he retired. Hence, he grew up practically living at the palace with us. He's like another sibling."

"Your sister doesn't seem to think so," I say.

"Bree used to have the biggest crush on Grady and would follow him around everywhere he went," Alistair says with a laugh.

"Did they ever date?" Because if they had and it didn't go well, that would explain her antipathy toward the captain.

"They did not." Alistair leads the way up a short flight of stairs to the first deck. "Not because my sister didn't want to, mind you." He explains, "Grady is very proper and has always felt that his station is too far below hers for anything of a personal nature to occur between them."

"Does he *want* to date her?" I ask, knowing this isn't any of my business, but still wanting to hear the answer.

"Grady has always had a soft spot for Bree. It wouldn't surprise me if he had feelings for her."

"But he's never said so?" I push.

"For someone who dislikes being flirted with, you certainly seem to be interested in other people's romances," he says.

I feel myself blush. "It's not that I don't like to be flirted with. I just don't want to be toyed with. There is a difference," I tell him.

"Who's toyed with you? Because if you're talking about me, I did nothing more than appreciate a beautiful woman. But now that I know how distasteful you find me, I promise to keep all my future opinions to myself. How does that sound?"

"That sounds fine," I say, even though I'm inexplicably filled with disappointment at the very idea. I don't find Alistair distasteful; I just can't let myself fall for one more unavailable man.

Alistair leads me over to a loveseat which is facing the sunset. "Why don't you sit down, and I'll get us something to drink. How does champagne sound?"

"That would be fine, thank you," I tell him primly.

As he walks away, the yacht starts to pull away from the dock. I can't suppress the rush of excitement that flows through me. This is a beautiful boat, and I'm lucky to be here. Staring out as the first pink starts to creep up into the horizon, I am determined to have a good time tonight, regardless of who I'm here with. Plus, it's not like Alistair and I are alone. Bree is with us. She'll be a great buffer for any tension.

Alistair comes back with two champagne flutes. He hands me one before toasting, "To a lovely evening." Instead of sitting next to me, which I assumed he would do, he sits down on a chair adjacent to me. He proceeds to watch the sunset silently.

Part of me wants to say something to fill the air around us, but I don't know what that would be. I'm saved from uttering something stupid when Grady joins us.

"Would you like to sit down and have a drink with us?" Alistair asks him.

"No, thank you. I just wanted to tell you that Princess Aubrey had to leave the boat and she won't be able to join you for supper, after all."

"What?!" I practically scream. I can't be trapped here alone with Alistair.

"The queen needed her to return home," Grady says.

"I hope nothing is wrong," Alistair says.

"I'm sure everything is fine," the captain responds as a hint of grin crosses his lips.

I look out toward the dock and see Bree waving wildly at us. I return the wave while simultaneously surmising that she doesn't look very happy about being left behind. "Bree doesn't look very pleased," I say out loud.

"She's probably not, but I assure you," Grady replies, "I'm just following the queen's orders."

Chapter Twenty

Queen Charlotte

"Grady said you had a message for me and that it would be delivered on the dock," Bree tells her mother heatedly. "Then he drove off without me!"

"Really, a message from me?" Charlotte asks before saying, "I can't imagine."

"So, you didn't request that I be left behind?"

"Darling, why would I do that? I know how much you were looking forward to tonight's cruise."

"What is wrong with that man?" Bree demands with her hands on her hips. "I want him fired."

"I'm not going to fire Grady because of some little misunderstanding," the queen tells her daughter.

"Why not? You could find ten captains to take his place by tomorrow morning."

"Grady is like family, dear. I'm sure there's a very logical explanation for what happened."

"I doubt it," Bree tells her mother. "He just doesn't like me, and he didn't want me around."

"That's ridiculous. Grady thinks of you like a little sister."

The queen doesn't seem to notice the look of disappointment that crosses her daughter's face. She adds, "I know how much you've always liked him, so I'm sure you can find it in your heart to forgive him."

"I do *not* like him!" Bree snaps. "Why would you say that?"

"Don't be ridiculous, Aubrey. You followed that boy around like he was the Pied Piper through your entire childhood. Of course, you like him."

"Maybe I used to, but not anymore."

"I don't really have time to get into this now," the queen tells her daughter before asking, "Why don't you join us for supper?"

"No, thank you," Bree replies. "I don't think I'd be very good company tonight."

The queen shakes her head as her daughter storms out of her chambers. She mumbles, "What a mother won't do for her children. But just you wait, young lady. I've got plans for you, as well."

Alistair

As I've been warned away from any sort of liaison with Lutéce, I have no idea why my mother would entice my sister off the ship. I know one thing, though. Bree did not appear too happy being left behind.

"We'll eat our supper out here," I tell the bosun, who acts as the boat's butler.

"Maybe we should go back," Lu suggests with a note of panic in her voice. Who does she think I am, the Big Bad Wolf?

"My dear Miss Choate, Lu," I tell her, "I quite love being out on the water, and I see no reason why we shouldn't enjoy ourselves even though my sister isn't present."

"What will we do?"

"We'll do exactly what we'd planned to do when we thought Bree was joining us."

"You're going to help me plan my sister's bridal shower?"

"Well, no," I tell her. "But we can still have dinner and maybe then we'll play backgammon or something."

"I don't know how to play."

"I could teach you." My God, I'm starting to get the feeling she'd rather jump ship and swim through shark infested waters than spend any time with me. It quite crushes a bloke's ego.

"How long do you think we'll be out here?" she demands.

"I've instructed Grady to circle around once we reach the old lighthouse up the coast. We should be gone for about four hours." My companion looks horrified by the news. "Lu," I tell her, "I'm not going to molest you. I've quite taken the hint that you aren't interested in me, and I assure you, I'm no glutton for punishment. With that said, do you suppose there's a way we can simply enjoy the night without any weirdness?"

Her head bobs up and down and then side to side undecidedly. She looks like she's having a stroke. "Yes. Fine. Sure. As long as you know that I'm not looking to be romanced."

"Perish the thought," I tease. "Now, what would you like on your burger?" I signal the waiter standing nearby.

"I'll have whatever you're having," she replies.

"You know the way I like it, Thomas."

When the waiter walks away, Lu asks, "Do you come out here often?"

"At least twice a week. I feel like a different me when I'm on the water." *Now why would I go telling her something as personal as that?*

"How so?"

Shrugging my shoulders, I answer, "I can be myself without having to worry how others perceive me. The ocean doesn't care how royal my blood is. It doesn't expect me to be impressive."

Lu doesn't respond right away. Instead, she seems to drift off into her own thoughts for several moments. When she breaks the silence, it's to ask, "How old are you?"

"Thirty-two," I tell her, wondering at the oddity of her question.

"I'm thirty-six."

What am I supposed to say to that? If I go with, "You look great for your age," she might take it that I'm calling her old and no woman appreciates that. I decide not commenting is the best course of action.

"Men in Los Angeles tend to shy away from women my age because of our biological clocks."

"Really?"

"They don't want to feel pressured to have children right away, and let's face it, if a woman wants to have a baby, her window of opportunity is closing by the time she's in her mid-thirties."

"Do you want to have a baby?" I ask her.

"Very much." Her throat sounds constricted by emotion.

"Don't men in Los Angeles have biological clocks?"

She looks at me like I just suggested the earth is not only flat but still full of dinosaurs. "No. I mean, yes, some of them are dads. It's just that there's no urgency for them."

"Nature is unfair."

There is little talking when we dig into our supper. It's not an uncomfortable silence. In fact, I find it very pleasant enjoying one of my favorite pastimes with someone who doesn't feel the need for constant chatter.

After our dishes are cleared, Lu announces, "The last date I went on was with a fourteen-year-old boy."

I nearly choke on my champagne, which causes a bit of a coughing fit.

"I know, right?" She giggles as she rolls her eyes.

"Isn't that illegal?" I finally ask when my airway clears.

"I met him online. He was using his dad's information so he could find a woman to teach him the ways of love."

"Industrious fellow. Did you have any tips for him?" I imagine what my fourteen-year-old self would want to do with a woman like Lu and realize it's very similar to what my current self wants to do. To start, I'd like to pull her into my arms and kiss her for hours on end.

"My last date before Benedict was at a taco bar with a man who hated tacos but forced himself to eat them anyway. He had a purple goatee that he forgot to mention."

"Lu,"—I pick up the bottle of champagne and refill her glass—"I think the problem may not lie with you, but with the men in that city you call home."

"I've begun to think that as well," she replies. "Which is why I've decided to go ahead and have a baby without a husband."

"How's that?" I ask, wondering if she's planning on hooking up with random men in hopes of getting pregnant. Try as I might, I can't see her doing that.

"IVF. There's a place near where I live that has quite a good track record."

"Please tell me it's not the place the octomom went to." I can't for the life of me fathom what that doctor was thinking even allowing the possibility of such a birth.

She laughs. "No, I'm not looking into anything that extreme."

"What about twins or triplets?" I ask.

A myriad of emotions crosses her face before she answers, "Those are possible, but the odds are that if I can get pregnant, it will only be with one baby."

I decide a change of subject is in order. "Bree mentioned you were going to stay here in Malquar for a while. I'm sure she can introduce you to some nice men." I'm not going to offer to do it for the obvious reason that I'd like to date the woman myself.

"Your sister seems to be having as much trouble finding a decent relationship as I am."

I can't believe I'm saying this, but I tell her, "I've invited Bree to come to the next party I throw on the yacht so she can expand her horizons outside of her normal social circle. Maybe you should join her." At least that way I can keep my eye on her and invent stories to warn her away from anyone that catches her eye.

"Maybe I will." She stares at me like I'm a calculus equation she's trying to solve. "Are you dating anyone special?" she finally asks.

"I'm not. Much like you, I find women make assumptions about me that aren't correct. I'd like to meet someone who sees me and not just my title." Look at me, spilling all my secrets. There's something about Lu that makes me want to tell her everything. "You know, no one would believe me if I told them about the orphanage. Most assuredly, not my family. They would tell you that it doesn't fit my image."

"Tell me about the orphanage," Lu says. "Have you been visiting there for long?"

"Five years," I tell her. "I'm their patron, but I like to do more than simply write checks."

"Do you think I could visit there sometime?"

"I'm sure Sister Hennepin would be delighted to show you around." I would offer to do it myself, but I don't want Lu getting all weird around me again. She's finally showing some signs of softening, and I don't want to go back to her feeling like she's being hunted.

Nodding her head, she replies, "Which days do you go?"

"It depends entirely on my schedule that week." I'm guessing she wants to know when I'll be there so she can avoid me, but I'm not going to make that easy for her. While I've decided not to openly pursue her, I am still going to see her every chance I get.

Chapter Twenty-One

Sharon

"I can't believe it's almost time for us to go home," Sharon grumbles.

"Why don't you stay for a while?" Tooty props her feet up on her sister's lap. "I'm sure Charlotte would love to have you on hand to plan the upcoming shindig."

"If I do that, then Lu won't stay. The only reason she agreed to extend her trip was because she wanted to avoid me."

"How are you going to track her progress with Alistair if you're not here?"

Sharon replies, "The queen is going to keep me up to date."

"But how will she know what's going on if Lu is staying out at Bree's cottage?"

"Maybe she has spies or something. All I know is that Alistair's cottage is right next door, and I'm guessing that daughter of mine will see a lot more of him over there."

"I'm not sure pushing Lu at him is the right thing to do. She's had such bad luck with men, what if she and Alistair get together and things fall spectacularly to hell? That wouldn't be good for Claire."

"Claire is a big girl and can handle herself. Lu is the one who needs my help now. Kids are a blessing and a curse, aren't they?"

"You've got that right, sister of mine," Tooty answers. "We're blessed to have them, then cursed with constant worry for them."

Lutéce

I can't believe what a nice time I'm having with Alistair. I keep expecting him to say something provocative like he has in the past, but he doesn't. Instead, he's treating me like a friend, and I feel like I'm getting to see the real him. As much as it pains me to say so, I like what I see.

"Thank you for a wonderful evening," I tell him as we lean over the railing and watch as the dock comes into view.

"Any future family of my brother's is a friend of mine," he replies. "Next time we go out, I promise to regale you with stories of my failed romances."

"Please, I'm sure they all failed because you weren't interested." Why did I say that? I sound mean and defensive at the same time.

He ignores my rudeness. "You might think so, but there was Elissa Frahn from my primary school. I may have only been eight, but I loved her beyond reason. She broke my heart." He arranges his face into an exaggerated pout.

"You poor thing," I joke back. "What was young Elissa's reasoning for not returning your love?"

"She told me point blank that she was in love with my brother. I informed her that she'd never even met my brother, but she didn't care. Her heart was set on being queen one day, and the only way that could happen was if she married Andrew."

Even though his tone is light and playful, I start to wonder if maybe that isn't the only time Alistair's affections were rebuffed in favor of a hopeful gal wanting to be queen. "I'm sorry, that's horrible," I tell him sincerely.

Alistair inclines his head slightly. "I'm happy to say that I've fully recovered. Elissa went on to marry the boy who grew up next door to her and they are happily expecting their fourth child."

"If it makes you feel any better," I tell him, "I would hate to be a queen. Too many eyes on me. Too much responsibility."

"Yet I have a feeling you enjoyed my brother's attention the other night. Are you sure you might not overlook the spotlight if it means being with the person you love?"

"I'm not in love with your brother, so I don't think I'm in any jeopardy of needing to make that decision." The look on his face suggests he might not be referring to his brother.

"I predict that when you go back home, you'll meet the perfect man who will help you make all of your dreams come true," he says.

"What about you?" I ask.

"I'm not looking for a man to make my dreams come true," he teases.

"That's not what I meant. What about finding the woman of your dreams? She must be out there." As much as I claim I don't want Alistair flirting with me, I seem determined to flirt with him.

"If the woman of my dreams exists," he says, giving me a look that causes tiny shocks to ripple through my nervous system, "she may not be as easy to find as you'd think. She has to be willing to put up with an awful lot of public scrutiny. She also needs to be game to mother the six children I want."

"Six? Why so many?" I swear I begin to ovulate at the thought of a man excited by the prospect of having a big family. Especially if that man is Alistair.

"I loved having so many siblings, and I'd like for my children to have a similar experience."

"I'd have to adopt if I were to have that many children," I blurt out. I immediately regret doing so when Alistair's eyes pop open like he's run headfirst into an electric fence. "I don't mean with you," I hurry to say. "I just meant in general. I'm too old to have a big family naturally." I need to stop talking. Now.

"There's nothing unnatural about adoption," he tells me. "Every time I visit the orphanage, I yearn to take the children home with me and give them the same opportunities and love that I've had."

"Why don't you?" I ask.

"I probably will adopt part of my brood, but I'm waiting until I'm married. I'm not sure I'm up to the task of fathering without a solid support system." He looks at me so tenderly, I want to crawl right into his arms. Alistair is turning out to be very different from the man I thought he was.

"Would your parents be okay with you adopting?" I'm not sure why I care but I do.

"Why wouldn't they be? My parents obviously love children. I can't imagine it would matter to them who their grandchildren's biological parents are."

"I've never thought about adopting," I tell him. "And I'm a

woman who's running out of time."

"That may be an option you want to keep open for yourself," he says. "I don't know what your laws are in America, but here in Malquar a single person is allowed to adopt as long as they have a stable income and can pass the interview process."

"My friend Ally and her husband adopted. It took them nearly three years before they got their son. That's a long time to wait."

"I would think the wait would be a great deal shorter if you didn't need to have a newborn."

Why have I never thought of this before? "That's a good point. I'll definitely have to research this when I get home." And I will. I suddenly feel like a world of possibility has opened for me and the constant pressure I've been feeling eases a little. "Do you think you could show me around the orphanage sometime?"

He inclines his head slightly before saying, "I would be delighted to. I'm going in the morning, if that works for you."

"Should I meet you there?" My stomach feels like a swarm of vulture-size butterflies are flapping around in anticipation of seeing Alistair again so soon.

"I'll pick you up at the palace at ten. We can drive over together." He stares at me so intently I expect him to lean down and kiss me. But after several moments of scrutiny, he looks back out to the water, his voice wistful. "I think I could live on this boat if my parents would allow it. I'm glad you decided to join me."

I feel like I've seen a whole new side of Alistair. One that I like very much. "Thank you for tonight, Alistair. I had a very nice time."

He gives me a look that I can only describe as longing. As the boat glides into its slip, I ask, "How are we going to get home from here?" Bree was the one to drive us and she's long gone.

"I suppose we could ask Grady to lend a hand." He pulls his phone out of his jacket and calls the captain. "Grady, would you be free to drive Lutéce back to the palace?"

When he hangs up, I ask, "Aren't you coming with us?"

"I'm going to spend the night here. I always sleep better on the water."

I don't know why this disappoints me so much, but it does. Moments later, the captain joins us on deck. "Miss Choate, I'm at your service."

Alistair takes a step back and says, "I'll see you in the morning, Lu. Sleep well." Then he turns and walks inside.

I'm suddenly so sad I could cry. What in the world is wrong with me? I can't be mad that Alistair didn't make a play for me when I've spent every moment that I've known him pushing him away. It's just that tonight felt different, and special, and I wanted to commemorate that in some way.

"No, Lu," I tell myself sternly. "Alistair is not for you. Be grateful he's no longer treating you like his prey."

The problem is, I'm starting to wonder if that's what I want.

Chapter Twenty-Two

Queen Charlotte

"I received a note from Ellery Pasteur today," Charlotte tells her husband while they prepare for bed.

"Dear God, what does she want?"

"She wondered if she might pay us a visit in a couple of weeks."

"Why?" Alfred demands as he pulls the covers down and crawls into bed.

"Why do you think? I'm guessing she's sniffing around after one of our sons again."

"She left a mess in her wake the last time she did that. I truly started to think Alistair was falling in love with her, but then she turned her affections toward Andrew. I'm sure you haven't forgotten the tension that created between our boys." Releasing a sharp grunt, he adds, "You should tell her she's not wanted."

"How can I do that, Alfred? She's the daughter of my dear friend. I'm her godmother for heaven's sake."

The king plumps the pillows under his head. "Do you relish the thought of making our sons uncomfortable?"

"Of course not. But I'm sure they're both firmly over her."

The queen sits down on her side of the bed and takes her slippers off.

"Yet neither of them has dated anyone seriously since she was here last. I find that quite telling."

"Maybe they just need to be reminded she's not the woman either of them once thought her to be. After that, they can finally move on."

"Or one of them might wind up marrying her. Do you really want Ellery Pasteur as a daughter-in-law after all the trouble she caused?"

Charlotte slides into bed next to her husband. "You're not giving Andrew and Alistair enough credit. Our boys aren't stupid."

"Nor are they married."

"Sometimes you need to make peace with your past before you can proceed with your future," the queen decides.

"Nothing I say is going to change your mind, is it?" Alfred asks his wife.

She simply laughs and tells him, "Darling, a mother knows best. You have to trust me on this."

Alistair

I sip my brandy as I sprawl out on a deck chair. Tracing the lines of the Big Dipper with my mind's eye, I replay the evening in my head. Once Lu realized I wasn't the enemy, we had a wonderful time.

I discovered something about her that she may not even know about herself. While she claims to be looking for love, she's afraid of it at the same time. Her past has left her injured, which is a circumstance I can relate to.

The only woman to break my heart did such a fantastic job of it, I gave up dating altogether. That was over two years ago. I haven't been tempted to put myself out there with anyone else since. Until now. Too bad the lady I'm interested in is as damaged as I am.

Grady joins me as soon as he gets back from taking Lutéce home. "She's lovely, isn't she?" I ask while pouring him a drink.

"She is." He sits down on the chair next to mine. "But she's American and she doesn't live here. That might make pursuing her a bit difficult."

I release a snort of laughter. "That's the least of my troubles. The biggest obstacle is that she doesn't *want* me to pursue her. She's made it perfectly clear she doesn't think of me in that way."

"Yet she couldn't keep her eyes off of you," my friend says.

"I'm not sure if that's true or not. She's staying in Malquar for a while. She's going to help my sisters plan Claire's bridal shower."

"Well then, you may have a shot after all."

I change the subject. "Why did my mother want Bree off the boat?"

"She didn't say, but I got the feeling she was trying to give you and Miss Choate an opportunity to get to know one another better."

"That's not it," I tell him. "I've been warned that I'm not to get involved with the bride's sister. The queen doesn't think it would be conducive to keeping family harmony."

"How so?"

"Mother is convinced I'll break Lu's heart, making future family functions awkward for Claire."

"Interesting." He doesn't offer anything more.

"How so?"

"The only reason I can see her wanting your sister off the boat is to give you time alone with Lutéce. Also, I'm pretty sure Bree will never speak to me again after tonight."

"The two of you are ridiculous," I tell him. "Bree has worshipped you since she was a little girl, and you go out of your way to antagonize her by treating her like she's your employer."

"What can I say? Her family *does* employ me."

"I'm part of that family too, and you and I have maintained a close friendship. Why is it different with Bree?"

"I don't want to kiss you," he says plainly.

"And thank God for that. My point is, why can't you kiss my sister? So long as you don't toy with her affections, I don't see what the problem is."

"Say I ask Bree out on a date and she says yes. It would be terribly awkward if things didn't work out."

"You're not even going to try because you're afraid?" I might as well be calling him a coward to his face. But if the shoe fits…

"I don't think you're the one to lecture me on the subject of women."

"Why, because I'm not involved with anyone?"

"Because when you got your heart broken, you gave up on love entirely."

"Well, that's a mean thing to say." Sounding as hurt as I am, I say, "Ellery didn't just break my heart; she chose my brother over me. She played us both like fiddles until she made her choice. I can't believe we never knew she was leading us both on at the same time."

Grady pours himself another brandy. "She may have chosen Andrew, but he dropped her once he found out she was involved with you, too."

"He still loved her," I say.

"And so did you."

"What's your point, Grady?" I slam back the rest of my drink before refilling it.

"My point is that you aren't in a position to give me advice until you take that advice for yourself."

"If I asked Lutéce out on a proper date, she would say no," I tell him.

"Have you tried?"

"No, but I know she wouldn't accept."

Grady turns so he's looking at the night sky instead of me. "Using that same stellar reasoning, I'm telling you that no good can come from my asking your sister out on a date."

"Do you have a crystal ball that I don't know about?" I demand.

"Do you?"

We consume our drinks quietly from that moment on. I can't help but wonder if part of what Grady says is correct. Am I afraid to ask Lu out because she'll reject me? Or am I just afraid of opening my heart to love again? The truth is that while I have pursued Lu in the past, it was never with the intention of something serious happening between us.

Yet, after tonight, I want to get to know everything about her. I have a feeling this strong pull I feel toward her is much more than just a passing fancy.

Chapter Twenty-Three

Sharon

"I'm going to require regular updates," Sharon tells the queen over breakfast.

"When I know something, you'll know it," Charlotte assures her.

"I wish I could stay."

"Why can't you? With Lutéce out at Bree's cottage, she never even has to know that you're here."

Sharon immediately perks up. "Does Bree come to the palace often?"

"Not usually, and even if she did, this place is big enough that she'd never need to know you're here."

"What if someone tells her?"

"Are you forgetting that I'm the queen?" Charlotte asks with a smile. "If I tell people that your continued visit is to be kept quiet, I assure you, it will remain our secret."

"I'm gonna do it!" Sharon declares. "Phillipe is leaving on a business trip, so he won't miss me. And even though I won't be able to see Lu while I'm here, I'll feel better being close by."

"Well then, my friend," the queen tells her, "it looks like you and I are going to have some fun."

Lutéce

I have no idea what to wear to the orphanage. I'd feel most comfortable in jeans and a sweater, but I don't want to make Alistair look bad if I'm expected to dress nicer than that. I finally settle on a pair of gray wool slacks and a cream-colored sweater. I'm not overdressed, and I'm not underdressed. Like Goldilocks, I declare myself just right before getting busy doing my hair and putting on makeup.

It took me ages to get to sleep last night. My mind was busy replaying scene after scene of my time with Alistair. The result is dark circles under my eyes which take a bit of effort to hide. I'm tempted to go full drag queen on the concealer, but decide that might not be the best look on me.

When I walk into the dining room, I discover Alistair sitting at the table with both of our mothers. He stands when he sees me. "Good morning, Lu."

"Hi there," I return his greeting, feeling a bit shy after all we shared about ourselves last night.

"Did you two kids have fun out on the boat?" my mom wants to know.

"It was very nice," I tell her, hoping I sound casual. I don't want her to pick up on my newfound attraction toward Alistair. The last thing I need is for her to say something that will embarrass me. She has specialized in that bit of mothering for as long as I can remember.

"I understand Bree didn't join you," Queen Charlotte says.

"I believe that was your doing," Alistair tells his mom.

"What? No. Wherever did you get that idea?"

"Grady," he tells her.

"There must have been a misunderstanding. I called Grady to tell him I was having something delivered to the dock for Bree. He must have thought I meant for Bree to stay on the dock." Then she executes a forced-sounding laugh and tries to change the subject by asking, "What did you have for supper?"

"What were you delivering to her?" Alistair ignores her question.

Queen Charlotte looks up with a startled expression on her face. "I was… she was… it was…"

We have no idea what she's about to say because my mom stands up and announces, "What a wonderful breakfast! Charlotte, are you ready for our walk in the garden?"

The queen pops up like a jack-in-the-box. "Absolutely! I can't wait to show you my salmon-colored Floribunda."

As soon as our mothers leave the room, Alistair announces, "My mum is up to something."

"My mom is always up to something," I tell him. "Welcome to the club."

While arranging some scrambled egg on his fork, he says, "It was almost like she was trying to give us time alone, but that can't be because she's already warned me that I'm to stay away from you." He looks up from his plate and gives me a look that causes the butterflies to come back en masse.

"Why did she warn you to stay away from me?" *Is there something wrong with me?*

"She thinks I'm a player and she doesn't want me toying with your affections."

"Meanwhile, my mother is convinced that I should either marry you or Andrew."

"My brother is quite a catch." His tone takes a serious turn. I'm guessing because he doesn't identify himself as a catch, he's not trying to sell himself on me. More's the pity.

Deciding a change of topic is in order, I ask, "What do you do when you're at the orphanage?"

"I either play with the kids or read to them. As wonderful as the nuns are, they're so busy keeping everything running they don't have time to toss a ball around or read books that are outside of the school curriculum."

"That sounds like fun. I haven't played in a very long time." I've been too busy being an adult to take time to nurture my inner child. Maybe that's part of my problem.

"It's good for the soul," he tells me.

After we finish our breakfasts, Alistair stands up and walks over to the sideboard. He starts packing the sweet-tasting breads and muffins into a large basket that's sitting on a nearby side table. "Are you worried you're going to get hungry?" I joke.

"I bring leftovers for the kids. While they always have plenty of food, they love to get treats from the palace."

That is so sweet that I'm once again struck by how different Alistair is from the man I thought him to be. "Do you have enough for everyone?" I ask.

"The cook makes extra on days when I visit. We'll need to stop off in the kitchen and pick up the rest."

After retrieving another basket, we exit through the kitchen door. Alistair's car is right outside. "I have to warn you," he tells me as soon as he puts the car into gear. "The nuns will not let you date any of the boys."

I slap him on the arm as I burst out laughing. "I should have never told you about Benedict."

"Benedict is my new hero. Imagine having the guts to perpetrate such a deception, all in the hope of finding love at the tender age of fourteen."

"He told me he'd look me up in four years when he turns eighteen. It's the best offer I've had in a long time," I joke back.

The drive into town only takes five minutes. The rolling farmland is dotted with a forested area and even a small lake. It's like being inside a painting from the eighteenth century. As soon as Alistair pulls up at our destination, the front door blows open and several children come running out.

"You're here!" a young redheaded girl calls out as she jumps up to see what's in Alistair's basket. "Did you bring the chocolate ones?"

"I only have a few of those," he tells her before taking out a pan au chocolate and handing it to her.

A short nun hurries forward and announces, "No treats until you wash your hands. Hurry now." She shoos them back through the front door before turning to Alistair. She sternly admonishes, "You know you're not supposed to hand out any food outside of the dining hall."

"I'm sorry, Sister." He lets his head hang like he's contrite, but I'm pretty sure the nun and I both know he's not. Then he says, "Sister Hennepin, this is Lutéce Choate. Her sister is marrying my brother."

The small nun looks up at me and studies me in a way that makes me feel decidedly uncomfortable. Then she looks down at my feet and announces, "The little girls will be happy to see that you don't really wear potato sacks on your feet."

I have no idea what that's supposed to mean, but when I look at Alistair his face turns red, and he says, "Bugger. I forgot all about that."

Chapter Twenty-Four

Queen Charlotte

"That was a close one," Charlotte tells Sharon as they stroll through the halls of the palace in the direction of the courtyard.

"Hopefully Alistair will forget all about why you wanted Bree off the boat."

"I doubt he will, but there's no way I'm going to tell him the truth." Sliding open a large glass door, the queen leads the way out onto a rock-paved terrace.

"Lu seemed happier this morning than I've seen her in a long time," Sharon announces. "I wonder if something interesting happened last night."

"I have a feeling that if it did, we'll never know about it. At least until the two of them are ready to come out as a couple."

"We need to prepare ourselves for the chance that something might not happen," Sharon says. "My daughter isn't the most warm and fuzzy person. Chances are that even if Alistair is the one for her, she'll fight it just to prove me wrong."

"Kids," the queen commiserates. "If they'd only realize we weren't the enemy." Leading the way into the rose garden, she adds, "I was thinking we could pick the flowers for the bridal

147

bouquet right from our garden, depending on the time of year Geoffrey and Claire decide to get married, that is."

"When do you suggest they set the date for?" Sharon asks.

"Next week would work for me," the queen laughs.

"Everyone would think it was a shotgun wedding. Plus, both Claire and Geoffrey have to go back to Oregon and pack up their houses for the move. I don't think we should expect the big day before spring."

"It's a good thing we have another romance to focus on then." Queen Charlotte grins slyly.

Alistair

"Language, young man," Sister Hennepin admonishes.

Crap. This time I say it to myself. "I'm sorry, Sister." Maybe my getting reprimanded by a nun will be enough to distract Lu from what she just heard.

"Why would I be wearing potato sacks on my feet?" she whispers to me as we follow Sister Hennepin into the abbey.

So much for distracting her.

"That's just an old Malquarian saying. It means, the children will be happy to know that you're well off enough to be able to afford shoes." I'm the worst when it comes to lying, but I hope she'll just chalk the whole thing up to cultural differences.

We become the center of much attention as soon as we walk into the dining hall. Millicent walks over and looks up at Lu and demands, "Hello. Who are you?"

"My name is Lutéce," my companion tells her. "My sister is marrying the prince's brother."

"Lutéce?" She looks down at Lu's feet and then up at me. "Is she the one from your story?"

"What story?" Lu wants to know.

"Just an old fairy tale I was telling the children the other day."

"It was a story about a prince named Alistair and a princess named Lutéce. The princess didn't like the prince."

"Really?" Lu asks, giving me the side-eye.

"The Lutéce in the story was as beautiful as you are, but she was always mean to the prince. She had a horrid disposition."

"Interesting," Lu replies. "Where do the potato sacks come in?"

"Oh, that." Millicent has her hands on her hips as she looks at Lu's feet. "Apparently Princess Lutéce had feet so big, they couldn't fit into real shoes, and she had to wear sacks. But you have on very nice shoes and your feet look normal, so I guess the story isn't about you after all."

"It certainly isn't," I tell Millicent.

"Is Lutéce a common name around here?" Lu asks.

"Yes, of course," I answer at the same time Millicent shakes her head and announces, "I had never heard it before Prince Alistair's story."

I half expect Lu to storm out of the orphanage and never speak to me again, so I'm delightfully surprised when she starts to laugh instead. She tips her head back, closes her eyes, and clutches her belly. It's the most beautiful thing I've ever seen.

She tells Millicent, "I think I've heard that fairy tale before."

"Really, how does it end? Prince Alistair didn't tell us," Millicent declares.

"Princess Lutéce went to a witch and got a potion that turned

Prince Alistair into a frog." Her eyes are sparkling with mischief.

"Does the princess have to kiss the prince to turn him back?" Young Beatrice joins in the conversation.

"Oh, no," Lu tells her. "There's no kissing because Princess Lutéce doesn't kiss frogs."

"The princess always kisses the frog," Curtis says.

Lu tells him, "This particular princess had already kissed more frogs than she could count, and they never turned into handsome princes. That's why she made a sacred vow to never kiss another frog as long as she lived." Lu sounds very determined on this count.

"I know, I know," another girl declares excitedly. "I bet it's like it was in *Shrek* where Princess Fiona became an ogre like Shrek. I bet Princess Lutéce becomes a frog so she and Prince Alistair can live happily ever after!"

"That's not how I heard the story." Lu tugs on the little girl's braid.

"What did you hear?"

"I heard that Princess Lutéce went back to the witch to buy another spell to shrink her feet, but the potion she got made her feet even bigger. They got so big, her parents had to add on to their castle just to fit them. But even that wasn't enough. Her big toes alone grew bigger than hundred-year oak trees and she was banished to the woods to live out her life alone."

"That's a bad fairy tale," Millicent announces indignantly.

"I have to agree." I finally decide to add my two cents. I tell Lu, "Fairy tales by their very nature are contractually obligated to offer a happy ending."

"Contractually obligated?" she asks with a snort. "Who draws up a contract like that?"

"The fairy tale king of course," I tell her. Walking over to my favorite chair, I sit down and address the group of children who follow me. "I have an idea," I tell them. "Anyone who wants to can write a new ending for this fairy tale. We'll have a contest, and when we have all your entries, we'll pick a winner."

"What does the winner get?" Millicent pipes up.

"What do you think would be a good prize?" I ask.

"I want to be invited to the palace for tea," she decides.

"I want a new baseball mitt," Curtis says.

"I want a pretty new robe with an extra-long sash so I can wrap it around my waist three times like a ninja," Beatrice decides.

"Okay," I tell my audience, which includes all the children as well as Sister Hennepin. "Anyone who wants to enter, can. All they have to do is write a new ending to the fairy tale about Prince Alistair and Princess Lutéce. The winner will be able to choose their own prize."

"You have two weeks," Sister Hennepin announces, "and you will be graded on your story for your writing class."

"Noooooo …" several of the children groan at the same time. A stern look from Sister Hennepin causes them to visibly shrink. I know just how they feel. My childhood was spent wishing there was a hole in the floor I could crawl into, so I didn't have to suffer the nun's death stare.

"But you get to pick your own prize," I tell them.

"Within reason," Sister Hennepin counters.

"Anything you want!" I assure them.

"Alistair," my old tutor cautions, "you may be a prince, but you don't make the rules for the children. *I* do that."

"We'll have to get the sister's approval, but I assure you, the prize will be a good one," I tell the kids.

I look for Lutéce, but she's not standing where she was. She's currently sitting on a chair across the room with Beatrice on her lap. The little girl is petting Lu's hair and whispering something into her ear. Lu's expression is so loving and raw it breaks my heart. She looks so natural with a child on her lap, I say a quick prayer that her dreams of motherhood come true.

Every child in this orphanage deserves to be loved and nurtured and spoiled. Lu wants a child so badly, I wonder if maybe one of these kids wouldn't just be a perfect place for her to start. I'd have to talk to my parents about the logistics. I'm not sure if you have to be a Malquarian citizen to adopt a child from here, but it's definitely something worth looking into.

I stand up and walk over to Lu and Beatrice. When I arrive, I ask, "Are you going to write an ending for the story, Beatrice?"

Her eyes fill with tears as she answers, "I want to, but I don't write so good yet."

"Maybe instead of writing your story, you could tell it to us," I offer. "What do you think about that?"

"I'm going to do it!" she says excitedly. "I'll make up the bestest ending in the whole wide world."

That's when I realize there is no way we can pick one winner. This isn't like a sporting competition where there's an obvious victor. These are children's hopes and dreams they're competing for. They've had enough of those dashed that I vow each and every one of them that puts forth an effort on this project will win the prize they ask for.

If it's something I can give them, that is.

Chapter Twenty-Five

Sharon

"Charlotte thinks she can keep my presence quiet so I can stay on in Malquar. Why don't you join me?" Sharon asks while sitting on Tooty's bed and watching her pack.

"Can't," Tooty tells her. "I'm due in the studio to start recording my new track."

"I'll miss you."

"I'll miss you too, hon. Depending on how long you're going to be here, maybe I'll come back for a visit," Tooty says.

"You could bring that daughter of yours along. Maybe we can set her up with Andrew and she could be queen someday."

"Unless Andrew has a hundred tattoos under his clothes and rides a Harley for kicks, I don't think Reagan will go for it. She likes bad boys."

"She gets that from her mama," Sharon says, while pulling out a sweater from her sister's suitcase and holding it up to herself.

Tooty grabs the sweater back and returns it to her bag. "Unfortunately, that's true. I shudder to think that my daughter might turn out like me one day. Being in your sixties and all alone is not for the weak."

"Maybe once I'm done with Lu, I'll work on finding you your knight in shining armor. What do you think about that?"

"I say do it. But keep in mind if you find him, I'm going to be mad you didn't help me sooner."

"There's always been someone by your side," Sharon says. "I didn't want to be the one to suggest it was the wrong one. You needed to figure that out for yourself."

"Ah, so that's it. Lu has used up her strikes so now you're benching her and taking over."

"Something like that, but I think it might be more accurate to say that my daughter has been swinging with a ping pong paddle instead of a bat. She's been playing the wrong game."

"What am I playing, tennis?"

"Golf," Sharon tells her. "You're hitting low and hard which is why you keep taking fastballs to the head."

"Ew …" Tooty scrunches up her face in disgust. "And don't even tell me you didn't mean it like that. You got your sense of humor from me."

Sharon doesn't even try to defend her comment. She merely smiles at her sister knowingly.

Lutéce

I think it's funny that Alistair made up an unflattering tale about me to tell the children. If I had a bunch of kids to tell stories to, I might have done the same thing. But even so, I'm not sure I'm going to let him off the hook. *My feet were so big I had to wear potato sacks? That's the best he could do?*

Alistair takes a bunch of children outside to play cricket while I stay inside to draw with another group. An older girl named Marcelle asks, "What's it like, living in America?"

"Busy," I tell her. The look on her face suggests she's looking for more, so I tell her, "It depends where you live. I live in Los Angeles, and it's a very crowded place."

"But that's where all the movie stars are, isn't it? It must be wonderful." Her eyes glaze over like she's lost in a particularly lovely fantasy.

"Maybe you'll visit there one day," I tell her. "Then you can see for yourself."

As she shakes her blonde head, her narrow shoulders seem to sink into themselves. "I don't think so. Once I turn eighteen, I need to get a job and start paying my way here at the abbey until I can find another place to live. I won't have any money to travel."

"Maybe one day when you're grown and have your own career, then," I suggest, trying to bring some optimism back to this young girl's life."

"I'm hoping Sister Hennepin will be able to find a job for me here. Maybe in the kitchen or cleaning. I've never thought much about what my life would be like if I left."

"How long have you been here, Marcelle?"

"Ten years. I never knew my father and my mum died from cancer when I was six. She didn't have any family that would take me, so I was brought here."

My heart breaks for her. I can't imagine being so young and not having a family member take me in after losing my only parent. These children have grown up in a way that is totally foreign to me.

I spend the rest of the morning getting to know the ones who stayed inside with me. Some of them share their stories, while others stay quiet. When lunch is announced, I stand up and declare, "I'm so hungry I could eat a horse."

Several children stare at me with looks of concern. "We don't eat horses here," Millicent says. "Horses are our friends."

"We don't eat horses in America either," I assure her. "That's just a saying. It means I'm very hungry."

"Can I sit next to you at lunch?" I feel Beatrice's small hand slide into mine.

"I would be honored," I tell her. Then, with a wink, I add, "You can show me the ropes so Sister Hennepin doesn't think I eat like a wild animal."

My little friend's long curls bob around as she nods her head. "I will. Sister gets very mad if you don't use your best manners."

Alistair and his crew join us in the dining room looking worn around the edges. Hair is tousled and shirts untucked, but the most obvious signs of hard play are the smudges of dirt across faces and clothing.

Sister Hennepin greets them with a stern sounding, "Did you all roll across the grounds then?" You'd think she was a real drill sergeant if not for the twinkle in her eye.

"Children need to play. You've said so yourself," Alistair tells her.

"So I have." The nun stations herself at the head of the largest of the three large dining tables. "There are enough sandwiches and fresh fruit for everyone, so please use your best manners. You don't want Prince Alistair going back to the palace and telling the king and queen what barbarians you are."

After the prayer is said, everyone quietly passes the platters around the tables. I'm not sitting at the same table as Alistair but when I look up, I find his eyes are on me. Tingles of awareness shoot through my body causing my temperature to seemingly rise and fall at the same time. He has always caused me to have a physical reaction to his presence. Even though it's not always been in a good way. The power he has over me makes me nervous.

Once lunch is over, the older kids clear the table, and Sister Hennepin announces, "It's time for school, children. Say goodbye to our guests and report to your first class." Groans of disappointment fill the air as two lines form—one in front of me and one in front of Alistair.

The children curtsy and bow, and declarations are made. These include thanks for our visit, excitement over the fairy tale writing contest, and sadness that we have to leave. Beatrice is the last child to say goodbye and instead of curtsying, she wraps her arms around my waist and hugs me tightly.

"I enjoyed meeting you very much, Beatrice. Would it be okay if I came back some time?"

"Yes, please," she says, her voice muffled against the wool of my sweater.

"Beatrice, dear," Sister Hennepin says in a soft manner, "please release Miss Choate and go to your schoolroom."

Beatrice looks up at me with haunted eyes. "Promise you're coming back."

"I promise," I tell her, while giving her one last squeeze.

She's the last child to leave the room, and once she's gone,

Sister Hennepin tells Alistair, "You know the way out."

"I'll be back soon," he says with a grin that indicates her curt manner has no effect on him.

"I expect you will. Now get going, I'm needed in the classroom."

"Thank you for your hospitality, Sister," I say.

"You are most welcome to come back at any time. With or without His Highness here." She says the last part like Alistair has a contagious disease she's afraid of contracting.

When she leaves the room, I turn to him and declare, "She doesn't seem impressed by your title, does she?"

"Oh, good lord, no. The only thing I do that the sister appreciates is visit the children. Even then, she usually treats me like I'm one of them."

"Yet you like her, don't you?"

"I quite adore her," he answers. "Sister Hennepin is a stern little bag of goods, but she's the most kindhearted and dedicated woman I know. Swear you won't tell her this, but she's one of my most favorite people."

"You're a glutton for punishment, huh?" I tease.

Leading the way out of the dining hall, Alistair answers, "I appear to have a soft spot for women who give me a hard time." I know immediately that he's lumped me in with the nun and I don't mind it a bit.

On the drive back to the palace, Alistair says, "You can take my car anytime you want to visit the children."

"You're not coming back with me, then?" I don't know why, but I find that thought rather disappointing.

"I have a very full schedule, but I promise to let you know

when I'm going so we can drive over together."

"It's a date," I tell him, immediately regretting my choice of words. "What I mean to say is, that sounds like a plan."

Alistair laughs. "Don't worry, Lu, I know you don't want to date me. Once again, I promise not to make any unwanted advances."

The only problem is, I don't think I'd mind if he did. The Alistair I've been getting to know in the last couple of days is worlds apart from the man I thought he was.

I silently vow to see as much of him as I can, on the outside chance that he might be the prince in my fairy tale after all.

Chapter Twenty-Six

Queen Charlotte

"Now that Phillipe and your sister have left, I think our first course of action is to plan a dinner party," Charlotte tells Sharon over breakfast.

"What for?"

"My goddaughter is coming to visit in a couple of weeks. Ellery is quite a force of nature, and I'd like to give her something other than my sons to occupy her attention."

"It sounds like there's a story there," Sharon says.

The queen takes a sip of her grapefruit juice before explaining, "Ellery led my older sons on a merry chase. She dated both at the same time unbeknownst to either Andrew or Alistair."

"How in the world did she do that?" Sharon wants to know.

"She asked each of them to keep their relationships a secret. She cited the awkwardness of having to tell their parents until there was real news to share."

"Oh, boy. What happened?"

"Ellery had her eye on taking my place one day, but she didn't receive interest from Andrew fast enough. She started a relationship with Alistair as her backup plan. Alistair fell for her, completely. But by then she'd gained some traction with Andrew, and she ended things with Alistair. When Andrew found out, he broke things off with her."

"The world is full of users." Sharon shakes her head. "Is Ellery the reason Alistair has become something of a playboy, or was he that way before her?"

"It all started after Ellery. I don't mind as much as I pretend to though. I'm sure my son is just blowing off some steam and recovering from his broken heart. I just think it's high time he puts the past behind him and finds a wife."

After wiping her mouth on her napkin, Sharon asks, "Aren't you worried how your sons will react when they see your goddaughter again?"

"Of course, I am. But even if they're still attracted to her, I'm confident nothing will come of it. They both put family above all else."

"It will be interesting to see how Lu acts around her, especially if she flirts with Alistair."

The queen laughs. "Yes, it will, which is why I'm not telling my sons that Ellery will be here. I don't want to give them the opportunity to back out. I'm hoping my goddaughter's arrival will force Lu into realizing that she has feelings for Alistair herself."

Alistair

I haven't seen Lu since she's moved in with Bree, and that was a week ago. My sister is keeping her guest busy with social engagements as well as supposedly planning Claire's bridal shower. I say supposedly because really, how much work could one of those events be? My sisters have thrown enough of them that they've got to be old hat by now.

With their guests, along with my brother and his intended, gone, my parents have gone back to their routines. Geoffrey and Claire are expected back in Malquar right before Christmas. At which time I expect excitement will start to pick up in earnest as the wedding planning gets under way.

My life is quite back to normal with the exception that Lu is next door. The image of her curled up on my sister's couch reading a book, or sitting by a roaring fire at night, quite haunts me.

I've purposely stayed away, hoping that there's some truth to the adage, absence makes the heart grow fonder. It has certainly worked out that way with me. I spend a good portion of my days dreaming about my new neighbor.

I decide to have my breakfast on the back terrace this morning. It won't be much longer before winter comes, and I won't be able to enjoy dining al fresco. Once I finish scrambling my eggs, I pour a mug of coffee and walk outside.

My garden abuts Bree's, so I shouldn't be surprised to see Lu walking among the flowers. But I am. I've been spying on my sister's grounds in hope of catching sight of her all week, but this is the first time I have.

When she approaches a willow tree between our grounds, I call out, "Good morning, neighbor!"

Her head pops up and she smiles brightly. "Good morning to you, Alistair. I haven't seen you in ages." She walks into my yard.

"Would you like to join me for breakfast?" I ask. "I made more than I could possibly eat all by myself."

She hesitates for a moment like she might bolt, but she suddenly strides forward with enthusiasm. "That would be very nice," she says as she reaches my terrace.

I get up and pull her chair out for her, then slide my plate across the small table to her. "I'll just go dish some up for myself."

When I come back out, Lu is feasting hungrily on her breakfast.

"You're quite proficient in the kitchen," she says. "Unless someone comes in and cooks for you." Her eyes twinkle with humor.

"Alas, no. I was taught how to make my own breakfast and lunch at a very young age. If you think my eggs are good, you really owe it to yourself to try my peanut butter sandwiches some time."

"Just let me know when, and I'll be here." She's quick to add, "But it better be the best I've ever had, or I'll be disappointed."

"I've missed you, Lu," I abruptly announce. Trying to make my declaration less awkward, I add, "No one puts me in my place quite as effectively as you do."

"Not even Sister Hennepin?"

"You run a very close second. Speaking of the sister, have you been back to visit the children at Shepherd's Home?"

"I've been back twice," she says. "But I haven't stayed as long as I would have liked. Bree's been eager to introduce me around to her group of friends."

"You poor thing. They're a frightfully boring bunch, aren't they?" I'm not even joking.

"Alistair, that's a horrible thing to say. They've all been very nice."

I offer an exaggerated yawn before imitating what I imagine a get together with them would be like. In a forced falsetto, I say, "Would you pass the crumpets, Victoria? Oh dear, I've gotten scone crumbs all over my best frock. I wonder if Baron Fierre is going to be at the next garden party? Do tell me where you got this remarkable tea. It's positively life-altering."

Lu bursts out laughing and confesses, "You know them well."

"I knew you were bored! You're much more adventurous than the whole lot of them combined."

"Why in the world would you think I was adventurous?"

"None of my sister's friends would ever think about becoming mothers unless they were married for at least a year. You know what you want and you're not afraid to go for it. In my book, that's adventurous."

"I wanted to do things the old-fashioned way too, but that doesn't seem to be what the universe has in store for me."

"I take it that my sister hasn't introduced you to any eligible men …" I try to make my comment seem casual and not like I'm dying to know the answer. Which I am.

"I've met a few," she says without offering further clarification.

"And? Is Prince Charming among them?"

"Alas, no. Fredrick Harcourt did ask me out on a date though. But being that he's the brother of your sister Sophie's ex-fiancé, I decided it would be best to turn him down."

"Ah, so your disregard had nothing to do with the fact that Freddie is half a foot shorter than you and his middle is as big around as he is tall?"

"You must think I'm terribly shallow to suggest such a thing." The humor in her tone belies the severity of her words.

"Not at all," I assure her. "I'm sure you and Freddie would make beautiful babies together."

Lu stares at me in such a way that I become more than a bit discomfited. Then she asks, "How about you? Have you had any interesting encounters with the opposite sex?"

None, but only because I haven't seen her in seven days. I don't say that though. Instead, I offer, "Alas, I've been too busy to keep up with my wicked ways." Then I add, "I don't suppose you'd like to have a picnic with me later?" I stare right into her eyes while I wait for her response.

A myriad of interesting expressions cross her face before she answers, "It would all depend on whether or not you're going to make your famous peanut butter sandwiches. I will have to decline if you're planning to bring ham and cheese."

"As luck would have it, I have all the necessary ingredients for my specialty. Why don't I pick you up at noon?"

"You might want to bring enough for Bree then. I don't think she has plans until later this afternoon."

As I don't want my sister joining us, I suggest, "Why don't you come over here at noon and then I won't have to risk running low on sandwiches."

Expecting her to shoot down my idea on the basis of not wanting to spend that much alone time with me, I'm surprised when she says, "That sounds lovely. Can I bring anything?

"Just your appetite."

I don't clarify what her appetite should be for.

Chapter Twenty-Seven

Sharon

Sharon: How are things going in Malquar, dear? Are you coming home soon?

LuLuBug: Things are good. No plans to come home yet.

Sharon: What are you doing to pass the time? Have you met any nice young men?

LuLuBug: I've been spending time at the church's orphanage in town. The kids are amazing.

Sharon: Really? How did that come about?

LuLuBug: Alistair is their patron. He took me there once and I've been going on my own ever since.

Sharon: Alistair, huh?

LuLuBug: Don't get any ideas, Mother.

Sharon: As if I would …

Lutéce

I fuss for way too long over what to wear on a simple picnic. I finally decide on a pair of yoga pants and a sweater. I'm ready twenty minutes before I'm due at Alistair's.

When I walk down the stairs, I run into Bree, who's on her way up. "I was just coming up to see if you wanted to go into town and have lunch today," she says.

"Oh … well … that sounds nice, but I've already made plans."

"With who?" she wants to know. "Not Freddie Harquart, I hope."

"No, no, no… not with him. I'm going for a walk by myself. I thought I'd take my sketchbook and spend time capturing the countryside."

I'm sure that sounds as lame as it is untrue, but it's the only thing to pop into my mind. I don't want to tell her I'm having lunch with her brother because I don't want anyone getting the wrong idea about us. *Even though I've started to.*

"Where's your sketchbook?" she asks, looking at my empty hands.

"It's in the parlor," I lie. "I'll pick it up on my way out," I say quickly, hoping she doesn't invite herself along. *Because how can I flirt with her brother if she's watching?*

I hurry to suggest, "Why don't we have supper together tonight?"

"I have to go to that tedious charity auction I told you about. I'd ask you to join me, but there are only so many tickets available, and they've been sold out for weeks."

"We'll do something tomorrow for sure," I tell her, thrilled to have a night in. While I really like Bree, I find her daily routine something of a grind. There's only so much socializing I can handle. In the week I've been staying with her, I've already surpassed my yearly quota of get-togethers.

I hurry out the front door, without my sketchbook, and practically run over to Alistair's house. After knocking on the door, I hear him call out, "Come in!"

Even though I had breakfast with him just this morning, I've never actually been inside his house. It's as masculine as Bree's is feminine. There are a lot of burgundies and dark greens, with dark mahogany furniture. It's quite stunning and more than a little intimidating.

Alistair walks out of his kitchen holding a large picnic hamper. Even though he's dressed casually, it's easy to imagine him starring in a Masterpiece Theater production.

"Is that bacon I smell?" I ask him.

"I refuse to answer and prejudice your opinion of my famous sandwich."

"Peanut butter and banana with bacon was one of Elvis's favorite combinations," I tell him.

"Interesting…" Yet, he still doesn't confirm or deny it as an ingredient in our luncheon.

"Where are we picnicking?" I ask.

"Follow me and I'll show you." As soon as we're strapped into his James Bond car, he says, "You didn't seem to have a very nice time at the beach when I took you last. I thought we'd revisit that destination."

"I really do love the ocean," I confess. "I was just a little skittish that day."

"Ah, because you were worried I had an ulterior motive for spending time with you."

"Something like that," I mumble my response.

As we pull out of his driveway, he says, "Now that you know I don't have any romantic designs on you, we can have fun."

"Yes, I suppose." I'm not sure how to go about letting him know that I've changed my mind about a possible romantic development. I'll just have to let things unfold and hope for the best.

We ride the rest of the way in relative silence. It's not an uncomfortable one though. It's quite pleasant. When Alistair pulls into the parking lot, his car is the only one there.

"Where is everyone?" I ask.

"It's Tuesday, so probably at work. Although even the weekends tend to be empty this time of year." He gets out and walks around to open my door before adding, "I have blankets in case we get cold."

He pulls the hamper out of the backseat and then retrieves a couple of throws which he hands to me. "You must have been a Boy Scout," I tell him.

"I'm not sure what that is, but I never was."

"It's a kind of club for boys in America. They learn how to hike and camp and survive in the wilderness. They also raise money for charity and do a bunch of good deeds. Their motto is to always be prepared."

"Aside from the camping and surviving in the wilderness thing, it sounds like my childhood," he teases. When we reach a spot about twenty yards from the shore, Alistair stops and puts the basket down. "How is this?"

I lay one of the blankets out for us to sit on. "Perfect. Now hand me a sandwich so I can pass judgment on your specialty."

He rifles through his basket and hands me a cloth napkin and a glass plate. Then he gives me a warm sandwich wrapped in foil. "Warm peanut butter?"

"I'm not saying a word until you take your first bite." He watches me intently, making it clear that he's excited for me to try it.

I unfold the aluminum foil to discover the sandwich has been grilled. Grilled peanut butter? I've never heard of such a thing. I'm about to take it apart to examine the inside, but he orders, "No looking. Pick it up and take a bite."

"But what if you put slugs in it or something?" I semi-tease. I really hate the thought of biting into something without knowing what exactly I'm eating.

"There's nothing disgusting in there. Trust me." I do trust him, even though the smirk on his face is making me nervous.

I put the bread up to my nose and smell it before putting it into my mouth. The scent of cinnamon is quite pronounced, which is more than odd for a peanut butter sandwich. As soon as I take the first bite, an explosion of flavors hits my taste buds. Cinnamon toast and warm crunchy peanut butter run smack into bacon, but not just any bacon.

"Did you candy the bacon?" I ask, full of shock and awe.

"It's the secret to my success." He smiles proudly at my obvious delight.

"Is that banana in there too?" That's the fourth flavor to hit. This sandwich is the gift that keeps on giving.

"Sliced very thin, so as to enhance, but not compete, with the other flavors. It's mostly a texture thing," he explains like he's teaching a class.

"Sooooooo good." I hurry to take another bite and feel almost woozy with delight. "You need to patent this recipe. You could make a fortune."

He laughs. "Yes, but then everyone would know about it. I'd rather keep it as my own personal culinary coup."

I have nothing more to say until I finish my entire lunch. Somewhere along the line he pours and hands me a cold glass of milk, which, of course, is the only way to fully enjoy peanut butter.

As I crumple up the sheet of foil, which is the only thing left, I announce, "You're a genius. I don't even care if that compliment goes to your head. I have never enjoyed a sandwich more."

He bows his head very regally and says, "I knew you were my kind of people."

"Gluttonous?" I ask jokingly.

"Highly refined while still maintaining a connection to the simple joys of life. Here's to us." He holds up his own glass to toast me. When he's done, he pulls a frisbee out of the basket and asks, "Want to play?"

"We're going to play frisbee on the beach?" Talk about feeling like a kid again.

"Unless you prefer body surfing, but I think we might catch a cold if we do that." He gestures like he's about to take off his clothes.

"I think we're better off with frisbee." I immediately regret telling him that before seeing what's under his sweater. Note to self: if this prince ever offers to take off his shirt again, let him.

Alistair goes long, and right before he throws the frisbee, he yells, "Incoming!"

I jump up to catch it and totally miss. Then I turn around, pick it up, and hurl it right into the ocean. Alistair looks at me and then the frisbee, and finally back at me. "You're not very good at this, are you?" he asks after jogging back to my side.

"I'm tempted to tell you that I meant to do that, but I don't think you'd believe me."

"How about if we go for a walk?" he asks. "Maybe this time you'll even take your shoes off."

I kick off my shoes and roll up my pants and declare, "Let's do it."

We walk side-by-side as the tide rolls over our feet. I'm so at ease with Alistair I wonder why I ever rebuffed his advances. He's nothing like the man I thought he was, and I can't help but wonder if he's treating me differently because he's lost romantic interest in me, or if he's just become so comfortable around me that I'm seeing the real him. I'm hoping it's the latter.

"Walking on the beach like this makes me feel like I'm starring in a tampon commercial," I blurt out. *Oh, my God! Why did I say that?* Talk about too much information.

He laughs. "It makes me feel like I'm in an advertisement for a class action lawsuit. You know, 'If you or someone you love has been attacked by sharks while minding your own business, we need to talk to you. You may have restitution coming.'"

I giggle before saying, "Thank you for breakfast and lunch. I'm thoroughly enjoying spending time with you today." Now take me in your arms and kiss me. I don't say that last bit out loud, but darn if I don't think it.

"I made us some hot chocolate. It's in a thermos back at our camp."

"Are you trying to woo me with food?" I ask, trying to lead him down a romantic path.

"Absolutely not," he exclaims, almost too loudly. "Truthfully, Lu, I promised I would not subject you to any unwanted attention and I mean it. As far as I'm concerned, you're nothing more than a little sister to me."

His words hit me like a shovel to the head. "Who's actually four years older than you," I say, sounding hurt.

"Well, then, you're nothing more than a truly delightful older sister. How does that sound?" He nudges me playfully in the ribs.

It sounds horrible. Short of jumping into his arms and declaring that I've changed my mind about dating him, I have no idea how I'm going to let him know. He's clearly not picking up on my less-than-obvious signals.

Should I jump into his arms? I'm so intent on trying to plot a course of action, I trip over my foot and nearly do a header into the water. I say nearly because Alistair reaches out and catches me right before I fall.

And there I am, in his arms. Right where I want to be.

Chapter Twenty-Eight

Queen Charlotte

"Who else are you inviting to your ill-fated dinner party?" King Alfred asks his wife while sitting in his study and rifling through the day's mail.

"You don't have to sound like the harbinger of doom," she tells him before answering, "Other than our children, I have six other eligible young people on my list. I figure it will be a good distraction for everyone and should alleviate some of the awkwardness."

"I don't know why you want to make the evening any easier for Ellery. She invited herself into the lion's den. It's on her if she gets bitten."

"She's not the one I'm worried about. I don't particularly want our sons angry at me for longer than needed. If there are other young ladies in attendance, it won't look like I'm purposefully causing them pain."

The king puts down his letter opener and demands, "Why are you doing this again?"

"Because, my dear, I think that Alistair and Lutéce would make a lovely couple and there's nothing like a little jealousy to push things in the right direction," Charlotte tells him enthusiastically.

"This again. I don't suppose I can talk you out of interfering, but please know that I do not support this foolishness."

The queen ignores her husband and asks, "How does salmon sound? We could serve it with a lovely basil and pine nut risotto …"

Alistair

Lu is in my arms, which is exactly where I've imagined having her ever since I first met her all those months ago in Oregon. She's looking at me so intently, I swear she wants me to kiss her, but that can't be right. She's made it more than clear—on multiple occasions—that she doesn't feel that way about me. And I don't want to ruin our truce by moving in an unwelcome direction.

After helping her back onto her feet, I step away from her and say, "Walking on sand takes a good deal of finesse, does it not?"

Her face flushes, and she won't meet my gaze. "You seem to be doing okay."

"Yes, well, walking on sand is actually one of my talents. As I have so few, I take a good deal of pride in it."

The corners of her mouth turn up slightly. "You make a good sandwich, too."

"Don't forget the scrambled eggs," I remind her.

"You're also a very good dancer."

"Yes, well, I'm afraid those are the only things I'm proficient at," I tell her with mock humility.

"Alistair, you don't have to try to make me feel better about being clumsy."

"As if I would …"

I like this woman so much. She's more than a beautiful face. She's kind to children, and funny. She even has a sense of humor about herself. Not only that, but she's playful, and she doesn't feel the need to fill every moment with inane chatter. She's practically perfect for me.

The real Lu is so different from the persona she puts out to the world. Yet with me, her shield seems to finally be coming down.

When we get back to our picnic site, we sit back down on a blanket, and I pull out mugs and a thermos full of hot chocolate. I hand her a cup. "I also make wonderful hot chocolate. I had to buy the biscuits, though, because I'm not quite sure how to turn my oven on."

Instead of commenting that I must be an idiot, she takes a sip of her drink and changes the subject. "I love being here in Malquar. I didn't even want to come and now I can't imagine ever wanting to leave."

"The good news is that you're close personal friends of the royal family, so I'm pretty sure you won't be forced out of the country for overstaying your welcome."

"Life is funny, isn't it?" she asks. "You think you know what you want, and you work hard to achieve those dreams, and then another dream comes along, and you realize that everything you thought was so important doesn't really matter that much."

"I'm afraid I'm not following you," I tell her. "Which one of your dreams no longer matters as much as you thought?"

"Having biological children. I used to think I needed to fall in love and get married before having them, and then when that didn't seem to be working out, I thought all I needed was a sperm bank. But now ..."

She doesn't finish her sentence, so I ask, "Now what?"

After taking another sip of her chocolate, she says, "Now I'm not sure that I even need biological children."

"Does this have something to do with the orphanage?"

She nods her head. "All of those kids are remarkable and wonderful in their own way, and they all deserve to have parents who will love them. The biggest part of the equation is that they're already here."

"So, you want to move to Malquar and adopt forty plus children?"

"You're making fun of me," she says.

"I am most certainly not making fun of you. As you know, I think adoption is a very admirable endeavor."

"I know I've only been here for a couple of weeks, but I've wanted to be a mother for as long as I can remember. I'm not saying that I want to adopt a child from the orphanage, but I definitely think that adopting could be my first step into parenting."

"Yet you're particularly drawn to a certain child, aren't you?" It doesn't take a crystal ball to see how she and Beatrice bonded when they were first introduced.

"Beatrice is quite special," she says dreamily. "I'd like to spend a lot more time with her to see if we're as good of a fit as I think we are. The problem is, I'm not sure I'd be allowed to adopt her. Some countries won't let foreigners do that."

"Why don't we look into the logistics and see if there isn't some way?" I propose.

"Which of the children at the home are you particularly drawn to?" she asks, before adding, "I'm not sure that's even a fair question."

"I have a soft spot for Curtis and Millicent. Curtis is the freckle-faced rascal who always seems to find himself cursing in front of Sister Hennepin. I've been there, so you know, we're birds of a feather. Millicent is the bossy business who treats me like her own personal servant."

"How so?" she asks with a laugh.

Doing my best to impersonate the youngster, I raise my voice and say, "Prince Alistair, I would like to dance, NOW. Prince Alistair, I would like a new hairbrush and Sister says I don't need one. Prince Alistair, why don't you bring more pan au chocolate when you come? You are a prince, after all."

"She does seem to have you wrapped around her little finger," Lu says. "She was the one you were dancing with in front of the orphanage, wasn't she?"

"She was," I tell her. "The problem for me is that being a royal, I'm expected to marry before having children. The next challenge would be convincing my wife that I want to adopt. And finally, how in the world would I ever take only two of them? I'd never be able to show my face around there again with all the hurt feelings I'd leave in my wake."

"Yet, they're already a family of sorts, aren't they?"

"In a way. But each one of them desires parents to dote on them especially. The sisters do their best, but I'm afraid it's not quite enough for the children."

"Alistair," Lu says. "I think you're a remarkable man."

I mock bow. "I shall endeavor not to let your compliment go

to my head." Even though it already has. Pleasing Lu is about the best thing I can imagine ever doing.

"I'm serious. I don't know any other man who would spend as much time with orphans as you do, and the fact that you'd like to make a couple of them your family makes you truly special. You are a lovely man, Alistair."

"You are quite exceptional yourself, Miss Choate," I say sincerely. "I'm quite pleased that our families are going to be united."

"I suppose you can call me your sister-in-law," she teases.

"I would be honored to be your brother." Well, that didn't quite come off the way I meant it to.

"Hardly my brother." The look she gives me starts my blood heating to a low boil, as it's not a very sisterly expression.

"I guess it's time we start to pack it up," I tell her. Because, hand to God, if we don't leave here soon, I'm going to go back on my word, and I'm going to wrap my arms around her and never let her go.

Chapter Twenty-Nine

Sharon

"I wish I could be a fly on the wall when your goddaughter is here," Sharon tells the queen.

"Ah, but you can." Charlotte stands up and walks out of the parlor. Motioning for her friend to follow her, she explains, "The walls really do have ears here."

Sharon hurries after the queen into the dining hall.

Charlotte approaches the far corner of the wall, then taps on it in several places before leaning her body into it. The panel pops open, revealing a small secret room. "These are all over the palace," she says. "They date back to times when the court was full of plots and intrigue." With a laugh, she adds, "Luckily, now that we're no more than figureheads, no one seems that interested in killing us."

"How exciting!" Sharon exclaims. "Not the part about people wanting you dead. The part about me getting to be in the same room as the action."

"You get to do more than be in the same room." The queen shuts the door so they're both inside. Then she flips a switch to illuminate the space. Pulling over a step stool that's been propped up against the wall, she instructs, "Climb up to the second step. There's a peephole that looks out of the eye of the horseman in the painting on the other side of the wall."

Sharon giggles, "It's like an episode of *Scooby Doo*. They always had paintings with peepholes."

The queen smiles. "I remember watching that show as a young girl. My brother used to love American cartoons."

Sharon releases a squeal of delight when she finds the spyhole. "I can see the whole room! But now I want to hear what's going on as well. How will I do that?"

"I don't have access to any bugs," the queen tells her. "And I'm not sure I could get any without raising suspicion, but I could give one of the servants a telephone to hold under their tray. That way you could hear the conversations of guests they're near."

"That's better than nothing," Sharon decides. "I feel like we're the main characters in an old spy movie."

Charlotte smiles enthusiastically. "This is the most fun I've had in a very long time."

"If things work out like we think they might, I have an eligible son and you have two single daughters. Who knows what might happen?"

Lutéce

The sun is nearly setting by the time Alistair takes me back to Bree's house. "I cannot thank you enough for saving me from a dull day of scheduling meetings," Alistair says as he pulls into his driveway.

"What is it you do, exactly?" I ask him. "I mean, do you have a specific job?" As an American, my knowledge of royal life is limited to what I see in the movies or read about in *People* magazine.

"I'm what you call a working royal," he tells me. "I chair several committees on my parents' behalf. I raise money for charity, and I act as the playboy prince to give the young women of the country a fairy tale to dream about." He says the last part with an edge to his voice.

"I'm starting to think you're nothing like how you allow yourself to be portrayed," I tell him.

He turns the ignition off. "I have no say in how the press treats me. They write what they want, and the truth has very little do with it."

"Yet, you seem to be photographed with an inordinate number of women." I look at him out of the corner of my eye.

"Are you following me in the press?" he asks. "Because if so, I can assure you that you learned more about who I am today than you will ever learn from the tabloids."

I feel like a kid who just got chewed out by the principal for spreading rumors in class. "It's very hard to pick up a paper in this country and not see your face," I tell him.

"Yes, well, how does the saying go? Don't believe anything you hear and only half of what you see. But in my case, don't believe anything you see, either."

Our wonderful day together seems to be ending on a sour note. "I'm sorry if I offended you," I tell him.

He turns toward me and his expression softens. "You didn't. It's just that in the short time I've known you, you are one of the few people who has made me feel like a normal person. I suppose

I don't want you thinking badly of me."

"Would you like to come in?" I ask him. "You could teach me how to play backgammon." *Way to entice him, Lu.*

"I would like that very much," he says, "but unfortunately I have a function to attend tonight."

"The charity auction?" I ask. His surprised expression has me adding, "Your sister is going as well."

"Ah, I see. If that's the case, why aren't you joining her?"

"She only had one ticket. But to be honest, I've had my fill of events for a while. I think I'm going to start bowing out so I can spend more time at the orphanage."

"Smart girl," he says. "Sadly, the auction is only one of three places where I'm expected to show my face tonight. My mother keeps our calendars quite full."

I open the car door as he asks, "How about a raincheck?"

"Absolutely," I tell him. "Just name the *date*." I emphasize the word date in hopes that it might actually become one.

"I'll consult my calendar," he says. "But in the meantime, I will be breakfasting on my terrace every morning this week at eight. Please feel free to wander over and try my toaster waffles. People rave about how I get them to the perfect crispiness without crossing the line into dryness."

"Maybe I will," I say with a chuckle. "Thank you again for a wonderful day, Alistair."

"It was entirely my pleasure, Lu."

I walk up to Bree's front door feeling like a giddy teenager. It's been so long since I've enjoyed spending time with a man without feeling pressure to decide whether or not he's worth investing more of my time.

Alistair is fun, interesting, and very kind. On the face of it, he's the perfect man. As I walk into the house, my phone pings.

Busybody: Hey, hon. I just wanted to check in to see how you're doing.

Me: Hi, Mom. How was your flight home?

Busybody: You know, it was flying. What have you been up to?

Me: I'm spending a lot of time with Bree. I'm also spending more time at the orphanage in town.

Busybody: Really? What do you do there?

Me: I talk to the kids. I was thinking I might give piano lessons if I can find anyone who's interested in learning.

Busybody: Well, that sounds wonderful.

Me: Mom …

Me: …

Me: …

Busybody: What, hon?

Me: What would you think about me adopting?

Busybody: A baby?

Me: No, a four-year-old.

Busybody: I think that would still be a lot of work for

*a single parent but it sounds like you might have
already met that child.*

Me: Her name is Beatrice.

Busybody: Should I fly back over and meet her?

Me: No!!! How about if I just keep you posted?

*Busybody: Okay, but the minute you need me, I'll
be on my way.*

Me: Thanks, Mom.

*Busybody: I love you, LuLuBug. There's nothing I
wouldn't do for you.*

While I know that's true, the thought of my mother coming
back to Malquar so soon is enough to cause the hair on my arms
to stand on end. I need this time away from her as much as I
need the break from my old life.

I decide to take a bubble bath and then settle in with a good
book. Even though I've been busy while I've been here, the knot
of stress I've been carrying around for so long has finally begun
to shrink. I feel like a different person in Malquar. I might
actually be turning into a person I enjoy spending time with—
one that isn't a perpetual ball of worry and anxiety.

Then, of course, there's Alistair. What in the world am I
going to do about him?

After thirty minutes in the bath decompressing, I wrap myself
in a robe and walk into my bedroom. Through the open window
I hear Alistair's voice from outside. He sounds stern. "I'm not

going if *she's* going to be there."

I can't hear the response which leads me to believe he's talking on the phone.

"I'm sorry Mother, count me out. I'll go straight to the gala at the museum." He's quiet for a moment before adding, "Yes, I know I should be over her by now, and I am, but that doesn't mean I have to put myself within five kilometers of her if I can help it."

I have no idea who Alistair is talking about, but I do know one thing. He doesn't sound the least bit over whoever she is. My heart sinks into a pit in my stomach.

Maybe Alistair isn't interested in me because he's in love with someone else.

Chapter Thirty

Queen Charlotte

"Why in the world did you warn Alistair that Ellery was going to be at the auction tonight?" the king demands.

"Because I want to remind him how much he loathes the girl."

"Yet, you've invited her to supper in a few days, and you aren't telling him about *that*."

"Alfred, my love, you are just going to have to trust that I know what I'm doing."

"I do trust you, but at the moment, I also find you scary." The king finishes tying his bow tie in the mirror. "You've never been quite so involved in our children's love lives before. It's a little unnerving."

"They've never been so old before," she says. "If I'm going to get those grandchildren I have my heart set on, I need to be more proactive."

"Yes, but what if one or both of our sons aren't over Ellery, and they start something up with her again? Do you really want her to be the future mother of our grandchildren? Or the cause of our sons not speaking to each other?"

Charlotte picks up her perfume atomizer and sprays it in the air in front of her before walking through it. "I have always liked Ellery, and so have you. She made a horrible mistake leading on both of our sons, but if one of them genuinely forgives her and falls in love with her, I would welcome her into the family."

"You would welcome a social climbing user?" Alfred demands angrily.

"I thought you were the one telling me to stay out of our children's love lives," the queen retaliates.

"My point is, Charlotte, that if you're not going to take my advice, at least do your best to protect our sons from their past mistakes."

The queen shakes her head. "I know what I'm doing, Alfred." Then she picks up her phone and makes a call. "Ellery? It's Aunt Charlotte. I'm not going to be able to go to the museum gala tonight, and I wondered if you would stop by and make my apologies for me."

"Charlotte …" the king warns.

His wife motions for him to be quiet. "Yes, just tell the curator, Mr. Heinrich, to direct any questions to Prince Alistair. I just tried calling that son of mine and he wouldn't pick up his phone …"

Alistair

I suppose the good news is that by skipping the auction, I'll only have two stops tonight instead of three. That ought to put me home an hour or two earlier.

All I can seem to think about is what a wonderful day I had

with Lu. First breakfast, and then a picnic. I could have spent the evening with her as well if not for my prior commitments.

The National Museum Gala has always been a favorite event. The guests pull out all the stops by dressing to the nines. The mood is always festive and fun. I briefly toy with the idea of going over to Bree's and asking Lu if she'd like to join me, but I'm guessing no woman wants to be asked out to a formal affair at the last minute. Also, she already told me she was looking forward to a quiet night at home.

It only takes me twenty minutes to drive to the museum. Five minutes after handing my car off to the valet, I've had my photograph taken no fewer than twenty times. As soon as I enter the museum hall, a glass of champagne is thrust into my hand and my friend Harry has his arm around my shoulder.

"You got here early," he exclaims. "I didn't think you'd be here until after nine."

"Yes, well, it seems that Ellery is back in the country and has decided to go to the auction. As you know, I will move mountains to avoid seeing her."

"I don't think things are going according to plan," Harry says while pointing across the room. "Isn't that Ellery?"

I turn quickly to look before cursing under my breath. "My mother's intel must be off. Well then…" I hurry to drink my champagne and hand Harry my glass. "I'd best be going."

"Nice try. You're supposed to give the speech at the unveiling of the new impressionist wing."

I feel her presence before I see her. "Alistair," Ellery practically purrs.

My flesh reacts in such a way that it feels like it's covered in fire ants. My skin is positively crawling in disgust. "Ellery." That's all I say. Heaven knows I'm not going to kiss her hand and tell her how nice it is to see her. It's not.

"I haven't seen you in ages. One might think you were trying to avoid me." Ellery is slim and blonde and every ounce a lady on the surface. Too bad she's really a two-timing blight on humanity.

"One would be correct if that is what one assumes," I say dryly while going out of my way not to make eye contact with her.

"Alistair, I've apologized again, and again. Is it my fault that I was taken with two handsome princes?"

Harry decides to speak up. "It rather is, Ellery. You were the one who dated them both without coming clean about it."

"Oh, shut up, Harold," Ellery spits, drawing out his full name—the one he's forbidden anyone to use. "I've loved both Andrew and Alistair since we were children. It was nearly impossible to make up my mind over who I wanted to be with."

"Ah, so you decided to lead them both on. Not very sporting of you, I'm afraid."

"Worry not, Harry." I turn so I'm only looking at him. My back is toward Ellery. "Neither Andrew nor I are the least bit upset anymore. You have to care about someone to be hurt by them."

"If that's the case," Ellery says, "why are you avoiding me?" Before I can answer she signals a photographer, then leans into me and kisses me on the mouth. Flashbulbs burst all around us. Damn her. It would appear that she's trying to stir up talk that we're back together.

I spend the next hour acting like my ex doesn't exist. Unfortunately, she spends the entire time trailing around after me. How is it that I never saw her for who she really is?

After two hours, I finally turn to her and say, "I don't think Andrew is planning on coming here tonight, so you might want to head off."

"I will always be fond of Andrew," she tells me, "but you know as well as I do that you're the one I truly love."

My eyes dart around the room looking for an escape. If I respond to her the way I want to, I'll make a scene that will have my own mother putting me up for adoption. When I spot an exit sign, I grab her arm and order, "Follow me."

Ellery practically has to run to keep up with me, but I don't slow my pace. I am so infuriated with her at this moment, I worry my head might blow right off my shoulders.

I don't stop walking until I'm standing in the statue garden in the museum's courtyard. Even though there are several heaters to keep people warm, the lighting is still dim, which means that it's practically vacant. People come to this event to be seen, not to hide.

"How dare you suggest that I'm the one you truly loved? You left me for my brother."

"I still love you, Alistair," she replies passionately. "The truth is, my mother pressured me to pursue Andrew, but you were always the one for me."

"Listen to me closely," I tell her. "I will never enter into another relationship with you. Not a romantic one, not a friendly one. We are through. Now, if you'll please stop following me, I would appreciate it."

Then, like my words have summoned the devil, sparks of light start to flash around us. We are once again being photographed. It's no wonder Lu had a hard time believing me when I told her I wasn't a womanizer. The press is relentless.

I learned long ago that it's pointless confronting them. If I do that, the story they invent will only be worse. For that reason, I simply walk back into the museum. I don't stop to see if Ellery is with me.

After making a brief speech to officially open the new wing of the museum, I make my final stop of the evening—a cocktail party that my friend Helena is throwing to christen her new home.

My plan was to only stay for thirty minutes or so and then hightail it out of there. But when I got there, I discovered that it was so nice to see my old friends that I stayed longer than planned. I also drank more than I should have. But who could blame me after having to deal with Ellery? I decided to spend the night so I wouldn't be a danger on the road.

It isn't until I'm walking out the door at ten the next morning that I remember I invited Lu over for breakfast at eight.

Crap on a cracker.

Chapter Thirty-One

Sharon

"Lu is especially taken with a little girl at the orphanage. I think she might want to adopt her," Sharon tells Queen Charlotte while strolling through the rose garden.

"Oh dear. We're such a small country, we don't allow outside adoption."

"Poor, Lu."

Charlotte stops walking. "There might be a way though."

"What's that?"

"Being that Claire will soon become a Malquarian citizen when she marries Geoffrey, the same courtesy will be extended to members of her family. If they agree to spend at least six months of their year here, that is."

"You know I wouldn't mind Lu living here. I expect that's what will happen if she and Alistair wind up together. I'm just not sure she'll agree to that if things don't work out with your son."

"There's only one option then." Charlotte nods her head firmly. "We have to make sure things work out. That way, Lu can adopt her little girl, and you and I will have our first shared grandchild to dote on."

"I like the way you think, Charlotte."

"I expect you do, as it's exactly the way you think."

Lutéce

I fell asleep last night thinking about Alistair. I woke up thinking about him, too. If I were being truthful, my dreams were of him as well. That feeling of initial infatuation you have when you first meet someone of interest never gets old. Sadly, it's been a long time since I've felt that way about anyone.

There's something about Alistair that makes me feel hopeful. It's like I'm in my twenties all over again, back when I still believed in happy endings and fairy tales—at least as they pertain to me.

I roll out of bed at seven and take extra pains to look nice. After curling my hair and putting on my makeup, I get dressed. *In a dress.* By seven forty-five I'm strolling through Bree's yard trying not to look like I'm stalking Alistair. Which, of course, I am.

My plan is to wait for five minutes after he first walks out onto his terrace before joining him. But at eight a.m. when he still hasn't come out, I walk over and boldly look through his french doors. There are no lights on, which leads me to believe he's either sleeping in or he isn't home.

Disappointment flows through me as I walk back to Bree's. I make myself some toast and coffee, but I have no real interest in either. Bree walks into the kitchen and asks, "What are you up to today?"

"I was going to walk into town and spend some time at the orphanage. How about you?"

"Shopping with a friend. We'd be delighted to have you join us." Sitting down at the table, she pours herself a cup of coffee from the carafe.

"I wouldn't mind meeting you for lunch if you'll be anywhere near the abbey," I tell her.

"I'm not sure where we'll be. Keep your phone on you, and I'll give you a call." Then Bree says, "You look very nice today. Quite dressed up for a visit with the children though, don't you think?"

If she only knew it wasn't the children I was dressing up for. "You're right. I'll probably change before I go."

After Bree leaves for her shopping trip, I stare out the window hoping that by my will alone, Alistair will show up. Where is he? At ten, I finally give up and change clothes. Then I walk out the front door.

Alistair's sports car is pulling into his driveway as I pass. I can't help but wonder where he went so early this morning. Excited to see him, I stroll up his driveway to say good morning. But then he gets out of his car and he's still wearing his tuxedo from last night. At least I assume it's from last night and that he didn't put it on this morning.

His shirt is unbuttoned a couple of notches and his bowtie is hanging loose. I suddenly feel extremely uncomfortable. He steps out of the car and says, "Lu, good morning. I hope I didn't leave you high and dry without breakfast."

I don't want him to know that I practically broke into his house to find him, so I say, "Not at all. I made some toast." After an uneasy moment, I add, "It looks like you had a good time last night."

"I did, thank you. I caught up with some old friends, which is always nice."

I just bet he did. "Okay, then, I just wanted to say good morning. I'm off to spend time with the kids."

I turn to walk away, but he stops me. "Would you like a ride?"

"No, thank you. It's such a beautiful day, I'd like to walk." Then I do. I walk quickly and angrily, taking determined steps to get as far away from Alistair as I can.

Did he spend the night with a woman? How dare he? But after a few more steps I realize that if he did, how is it any of my business? It's not like he and I have started anything, which is all my fault. Had I shown interest in him instead of rebuffing him, maybe I would have been the woman he spent the night with.

Thoughts fly around my brain like a blender set on puree. Just because Alistair invited me on a picnic doesn't mean he's interested in me. In fact, he made it clear that he would no longer pursue anything other than friendship. Oh. My. God. I'm my own worst enemy!

Sister Hennepin greets me when I get to the abbey. "Good morning, Lutéce. The children are already at their studies, but they can come visit with you in the parlor when they have a break."

"I was hoping you might let me teach some of them to play the piano," I say.

Her eyes widen with interest. "That would be very nice. We have a piano and music books. Sister Margaret used to instruct them, but then she retired, and we don't have any other musicians among us."

"I could come whenever you want. Hopefully I can teach several lessons a day." Just because it doesn't seem that anything interesting is going to occur between me and Alistair doesn't mean that I'm going to give up on the kids, especially Beatrice.

As the nun walks out of the room, I remind myself that I didn't come to Malquar looking for love. I came looking for a break. I may also have stumbled upon a way to make my dreams of motherhood come true sooner rather than later. So what if Alistair isn't interested in me anymore? I'm used to not being the object of a man's desire. Yet even as I try to convince myself that I'm fine with that, the truth is, I'm not. I'm totally crushed.

Beatrice comes running into the room which brightens my mood considerably. "Good morning." She offers me a quick curtsy. "Would you like to go for a walk? Sister Hennepin says I can go if you'll accompany me."

"I would love to go for a walk with you, Beatrice. Should we see if any of the other children want to come?"

Her little face crumples in on itself. "Do we have to?" Ah, so Beatrice is looking for some one-on-one time.

"We don't. How about you and I take a stroll alone and then we can invite some of the other children for another walk later on?"

"Okay." She nods her head. "I want to go to the fountain and toss in a coin." She holds up a small copper penny.

"Ah, you have a wish, do you?" I used to love making wishes as a little girl. Wishing wells, fountains, dandelions, rainbows, lady bugs, you name it, I would wish on all of it.

"I might just make a wish myself," I tell her. Then I take her hand and we find Sister Hennepin to let her know we're leaving.

Crossing the square, we pass the same old woman who yelled at Alistair the last time I was at the fountain. She's busy feeding the birds with great concentration. As we walk by, I overhear her singing to them.

As we approach the water, I ask Beatrice, "What are you going to wish for?"

"I can't tell you that," she says very seriously. "Wishes have to be secret or else they won't come true."

"I think I remember hearing that," I tell her. I pull the wallet out of my purse and say, "I don't know about you, but I have more than one wish."

"Oh, me too. But I only have one penny. I don't think you can make more than one wish on it."

I hand her a quarter. "In America, this coin is worth twenty-five pennies. That means it's good for twenty-five wishes."

"Is it for me?" Her eyes shine with excitement.

"It sure is," I tell her as she gently takes it out of my hand.

With her eyes closed, Beatrice turns so her back is to the fountain. I watch as her lips start to move silently while she formulates her desires. Several moments later, her lashes flutter open and she tosses the coin over her shoulder into the water.

"Did you make your wish yet?" she asks me.

I shake my head. I was so intent on watching her that I didn't even think about my own wishes. Unzipping my coin purse, I take out a handful of coins. After taking a deep breath, I throw the whole bunch right into the water.

"Wow!" Beatrice says. "All of your wishes have to come true now." Ah, to be so young and open to the power of magic. I mostly threw the money into the fountain because I know the nuns will put it to good use.

But even so, maybe, just maybe, one or two of my wishes will come true.

Chapter Thirty-Two

Queen Charlotte

"Sister Hennepin, please. This is Queen Charlotte."

Seconds later, the nun picks up the telephone and greets, "Your Majesty, how can I help you?"

"I was hoping I might visit with you sometime this week regarding the adoption of one of your children."

"You want to adopt a child?"

"Not me, Sister. But I believe my new daughter-in-law's sister might be interested," the queen tells her.

"Ah, yes, Miss Choate. She and young Beatrice are out on a walk now. Are you thinking about bending the rules to allow this?"

"No," the queen says. "But circumstances can be manipulated in such a way that we could make it legal. I'd like to chat with you about that."

"Certainly," the nun says. "I'm available at your convenience."

"Thank you, Sister. If you should see my son, please don't mention this to him."

"Why would I? This has nothing to do with him."

"Exactly," the queen says before hanging up the phone.

It's not that Charlotte thinks Alistair would object; she just wants to make sure that he's good and smitten with Lu before he finds out she's going to become a mother. It's one thing to date a woman without a child, but it's another entirely to date a mother.

Picking up her morning paper from her breakfast tray, Charlotte once again reaches for the telephone. When her call is answered, she asks, "Is there something you want to tell me about you and Ellery?"

Alistair

After showering and shaving, I make a full pot of coffee, collect the three newspapers that are left on my sideboard by my housekeeper, and sit down to read the headlines.

Surprise, surprise, a good number of them are about me. There are no fewer than eight photos of me and Ellery. They range in setting from her kissing me in the entry hall of the museum to us hurrying through the corridor toward the outdoors. Finally, we're photographed in the Statue Garden where we look ready to embark upon a tryst. If I weren't there and didn't know better, I might believe the headlines myself.

"Prince Alistair and Lady Ellery are Back Together!"

"Love in the Garden"

And my least favorite, *"Are Those Wedding Bells We Hear?"*

Ellery must be reveling in all of this. It was obviously her intent from the start to link us together again.

I'm not surprised when my mother calls. "No, Mum, there's nothing to tell," I assure her.

"I didn't even know she was back in the country until you called to say she was going to the auction. Looks like you got your intel wrong, huh?"

"Well, it all worked out for the best if you're back together."

"I assure you, Ellery is the last woman on the planet that I'm interested in," I say heatedly.

She ignores me, and says, "I was dreadfully upset for both you and Andrew when all that nasty business came out. But being that I'm not one to get involved with your love life, you can do whatever you want with my blessing."

"You're not one to be involved with my love life?" I ask incredulously. "You are always commenting on my love life." *What game is she playing?*

"Darling, all I'm saying is that if you and Ellery get back together, it's fine by me."

"After what she did to Andrew and me?" Something isn't ringing true here. My mother was furious with Ellery when—as she then claimed—she played her sons like a couple of fools. Now I'm supposed to believe everything is forgiven? I'm not buying it.

"I just want you and your brother to settle down," she says, sounding like our social lives have the power to end world hunger.

"I can't speak for Andrew, but I have no interest in rekindling a romance with Ellery. Ever. That ship has not only sailed, it has also sunk."

"That's fine, dear. It's none of my business."

"Is there some other reason you called?" I'm not really interested in hearing what else she wants, but I absolutely need her to stop talking about my ex.

"I wanted to let you know that your presence will be required at a dinner party I'm throwing on Friday. Please bring your sister and Lutéce with you."

"Why is this the first that I'm hearing of it? You normally give me at least two weeks' notice."

"I'm sorry, dear, I totally forgot. But please know that it should be quite a nice event."

"Who's coming?" I want to know.

"Mostly family, but there will be a few eligible men. I wanted to introduce Lu to more of our friends in a smaller gathering."

"Bree has taken the role of social director to heart," I tell her. "I'm pretty sure Lu has been introduced to all of the inner circle at least once." *As to eligible men, is she trying to set up Lu now? My mother needs another hobby.*

"Well then, she'll enjoy the night even more. Be here at seven and don't be late," she says before hanging up on me.

I would normally not attend my mother's party on such short notice, but the thought of spending time with Lu is more of a lure than I can resist. Especially if my mother is trying to marry her off to one of our friends. I can't let that happen.

Seeing Lu this morning was rather awkward as I was still wearing my clothes from last night. But there wasn't much I could do about that.

I had wondered if she'd stopped by for breakfast, but she didn't come right out and say so, and I didn't want to draw attention to my bad manners for not being home when I said I would be.

I do want to see her today though. I hurry to finish up my breakfast and get into the car. I know she went to the orphanage this morning, so maybe if I hurry, I can spend some time with her there.

When I walk out of my house, I'm surprised to find my sister Sophie standing on my stoop. "Hey, Soph, what's up?"

"I want you to tell me to my face that you and Ellery are not back together." Her hands are on her hips, and she looks mad.

"I can assure you that we are not. Why do you care?"

"Because I found out that while she was in France last month, she spent a good deal of time with Charlie."

"Charles Harquart, your ex?"

"Yes. I don't know what happened between them, but according to Stephanie Franc, they were acting very lovey-dovey."

"That girl certainly gets around," I say before realizing how insensitive that might sound to my sister. "I'm sorry that Charlie is such a turd."

"I'm sorry that Ellery is one, as well. We both deserve better."

"Yes, we do, sis. Yes, we do."

Sophie's body language relaxes. "Well, then, that's all I wanted to know. I suppose I'll see you at Mum's supper party on Friday."

As she walks away, I can't help but wonder at the truly horrible luck my siblings and I have had in the love department. Geoffrey struck gold with Claire, but I'm willing to bet that can be attributed to his living away from home for so many years.

Dating as a royal is proving to be quite a treacherous affair. I half wonder if we wouldn't all be better off going to America for a couple of years. Of course, America seems to have come to me in the form of Lu.

I hurry down my driveway with thoughts of my new

neighbor. Everything about her seems a perfect fit for me. I just need to spend enough time with her to know that it's not wishful thinking on my part.

When I pull up in front of the abbey, I see Lu and Beatrice with their heads together across the road at the fountain. I'm about to go over to them and say hello when Sister Hennepin walks out. "We weren't expecting you today," she says.

"I had a free morning and I thought I'd check to see if there was anything you needed this month." Lies. But I'm not about to tell her that I'm there to see Lu.

"I have a list in my office," she says. "Follow me and I'll show you." This visit clearly isn't going as planned.

Following Sister Hennepin into the abbey feels eerily like that time I was called into the headmaster's office for gluing Cannon Allard's shoes to the ground. In my defense, he called my little sister a big dyke. Then, like now, I'm certain I've done nothing wrong. Yet, even so, I can't shake the feeling of trepidation.

"Close the door," Sister Hennepin announces as soon as I join her in her inner sanctum. The room is stark but intimidating with its ancient plaster walls that are the backdrop to equally-aged works of religious art.

Now I'm really nervous. Every time Sister had me close the door during one of our study sessions, it was to tell me things like, "Just because you're a prince doesn't mean you're smart." And "Don't think I'm going to put up with your nonsense just because you're a prince." The basis of our relationship seems to be her making sure that I know I'm not special.

"Is everything okay?" I ask as I sit down on the wooden chair across from hers.

"No, everything is not okay."

"Is the plumbing acting up?" *Please let it be the plumbing.*

"Curtis is acting out again." She slides a piece of paper across the table to me. "This is what he wrote for your fairy tale contest."

I pick up the piece of paper and read:

Prince Alistair decided to help Princess Lutéce by cutting off her giant feet with an axe. After she recovered, Princess Lutéce thanked him kindly, and they got married and adopted all the orphans at Shepherd's Home. The orphans never let the princess want for anything, so she never had to worry about not having any feet.

Shifting uncomfortably in my chair, I say, "I see. While the whole cutting off her feet thing is rather gruesome, it's no less horrible than many of Grimm's Fairy Tales. I think Curtis was just trying to come up with a logical solution for having big toes as big as oak trees." I wrap it up with, "I wouldn't worry about it too much, Sister."

"That's not the part I'm worried about, you dolt." You see what I mean? No deference to my title, whatsoever.

"What part are you worried about?"

"The part where Curtis thinks you and Lutéce will get married and adopt all of them. Alistair, it's hard enough managing the children's expectations without crushing them. Most of them dream about being part of a family again, and most of them are resigned to the fact that it isn't in their future. Curtis is ten, and he still yearns for a father figure."

"I'm not sure what you're suggesting here, Sister. Are you saying you want me to adopt all of the children?"

She rolls her eyes at me. Not at all subtly. "I think you need to stop visiting so frequently. When the children see you, it gives them false hope. I don't think that's fair."

"But I'm not even married. Why would they think I was looking into adopting some of them?" Like I told Lu, I've certainly thought about it, but I can't imagine doing it anytime soon.

"Curtis told the other kids that the whole plan behind the writing contest was for you to pick the child you were going to take out of here. That is currently all they can seem to talk about."

That would make a good fairy tale right there. "Where in the world did he get such an idea?" Sweat starts to bead on my forehead.

"From you, Alistair," she says sharply. "You're the one who told the children they could pick any prize they wanted. What do you think is the biggest thing they all want?"

"I didn't mean *that.*" I feel horrible for giving them false hope. "What do you want me to do?"

"Like I said, I want you to stop visiting. And then when you start again, perhaps you should only come every few weeks or so."

"That would punish both me and them," I tell her firmly.

"I'm not worried about you, Alistair. You are going to be just fine. These children, on the other hand, must be prepared for the reality of their lives. Dreaming of becoming your child is not at all realistic." She pushes her chair back from her desk and stands up.

"Can I at least say hello to them now?" I'm so stunned by her decree I feel like I've taken a sharp blow. I'm positively dizzy.

"I don't think that would be wise. In fact, I think Miss Choate should pick the winner of the contest. I'll tell the children that you're very busy being a prince and that you don't have time to stop by in the foreseeable future."

I stand up so abruptly, I nearly topple the chair. "They'll hate me if you say that!"

"It will be less painful for them in the long run," she decides.

"Don't I have any say in the matter?"

"What do you think, Alistair? In all the years that you've known me, have I ever given in to you?"

She hasn't. "Please let me know if you need anything," I tell her before turning to leave her office.

"Alistair," she calls after me. "It's for the best."

How taking away the one thing that brings me so much joy is for the best, I'll never know. While I peripherally understand her reasoning, I can't help but feel like I'm the one being punished here.

Chapter Thirty-Three

Sharon

"I feel like a caged animal," Sharon shouts across the room while pacing back and forth across her bedroom floor. She has Tooty on speaker phone.

"Then go out. If Lu is thinking about adopting a child from Malquar, she won't run just because you're there."

"You don't seriously believe that, do you?" Sharon snorts.

"I don't know what to think. I do know that I want to come back for a visit though. I'd like to see that orphanage. If Lu is spending a lot of time there, maybe it would be a good place to start my camp for underprivileged kids. Once I have a better idea of what I'm doing, I could expand it to the States."

"You *should* come back. That way you can be my eyes and ears and Lu won't suspect a thing."

"I'll do my best, but in the meantime you've gotta take a giant chill pill, sis. Read a book, learn to knit, do something other than worry about Lu."

"Easier said than done. Alistair's ex is back on the scene, and I'm not convinced she isn't going to get him back."

"Why do you think that?"

"There were some pretty salacious pictures in the newspapers this morning."

"You know enough not to believe what you see in the rags."

"I do, but I'd feel a lot better if I knew that Alistair and Lu had already made a connection."

"You've got to give them time. You want the man Lu winds up with to be a keeper. That man does not have to be Alistair and you know it."

"I just have this feeling is all…" Sharon says.

Lutéce

Beatrice and I are nearly run over as Alistair storms out of the abbey. He's moving so fast I barely sidestep him in time. "Alistair, are you okay?" I ask agitatedly.

He stops walking. "No." Then he looks down at Beatrice and asks, "Beatrice, can you tell me what you're going to ask for if you win the fairy tale competition?"

The little girl shakes her head solemnly. "I just wished for it at the fountain, and if I tell you, it won't come true."

"Is it something big?" He sounds concerned like she's going to ask for an automatic rifle or the Eiffel Tower.

"Very big," she tells him.

"What's going on?" I insert myself back into the conversation.

Alistair's gaze looks haunted. "Might you be free sometime this afternoon?" he asks.

"For what?"

"To spend some time with me," he says, like it's an obvious answer.

I'm still mad at him for not being home this morning when he said he would. I'm more concerned about who he was spending the night with than missing his toaster waffles though. A wave of nausea rushes through me at the mere thought. "I suppose I could be. *If* you'll be home."

He arches an eyebrow in question before answering, "You have my word. How does three o'clock sound?"

"That sounds fine," I tell him while taking Beatrice's hand and pulling the little girl to my side. I lead the way into the abbey without looking back.

The rest of the morning and early afternoon are spent giving piano lessons. The children are eager students, and I'm delighted to be able to help them cultivate a new skill. As I'm walking out the door, Alistair's young friend Curtis stops me. He says, "Please tell the prince that I'm pretty sure I'm going to win the writing competition."

"You've come up with a good ending, have you?"

"*You* might not like it, but as far as fairy tales go, it's pretty solid. Also, it's unexpected, which is something I think fairy tales could use more of."

"I can't argue with you there," I tell him. "If I were writing one, there would be fewer frog kissing incidents, and more forest creatures knowing how to clean a house."

Curtis lifts his hand up in the hair and slaps mine sharply. "You've got that right. We could sure use a few maid squirrels around here."

"And kangaroo butlers," I add with a giggle.

"And camel coachmen," he laughs.

"Are you sure you're done with your story?" I ask. "Because you've just added some pretty enticing elements. I'd be hard pressed not to vote for you if you could add some trained birds that know how to cook …" I tease.

Nodding his head, he says, "I think there might be room for improvement. I'll go back to work on it now."

As I walk home, I imagine what fun it would be to have regular competitions so that more children have a chance to win something. I'll have to bring that up with Alistair and Sister Hennepin and see what they think.

I've tried very hard not to obsess about Alistair today. But the more I try to steer my thoughts in another direction, the more he's front and center in my mind.

Who was he with? Why was he with her instead of me?

When I get to his house, I knock on the front door. He doesn't answer right away, and I immediately double check his driveway to make sure his car is there. It is.

"Lu." He finally opens the door looking like he just went twelve rounds with a sack of flour. And lost.

"Are you baking bread or something?" I ask.

"I'm actually making homemade Play Doh."

"Why?" I couldn't be more surprised if he said he was building a plutonium bomb.

He shrugs. "I was fooling around on the internet, and I read an article about forty innovative uses for flour. I thought I'd try some of them out. If they work, I thought Sister Hennepin might be able to implement them at the orphanage."

"What else can you do with it?" I ask.

He leads the way to his kitchen which looks like a flour bomb went off in it. "You can make a kind of kinetic sand, glue, an acne mask …"

I start laughing. "Alistair, you can't be serious. You must have something else on your agenda today."

He shakes his head, looking like a little boy whose puppy just got hit by a car. "Sister Hennepin has asked me not to come back to the abbey for quite some time." At my shocked expression, he explains, "It seems that Curtis thinks I'm going to adopt the winner of the contest. He's been telling the other children that and now they all have it in their heads that if they win, I will become their father."

"Oh, dear. Curtis wanted me to tell you that he thinks he's going to win."

"I read his story. It was quite brief, but the long and short of it was that I get married and adopt all of the children from the home," he tells me.

Oh, those poor kids. Poor Alistair. "What are you going to do?"

"It seems that I have two options. I can either stay away as I've been instructed to do, or I can marry and adopt forty-two children." I don't know whether he's joking or not, but he asks, "What do you think? Should we get married?"

Nervous laughter erupts out of me, even as a pleasant pulsing starts to rush through my extremities. "There has to be another solution," I say.

"I don't know what it is."

Looking at the newspaper on his kitchen table, I suggest, "Maybe there's someone else you could marry." I'm staring right at a photograph of Alistair kissing another woman last night. I try to tell myself that I shouldn't be bothered as we haven't so much as kissed yet *or* made any declarations to each other. But I am bothered. Very much.

"Do you remember the conversation you and I had yesterday?" he asks angrily.

"Which one?"

"The one about not believing everything you see?"

"I remember," I tell him without averting my gaze. Looks like we've just entered another staring contest.

"And yet, here you are believing. Why is that?" Before I can answer, he takes a step closer to me. I hold my ground. His next step has us practically touching, and my body responds like I've just fallen onto a live wire.

Alistair leans down so our faces are only a breath apart. Then his lips actually do touch mine. Firmly and possessively, he presses his mouth against mine, and it's all I can do not to throw myself into his arms and accept his joke of a marriage proposal.

He slides his hands around my waist, and he pulls me ever closer. With a low groan, I manage to say, "Alistair …"

I'm about to surrender to him totally when he pulls back. "You didn't ask for that, did you?"

What is he talking about?

"If a photographer were present and printed a picture of us just now, everyone who saw it would think we were a couple, wouldn't they?"

I nod my head slowly.

"But as you've made it perfectly clear that we are *not* a couple, and you don't feel that way about me …"

He's wrong. I most definitely do feel that way, and I'm pretty sure he does as well. No one kisses like that without genuine interest. If they do, they should be locked up to protect the innocent hearts they're bound to break with such callous disregard.

"So, you're saying you were an unwilling participant in those pictures," I manage to say, still breathless from his kiss. From his touch.

"That's what I'm saying."

"And what just happened here?"

"You were the unwilling participant," he says.

I was not. And I'm about to say so, but I'm more than a little peeved at him for thinking it's okay to toy with my emotions just to make a point.

"But you loved her once." I decide to push the envelope to find out as much as I can.

"I used to love mustard on my scrambled eggs as well. But I assure you, I've grown out of that."

"The woman in the picture doesn't mean anything to you?"

"All she means to me now is a load of trouble." He steps toward me again, but this time I step back. "I find that I'm much more interested in someone else."

"Lucky girl," I mumble.

"Unfortunately, she doesn't want anything to do with me. She thinks of me like a brother." He advances another step, causing me to retreat again. My back is literally up against the wall.

"Maybe she's changed her mind." Please let him be talking about me. *Please oh please oh please.*

"She's given me a hard enough time in the past, that if she has, I'm leaving it up to her to tell me."

This is my big chance to do just that, but somehow, I can't seem to force a sound past my lips.

Chapter Thirty-Four

Queen Charlotte

"I would love it if Tooty came back," the queen tells Sharon while shifting the basket of flowers she's collecting to the other arm.

"I'm sure she'd be happy to sing for her supper."

"Nonsense. As far as we're concerned, you're all family. Also, I love this idea of hers about starting a camp. I might even know of the perfect location for it."

"Where is that?" Sharon asks.

"We have several buildings that are underutilized. Some of them date back generations when the royal family moved around like nomads. These days, we like to stay home as much as we can."

"If I lived in a palace like this, I think I'd be a homebody, too."

"I don't care how much help you have, traveling with six children was always a challenge. I'm still recovering," Charlotte jokes.

"It's nice that you have most of your children around you. If Lu winds up here, either to secure citizenship to adopt, or if something happens between her and Alistair, I'm going to have to buy here. I can't have my grandkids growing up without me."

"Just say the word, and we'll find you a place. Of course, you know you're always welcome to stay with us."

"What do you think the chances are that something will happen between Lu and Alistair?" Sharon asks.

"I think we'll have a better idea after seeing them together at my dinner party."

"Those pictures in the paper have me worried," Sharon confesses.

"Ellery is proficient at getting what she wants, but I'm certain that won't work with either of my sons. Not again."

"Here's hoping …"

Alistair

"I really think I want to adopt Beatrice," Lutéce blurts out.

Well, that's awkward. I tell her that if she wants me to kiss her again, she's going to have to tell me, and she changes the subject. Maybe I misread her. On the other hand, her body language during that kiss seemed pretty telling.

Apparently not.

"Have you talked to Sister Hennepin yet?" I ask, trying to keep my tone bland. Also, I'm trying not to drag her into my arms again.

"Not yet. I'm worried I won't be able to take Beatrice out of the country. I thought maybe you could talk to your mother and ask her what the rules are."

I pick up my phone and call the palace. "Mum, it's Alistair. Do you have a few minutes?"

"I do. What do you need?"

"I'd rather talk in person, if you don't mind."

My mother says, "I'm on my way out, so if you're home, I can stop by for a few minutes before my appointment."

"I'll see you then," I tell her. I rarely invite my mother over, so I know she's probably itching to look around and make sure I'm not living like a wild animal. After hanging up, I tell Lu, "She'll be here shortly."

"I didn't necessarily mean now," I tell him.

"Why wait?"

"I guess." She does not seem at all comfortable being here with me after what just happened. Is she thinking of our kiss like I am? Does she want to do it again?

"Do you have any toaster waffles?" she asks.

Hm, apparently, she's thinking about toaster waffles. "You want toaster waffles in the middle of the afternoon?" She is certainly an odd duck at times.

"I'd rather have Froot Loops," she says, "But I don't suppose you have those here in Malquar."

"Of course, we have Froot Loops. What kind of barbarians do you take us for?"

She looks surprised, as she asks, "Do *you* have Froot Loops though?"

I turn around and walk into the pantry. I come out carrying a box of my favorite cereal. *Are we made for each other or what?*

I pour two bowls before pulling a jug of milk out of the fridge. Then I indicate that Lu should sit down at the kitchen table before saying, "You don't seem like the Froot Loop type."

"That's offensive." Yet she doesn't sound offended. "What

type do I seem like?"

"Something more sensible. You know, like Raisin Bran or Kashi or something." I'm just teasing her. Obviously, she's the Froot Loop type—fun, playful, sexy as all get out.

"I'm not eighty," she tells me before asking, "Do I really seem that dull?"

"You don't seem the least bit dull. Any woman who loves Froot Loops and peanut butter and bacon sandwiches is quite a catch." I stare at her with a look that I hope says, *let me catch you, Lu. Let go of your reservations and let yourself fall.*

She averts her eyes but not before I see the heightened pink tinge in her complexion. We eat our cereal in silence and are just finishing up when my mother strolls into the room. "I let myself in, dear. What would you like to talk about?"

When she sees my guest, she says, "Hello, Lu. Did you and my son have a sleepover?" *She did not just ask Lu if she was sleeping with me?* Good God, talk about uncomfortable.

"I… I… I just stopped by to ask Alistair a question, and he seemed to think you would have the answer," she manages to say, even though she looks like she wants to crawl under the table. Which makes two of us.

"Hmm." I don't think Mum believes her. And now I'm thinking about sleeping with Lu. Okay, fine, I think about that a lot, but usually not around my mother.

"I was wondering what the laws are regarding adoption in Malquar," Lu gets to the point.

"Ah yes, your mother told me you were interested in one of the orphans," Mum says.

"*My* mother told you? When did you talk to her?" she

demands like it's illegal for our mothers to speak to one another.

"Our children are getting married, dear. Of course, we're in contact."

"We were just eating cereal, not getting married!" Lu seems to realize her mistake as soon as the words are out of her mouth. There's no calling something like that back.

"I didn't mean you and Alistair, dear," Mum says.

"I think she meant Geoffrey and Claire." I give her a super bionic wink, and she blushes quite prettily.

"Yes, well, of course ..." She's clearly mortified. "About Beatrice. Is it possible that I'd be allowed to adopt her?"

"Not without some concessions." The queen pulls out a chair and sits down next to me. Then she takes in the mess in the kitchen and asks me, "Were you baking?"

"He was making Play Doh," Lu tells her.

"Of course, he was." Mum doesn't sound like she believes her. I don't bother offering another explanation.

"About Beatrice," Lu tries once again to keep my mother on task.

"You have to be a Malquarian citizen to adopt her. But being that your sister will soon become one, your family will be eligible to as well."

"That's wonderful." Lu claps her hands together excitedly. "Will Claire be eligible soon or does she have to wait until she's married?"

"She might as well wait. It becomes automatic then and she doesn't have to take any of the classes." Not that she could take the classes while living in Oregon, but I don't say that.

"Oh." Lu's disappointment is palpable. "So, I couldn't adopt

Beatrice until after the wedding."

"Correct," Mum tells her. "But for you to hold dual citizenship, you would have to live here six months out of the year."

"What? Why? I mean, I can't live here. I have a job and a house." This is clearly not what she wanted to hear.

"Then I don't think you can adopt Beatrice," Mum says. "Of course, if you married someone from here, you could adopt her and move out of the country. As long as your husband doesn't mind living elsewhere."

Lu's eyes dart to me and I briefly wonder if she's thinking about taking me up on my proposal. Of course, I wouldn't be up for living outside of Malquar. Not with forty-two children anyway.

Before I can ask her if she's rethinking my offer, her eyes fill with tears, and she starts to cry.

"I'm sorry," she mutters while wiping the back of her hand across her face. "I'm just very disappointed."

"I understand, dear," Mum tells her. "You might consider fostering Beatrice. I'm sure we could make a concession in the rules about that."

"You mean have her move in with me now?"

"That's exactly what I mean. Then you can adopt her when you become a citizen. If you become a citizen."

"I couldn't have her move into Bree's house with me. I don't want to inconvenience her."

"You could move back into the palace," Mum tells her. "I imagine that will give Beatrice some memories of a lifetime."

"But if I moved into the palace, that would mean staying in

Malquar at least until Claire got married. That could be a year or more." She stops to take a breath before adding, "I'll have to give it serious consideration. But thank you for your advice."

"Of course! We're family now so you just let me know if you need anything." She looks at me and asks, "Do you need me for anything?"

"I think I'm good, Mum. Thank you for stopping by."

As I walk her to the door, she leans in and says, "Be careful. I don't want you breaking Lu's heart."

"Breaking her heart?" I demand. "I assure you, Mother, if there's a heartbreaker in this scenario, it's Lu."

"Ah, so you do have a romance brewing, and against my wishes." She doesn't sound the least bit upset. In fact, the smile on her face suggests she would be quite pleased if something of a more personal nature occurred between me and the elder Miss Choate.

"Goodbye, Mum," I tell her right before shutting the door on her. If she's changed her tune and she's pulling for me and Lu, that can only mean she's going to insinuate herself in our business.

The funny thing is, if it results in Lu and me becoming a couple, I don't even mind. Talk about a strange turn of events.

Chapter Thirty-Five

Sharon

"Where will I go if she moves in here?" Sharon asks Charlotte after being updated on her daughter's adoption plans.

"Obviously, you can stay here as well. You'll just have to be more careful about walking around."

"Prisoner in the Palace... It sounds like a good, old-fashioned, bodice-ripping romance, doesn't it?" Sharon laughs.

"While we're nowhere as big as Buckingham Palace, we do have fifty-five thousand square feet of living space. We can certainly carve out a sizable chunk for you, so you don't feel confined."

"I appreciate that."

"So, do you think she's going to do it?" Charlotte asks her guest while readjusting the pillow on her favorite Queen Anne chair.

"I think the draw of a child—especially one she's already bonded with—will be too great of a temptation for Lu to resist. It will mean leaving her job though, so I'm sure she'll have to find some kind of work."

"Why? We're certainly not going to charge her rent."

"She still has a mortgage in LA," Sharon says. "Unless she goes ahead and sells."

"It sounds like Lu has a lot to figure out, but I'm sure she's going to make the right choice." The queen puts her teacup on the table next to her.

"The right choice being to move into the palace with Beatrice so that she and Alistair can fall in love?"

"That would be the one," the queen answers with a confident smile.

Lutéce

"I'm sure Bree wouldn't mind having Beatrice at her house," Alistair says when he comes back into the kitchen.

"It would be a lot to ask," I tell him. "Plus, I'm not even sure I can make that kind of time commitment."

"Because of a job and a house?"

"Because my whole life is in LA," I tell him, sounding surly.

"Yet, you've told me that the most important thing is for you to become a mother. You are being given that opportunity with Beatrice."

"I know that, Alistair." I abruptly stand up and put my cereal bowl in the sink. "I have a lot to think about." The least of which is Beatrice. My biggest concern is adjusting to life in a new country. It will help that my sister will be here, but I'd still need a home, a job, and a new circle of friends.

"I will help you in any way that I can," Alistair tells me as he walks over to me. He puts his hands on my arms and stares at me with what I can only describe as longing. Then he pulls me close and hugs me. That's it, just a hug, but it is singularly the most erotic hug I've ever been part of.

"Thank you." I don't know what else to say. The gratitude I feel toward him right now is nearly overpowering. One of the things I miss most about being in a relationship is feeling like someone has my back. A close second is getting a hug when I need one.

Of course, none of my relationships have worked out, and any feeling of stability I ever had was largely in my head. I cite my last three boyfriends cheating on me.

Alistair doesn't let me go. Instead, he holds on even tighter and says, "Thank *you*."

Can this all be happening? Could I really be on the cusp of becoming a mother who's met her own real-life prince? Not in the royal sense, so much as the personal.

I tentatively push Alistair away. I have some thinking to do and when I'm in his arms, my brain short-circuits. "I need to go," I tell him. Then hurry to add, "Thank you again for everything." I sound like I'm thanking him for cleaning out my gutters.

"You're welcome." He takes me by the hand and leads the way to the front door. *I'm holding hands with Alistair.* I feel like a twelve-year-old in the throes of my first real crush. My insides are a tornado of emotions.

After opening the door, Alistair once again pulls me into his arms. This time I take the lead and lean in for another soul-searing kiss. This man fits me. He's supportive, kind, funny, and drop-dead sexy. Is it possible that he's the one I've been waiting for my whole life?

Everything I've ever wanted might just be within reach, but going for it is not without risk. Unfortunately, great reward comes with great risk, and I need to assess the situation with a clear head, which means pulling away before I let this kiss go too far.

I walk toward Bree's like I'm sleepwalking. I get so caught up in my thoughts that I pass her house and don't consciously realize it until I near town.

Malquar is beautiful and if I lived here, Beatrice and I could travel Europe with ease. I could give her a totally different life than she has at the abbey. She would give me a totally different life as well. And it's not like I couldn't take her back to LA to visit...

Should I sell my house? Do I keep it and rent it? What kind of job would I get here? While Queen Charlotte has graciously offered to let me stay at the palace until I adopt Beatrice, I can't live off them without contributing something. Not to mention, once I adopt, I'll need to find a house of my own.

Then there's Alistair.

How has life gotten so complicated so quickly?

Before I know it, I'm standing at the fountain across from the abbey. I sit down on a park bench and watch my favorite old lady feed the birds.

Trying to give my mind a break from my own reality, I wonder again what her story is. Did her husband die? Does she have children somewhere? Do they visit her? Is she lonely or do the birds fill her life to a comfortable degree?

Before I can create a character sketch for her, a couple of well-dressed women walk in front of me and sit down on the bench next to mine. They've just come from the bakery and they're holding coffee cups. I overhear the tall brunette say, "Those pictures in the paper were quite telling."

The petite blonde replies, "Alistair and I are rekindling our relationship."

My ears perk up and I turn to get a better look at them. I don't know if Alistair is a common name or not around here, but I do know that *Prince Alistair* was in today's paper kissing someone. I need to know if this woman is her.

"He'd be a fool not to welcome you back," the brunette says.

Her friend, the one I'm most interested in, replies, "We had the loveliest night at the museum gala. I knew he wasn't over me when he dragged me out into the Statue Garden for privacy."

OMG, it *is* her! And what she's saying is remarkably different from the story that Alistair told. While my heart says to trust Alistair, I don't know if believing him is wishful thinking or not. My brain reminds me that I've been cheated on in the past. Several times.

One of my mom's favorite sayings pops into my head. "If it quacks like a duck, and waddles like a duck, it's no giraffe." Wouldn't that apply to Alistair?

He shows up in the newspapers regularly looking like he's romancing a bevy of women. Why would I think he was any different?

But in my gut, I know he is. I have never felt about anyone else the way I do about him. In all the relationships I've had in my thirties, I've grown to like the men I've dated, but I wasn't head over heels for them from the get-go. I also never thought about them as just them. They were always a means to an end—

to help me reach my goal of becoming a mother.

I suddenly realize how unfair that was to them. I'm sure they felt my intensity and I'm equally sure it scared the daylights out of them. What man goes out on a first, second, or even fifth date and wants his date questioning how he feels about private school vs. public school, or where he stands on a stay-at-home wife versus a nanny?

It's no wonder I was cheated on so many times. Even if the man I was with really liked me, I probably gave off such intense vibes that he felt suffocated by me.

I feel slayed by my bad judgment. Have I brought this loneliness on myself? I think I have.

I look over at blondie, who's still bragging to her friend about how she and Alistair are getting back together, and it's all I can do not to walk over to her and rip her hair out.

I don't do that. Instead, I send her a psychic message. It goes like this: "You had your chance, and you blew it. I am not going to do the same."

It may also involve a mental image or two of some definite follicle yanking.

Then I stand up and walk over to the abbey to talk to Sister Hennepin. I'm going to tell her what I talked to the queen about, then I'm going to ask for her counsel on the best way to start the process of fostering Beatrice.

With any luck, this time next year, I will be adopting her. And if the stars are truly aligning in my favor, I might have already started falling in love with her future father.

Chapter Thirty-Six

Queen Charlotte

"I ran into Lutéce over at Alistair's this afternoon," Charlotte tells her husband as she slips into bed.

"And?" Alfred asks.

"They were eating cereal at nearly four in the afternoon. I think they'd just gotten up." She shimmies with apparent excitement.

"I hope you're not jumping to conclusions."

"What conclusions? Who eats Froot Loops in the middle of the afternoon? They were probably regrouping their strength so they could go back to bed."

"We should not be discussing this," Alfred says sternly. "Also, if it's true that Alistair and Lutéce are starting something, what in the world are you going to do about Ellery? Did you happen to see today's papers?"

"If you're referring to that cozy scene at the museum, I saw it. But I don't believe what the papers are selling." Charlotte pulls the coverlet over her and smooths out the wrinkles.

"Since when? You always give Alistair a hard time about his press, and you're always ready to believe the worst."

The queen rolls her eyes. "Maybe, but I tell you, after seeing him and Lutéce together, I don't think for one minute that he has something going on with Ellery too."

"And yet you're having a dinner party where you've invited Ellery. How do you envision that going down, now that your son might have taken the bait and is interested in Lutéce?"

"I imagine Ellery will back off when she realizes Alistair is otherwise engaged."

"Then you don't know the girl as well as you claim to," Alfred says. "I'm quite certain she won't stop at anything if she's decided she wants Alistair back."

"Then you're not giving our son, or Lutéce, any credit. Lu isn't the kind of girl to sit back and let another woman make a play for her man. I expect it will turn into one of those country western songs of Tooty's. You know, a real brouhaha, as they call it."

"Be careful what you wish for, dear," Alfred says. "Because you just might get it."

Alistair

I can't stop thinking about Lu. I was committed to the idea of not pursuing her until she made a declaration that that's what she wanted. Well, in my eyes, she made that declaration when she kissed me before leaving my house. And what a kiss it was.

Although tentative at first, it was sweet and so full of possibility, I can't imagine ever wanting to do that with anyone else.

I'm tempted to go next door and see if she wants to have

dinner with me, but I think better of it and decide to give her some time. She has a lot on her mind with Beatrice, and whether or not she's going to pursue a future here in Malquar. I don't want to come on too strong.

I decide to go out on the boat, but I won't spend the night. You know, in case Lu stops by for breakfast in the morning. I start to plot the menu in my head and decide to make all my specialties—scrambled eggs, toaster waffles, and Froot Loops. If that doesn't show her how much I care about her, what will?

I call Grady before heading out to make sure he's available. "I'm on a bit of a date," he tells me.

"Bring her along. The more the merrier, right?"

"We're actually on my boat." Grady keeps a small cabin cruiser for his own pleasure even though I've told him repeatedly to use the yacht whenever he wants to.

"I've got an idea," I tell him. "Bring your date over to the yacht. I'll stay on half of the boat, and give you the other half, so I don't interfere with your game."

"I don't feel comfortable with that," he says. "What if your mother finds out?"

"What if she finds out what? That you have a life? Why would she care?"

"I'm her captain. I'm not supposed to be carousing while on duty," he says.

"Grady, you are the biggest stick in the mud. Just meet me at the yacht and quit giving me a hard time. That's an order."

"An order?" He doesn't seem to care for my choice of words.

"Yes."

I'm not actually trying to pull rank on my friend. I could

certainly just sit on the boat without going out, or heaven forbid, I could drive it myself. But I know Grady's date would be impressed by a cruise on the royal yacht. I'm only trying to help him.

As I walk out the front door, I run into my sister, Bree. "Have you seen Lu?" she asks.

"I think she went into town," I tell her. "She's been spending a lot of time at the abbey. Can I help you with something?" I ask her.

"I'm bored," she says. "I was looking for someone to hang out with."

"Well, then." I take her arm. "Hang out with me."

"Where are you going?"

"I want to go look at the ocean. I need to put my thoughts in order and there's no place like the Atlantic for that."

She nods her head. "That sounds like fun. Maybe we can even have supper out."

"Delightful." I lead the way to my car.

We drive peacefully until we pass the turn off for our favorite beach. "You missed our exit," she says.

I veer off at the next turn. "No, I didn't."

"There's no beach access from here." She sounds annoyed.

"Good thing I'm not going to the beach then," I tell her. "I'm taking the boat out."

"Turn around," she orders. "I want to go home."

"Why? I thought you wanted to spend time on the ocean."

Out of the corner of my eye, I see her shaking her head. "No. I wanted to go to the beach."

"Well then, we got our signals crossed. Being that you missed our last outing, why don't we discuss bridal shower plans tonight?"

"Can you believe Grady left me behind?" she practically screams. "How dare he? I should give him a piece of my mind." She sounds like she'd like to do that with boxing gloves instead of words.

Come to think of it, tonight might not be the best time for them to run into each other. I don't want to ruin my friend's evening.

"I'll take you home," I tell my sister.

"No. I'm going to talk to Grady. I need to let him know that his bad behavior is not going to be tolerated in the future."

Oh, boy. I'm not sure what to do now. If I take Bree to the boat, she might go off on Grady and totally wreck his date. Although, if things are as I suspect—that Grady has as much of a thing for Bree as she's always had for him—then maybe that would be okay.

I decide to let things play out however they will. I'll try to keep my sister distracted, but if she's determined to cause a scene, then sobeit. That will be on her, not me.

After parking, Bree and I walk across the dock to our destination. As soon as we step foot onboard, we discover Grady and his date cozied up together on the deck.

"Why don't we head down to the galley and see what's in the fridge for supper?" I ask Bree.

"What is he doing?" she demands while pointing at the object of her ire.

"He was on a date. I asked him if he wouldn't mind taking me out anyway. I told him to bring her along."

My sister stares like she's witnessing a murder—big eyes, look of horror, and all that. The tall blonde that Grady is canoodling with appears to either be a dominatrix or a stripper. Her dress, which is really more of a long shirt, is being held together by a series of leather straps. Her heels must be at least five inches tall. She is not my friend's usual type.

"As captain, Grady should know better than to bring someone like that out on the boat," Bree hisses.

"I told him he could, so let's leave them to it and see to our supper." I try to pull her toward the stairs, but she seems to have other plans.

"Grady!" she yells before pursuing him like he's a chunk of beef and she's a kabob skewer.

He jumps when he hears her and practically pushes his date to the ground. She grabs ahold of the railing in the nick of time. "Aubrey," he says. "What are you doing here?"

"What am *I* doing here?" she demands with her hands on her hips. "What are *you* doing?"

"I work here," he tells her dryly.

"I know *that*. I mean, what are you doing here with *her*." Her tone suggests that he was about to perform an unholy act. Which maybe he was, but that's none of my business.

"This is Brittany, my date."

Brittany scowls at Bree and says, "Yeah, I'm his date. Who are you?"

"Who am I?" Bree sputters. "I am Princess Aubrey. You might have heard of me?" Bree is not one to lord her status over anyone, so her comment is more than a little out of character.

"I'm American," Brittany says. "I don't know who any of your little country's royalty are."

"Where did you pick her up?" Bree asks Grady.

"We met in town today. Not that it's any of your business."

"None of my business? *None of my business?!*"

I join the party and say, "I'm pretty sure it's none of our business, Bree. Come on …" I practically have to drag her away from them. I call out to Grady, "We'll stay on the other side of the boat. Don't worry about us."

"Speak for yourself," Bree says. Then, in a louder voice, she declares, "This is my boat, I'll go wherever I want."

Oh dear, this might not be the peaceful evening cruise I had hoped for. Having said that, I don't think it's a total loss. My little sister appears to be ready to confront some of her feelings for Grady.

Either that, or she's going to kill him.

Chapter Thirty-Seven

Sharon

"I'm going to be a grandma!" Sharon tells her sister on the phone.

"When will you know for sure?" Tooty asks before saying, "I can't wait to meet the little girl!"

"According to Charlotte, the nun in charge of the orphanage is working on the best way to tell Beatrice."

"What best way? Just tell her and be done with it."

"It's a bit more complicated than that," Sharon says. "As Beatrice will be moving into the palace with Lu, the press has to be handled very carefully."

"At least Lu's going to get her," Tooty says. "When are you going to meet her?"

"I can't meet her until Lu knows I'm back in town. I don't plan on letting her know that until I find out where things stand between her and Alistair. I'm hoping that's soon though."

"Keep me posted."

"You know it, hon," Sharon says. "By the way, I talked to Charlotte about your idea for a camp, and she says she has a building you can use. It sounds like it's on several acres, or hectares as they call them here, so not only can it be your headquarters, but you can actually use it as your campsite."

"I can't wait to see it. I'm working hard to clear up my schedule. With any luck, I can be back in Malquar sometime next week."

"It's all coming together, Toots! Nothing can go wrong now."

"Sharon, do not jinx this by being too cocky," Tooty warns.

"I don't believe in that nonsense. I believe in happy endings."

"That sounds like a song title."

Sharon starts to hum a little tune, "Prince Charming, white weddings, happy endings … Hmm, I might be able to do something with that."

Lutéce

I crawl into bed early, thinking about Beatrice, Alistair, and how my life is about to change beyond anything I could have ever imagined. I am going to be a mom. This is huge.

I'm in the weird place between consciousness and sleep when I hear a car door slam. Bree yells, "Of all the nerve! He threw me overboard!"

"You had it coming," Alistair tells her. "Grady's date was none of your concern, yet you hounded him all night and made it impossible for him to have any time with her."

"Brittany," Bree spits. "What kind of name is that?"

"It's a very pretty name," he says.

I roll over in bed—automatically flipping my pillow to the cold side— still not sure if what I'm hearing is real or part of a dream.

"Grady should not be allowed to bring outsiders onto our boat."

"Enough, Bree. You either need to confront him and tell him how you feel, or you need to let him have his life."

"Oh, I'm going to tell him how I feel all right. Starting with how inappropriate I find his behavior. I'll follow that up with telling him that dating trashy women reflects badly on the royal family. Then…" Her voice becomes muffled, and I can't hear the rest of her diatribe.

When I wake up in the morning, my first thought is whether the conversation I thought I overheard was real or a fabrication. I'll have to ask Alistair.

I don't bother putting on clothes after getting out of bed. I just throw on a robe and slippers and make my way over to Alistair's house. The French doors aren't open, so I press my face into the glass and knock.

Alistair appears in my line of sight. His smile causes my heart to beat overtime.

"Good morning," he says after opening the door. Then he pulls me into his arms and gives me the sweetest kiss.

"Good morning to you, too." I inhale the spicy scent of him, and it's all I can do not to tackle him to the ground.

"How did you sleep?" I ask.

"Like the dead. I went out onto the boat last night. There's nothing like sea air to clear your head."

"Did Bree go with you?"

"She did. How did you know that?"

"I thought I heard you come home. She sounded madder than a wet hen."

"Oh, she was wet all right," Alistair laughs. "Grady was on a date and Bree was so green with jealousy, she followed him around all night yelling at him. He finally got so irritated with her that he picked her up and threw her overboard."

"Is she okay?"

"She's fine. We were almost to shore. Plus, he threw in a life preserver after her. She didn't need it though. Bree is the strongest swimmer out of all of us."

"So, Grady's date was a bust?" I ask.

"You could say that. Brittany told Grady that if she'd known he was married, she would have never gone out with him."

"Married?"

"She said that he and Bree acted like an old married couple, and if they weren't already hitched, they should look into it. Then she stormed off the boat telling Grady to lose her number."

"Oh, dear. Where do things stand with Bree and Grady now?"

"If I had to place a wager, I'd say that they kicked off World War Three last night. I can't imagine they'll be seeking each other out to fix things." Then he pulls me into a delicious hug and says, "But who cares about them? Let's talk about us."

"What do you want to talk about?" I ask. "Breakfast?"

He shakes his head as a slow smile overtakes his face. "Let's talk about how I want to date you."

"You do?" I tease. "What about all those other women?"

"You're the only woman I'm interested in," he says. And I believe him.

I think back to the conversation I overheard with his ex and say, "I'd better be." My tone is light, but there's a strong message behind my words. If I commit myself to Alistair, I will not tolerate a wandering eye.

Right now, though, both eyes are right on me, which is exactly where I want them. "What would you like for breakfast?" he asks. "You know my specialties."

"No offense to your eggs, but Froot Loops really is the breakfast of champions."

After two bowls, I run home and get dressed. After that, Alistair and I spend the entire day together.

We walk, we picnic, we snuggle on the couch. The day is pure bliss. At four in the afternoon, I ask, "Do you have plans tonight or can we have supper together?"

"Alas, I have to host the son of the British Ambassador. He's a real jackass or I'd invite you to join us."

"Why are you going out with him if he's such a pain?" I ask in a semi-pout that our day is ending.

"Our fathers went to university together. It's more of a family commitment than anything else."

"Well, then. Maybe I'll see if your sister wants to go out with me and paint the town red."

"Are you trying to make me jealous?" he asks.

Giving him my most innocent expression, I say, "Who, me?"

While I'm not out looking for men, I wouldn't mind if Alistair was a little jealous. A girl likes to know she has that kind of power over a man.

Chapter Thirty-Eight

Queen Charlotte

"I'm afraid your son is not very pleased with me at the moment," Sister Hennepin tells the queen.

"Which son?" Charlotte wants to know.

"Alistair, of course."

"Why would he be upset with you?" The queen's tone is full of confusion.

"Because I asked him to stop coming by so frequently." The nun shuffles through a stack of papers on her desk.

"Alistair visits the orphanage?"

"Your Majesty, he is our patron. Of course, he visits." It's Sister Hennepin's turn to look confused.

"I knew he paid the bills, I guess I didn't realize he was more involved than that." Then she asks, "What does he do here?"

"He reads to the children, plays ball with them, or just listens to them. He recently conceived of a fairy tale writing contest. That's the reason I asked him not to come back for a while."

The queen takes a sip of her tea before asking, "What does one thing have to do with another?"

"The children have begun to believe that Alistair is going to adopt the winner of the contest. It's part of the reason we need to be careful how we deal with Lutéce's conservatorship over young Beatrice. While the children will be happy for her, there will be some hurt feelings that it isn't them."

"I see." Charlotte's brow furrows. "I've been talking to a family friend of ours about starting a children's camp of sorts. I think I may have an idea …"

Alistair

Easton Hardcastle is a real dick. As much as I've tried to like him, I can see no redeeming qualities. We're currently at a club downtown, and his hand has not left the waitress's backside since she walked over to get our order.

"Easton," I tell him. "I don't think our server cares to be pawed while you explain that you want your martini *extra* dirty."

The waitress looks at me and blows a kiss. "Who says I have a problem with it?"

Okay. See if I try to play knight in shining armor again.

"When does your shift end?" Easton wants to know while pulling her down on his lap. "Because the prince and I would love to have you join us."

Yeah, no.

"I'm off in two hours, so if you can keep yourself occupied until then, I'll be all yours."

He pushes her off him. "Then you'd better hop to it and get me my drink." What a slime bucket. After she's gone, he says, "Your life must be like this all the time, you lucky dog."

"It's nothing like this," I assure him.

"That's not what the newspapers say. But hey, it's cool if you don't kiss and tell. I respect that as long as you don't mind me sharing the booty."

"Easton, while I promised to meet you for a drink, I'm afraid I can't spend the whole evening with you."

"I give you permission to leave as soon as my night's entertainment is off the clock."

I will lose my mind if I have to spend two hours with this man. I get up on the pretense of using the loo, but what I need is a breath of fresh air. Walking out the front door, I think about how much I wish I were home with Lu.

I used to enjoy clubbing when I was younger, but now that I'm nearing my mid-thirties, I'm ready for more grown-up pursuits. I'm ready to get married and have a family. It's one of the reasons I took Ellery's betrayal so badly.

While I loved her, it was nothing compared to what I'm starting to feel for Lu. We enjoyed spending time together, and we were both ready to take the next step. So it seemed a good choice that we settle down together. At least that's what I thought.

As though my reflections have the power to conjure, a red sports car pulls up and Ellery gets out. My God, did she install a tracking device in my car or something? How else could she know I'd be here?

She walks toward me wearing the tiniest black cocktail dress that I've ever seen. "Alistair." She throws herself into my arms. "What are you doing here?" She's hanging onto me like I'm her lifeline.

I gently try to push her away while answering, "I'm having a drink with a friend."

Ellery turns around and waves at someone. The next thing I know, cameras are flashing and she's full-on trying to make out with me. What in the actual hell?

I try to push her off me, but I'm pretty sure she must have slathered herself in super glue. "Darling," she purrs in my ear. "Quit fighting it. You and I were meant to be."

"Like hell," I tell her. "You need to step aside, Ellery, or things are going to get pretty uncomfortable for you."

"I'd love to go back to your place!" she says loudly enough that I'm pretty sure they heard her in Paris.

"I didn't invite you back to my place," I tell her angrily.

"Ah, hahahahahahaha! You rascal!" I feel like I'm trapped in a nightmare that I can't wake up from.

I finally give her a firm shove, which causes her to trip over her own foot and fall backwards. I reach my hand out to stop her from slamming into the ground.

More flashing cameras. I can only imagine how this is going to look in the papers tomorrow.

When she's back on her feet, Ellery leans in and says, "We're going to have a drink together, so turn around and walk into the club."

"I'm not having a drink with you," I tell her.

"Oh, I think you are."

"That's not going to happen."

"If you don't turn around and walk inside, I'm going to create a scene that your reputation will never recover from."

"What in the hell, Ellery? You're threatening me?"

She shrugs. "Don't think of it that way, Alistair. Think of it like I miss you so much that I need to spend some time with you."

"I don't want to spend time with you. How do I need to phrase this so you believe it?"

"Let me put it this way," she says. "Turn around and walk into the building with me or I will start crying. Then I'll accuse you of being the father of my baby."

"What?" She's pregnant? What in the fresh hell? I don't trust Ellery as far as I can throw her, so I turn around and walk back into the club. As soon as we're inside, I pull her into a dark corner and demand, "What are you playing at?"

"I'm not playing at all. I've just found myself in the family way, and I thought I'd better hurry up and secure myself a husband."

"Why not choose the baby's father?" I ask, full of disdain.

"He's not the most appropriate partner for me. You're much more respectable."

"Except for the small fact that I want nothing to do with you," I tell her.

"Alistair, you need to get married, and I need to get married. Why can't we just go back to the way things were? Surely we can make each other happy again."

"Except I don't love you. I don't even like you anymore."

"At least buy me a drink."

"You're pregnant and you're going to drink?" I know this shouldn't surprise me, but it does.

"Just one." Then she says, "See? You're already worried about our baby."

"I am not the father of your child, Ellery. I will not buy you a drink, and I'm done talking to you." I turn and walk back toward Easton, only to find that he has another woman on his lap. I don't have the energy to put up with him or Ellery. Instead, I find our server and give her a large bill. I ask her to tell Easton that I was called away. Then I leave the bar.

Instead of going home, I decide to spend the night on the boat. I need to figure out a way to shake Ellery once and for all. Why in the world does she think I'd take her back after what she did to me and Andrew? Why does she think for a minute that I would play the role of father to her unborn child?

Chapter Thirty-Nine

Sharon

"What do I wear to a dinner party that I won't actually be attending?" Sharon asks Charlotte.

"I say wear your jammies. You probably won't be in there for longer than a couple of hours, but still, you should be comfortable."

"I better not drink anything before I'm locked away," Sharon says.

"Good thinking. Now, do you want to go down and look at the room? I had the housekeeper put a comfy chair in there for you when you're not peeking through the spyglass."

Sharon waves her off. "There will be no sitting. Now, tell me who else you've invited. I know your kids will be there, Lu will be there, Alistair and Andrew's ex—I'm a little nervous about that one—but who else?"

"I've invited a couple of men that I have my eye on for my girls, and someone I think might be a match for Andrew."

"Wow, you're really going all out, huh?"

The queen laughs, "My only real targets are Lu and Alistair, but I like to keep my eyes open for the other kids."

Sharon says, "Nobody has any idea what we're really up to, do they?"

The queen shakes her head. "No clue, whatsoever."

Lutéce

I look down at my phone to see a message from Alistair.

> *Prince Charming: I slept on the boat. Do you want to meet me here for breakfast?*
>
> *Me: I'd love to, but I don't have a ride.*
>
> *Prince Charming: I could come get you.*
>
> *Me: You could …*

I reach over and pick up a newspaper that's sitting on the kitchen table. OMG. There is picture after picture of Alistair and Ellery, and they appear to be full-blown making out. I thought he was meeting some ambassador's son last night.

> *Prince Charming: Lu, are you there? I can be there to pick you up in ten minutes.*
>
> *Me: Sorry, I can't.*
>
> *Prince Charming: Are you okay?*

I am so not okay, but I really don't want to get into this with him right now. I have to think. I turn my phone off without responding to him.

I open the paper and spend several minutes dissecting the images of Alistair with his arms around his ex. The photos don't leave any room for interpretation. None. Obviously, Alistair is two-timing me with Ellery. Which means I should just accept that I'm meant to be single forever. Maybe I should chat with Sister Hennepin about joining the convent.

I can't believe I've done it again, falling for a man who can't commit. But this time it's worse than ever before because it's with my sister's future brother-in-law.

Why didn't I follow my instincts about Alistair? What is wrong with me, always chasing after unavailable men?

I hurriedly pack my things into my suitcases. I cannot stay here for another minute, because staying with Bree means living next door to *him*. As soon as everything is packed, I leave a note for my friend, and then walk outside her front door. Thank goodness for luggage with wheels or the hike up to the palace would be a much more arduous task.

The butler does his best not to look shocked as he watches me walk up the driveway with my suitcases. He hurries out and asks, "May I be of assistance, miss?"

"Yes, please," I say, trying to sound calm. "The queen was expecting me to move back into the palace." Then I motion to my things and add, "I'm here."

I'm not shown to the bedroom I inhabited when I first arrived in Malquar. Rather I'm taken to an apartment within the palace that has two bedrooms and two-bathrooms. This must be where the queen envisions me spending the next year with Beatrice. It's quite charming.

I'm not here for long when Queen Charlotte herself knocks on my door. "Hello, Lu. Are you getting excited about tonight's dinner party?"

"I'd actually forgotten about it," I tell her. And I really, really don't want to go.

"My goddaughter Ellery will be there. I'm sure the two of you will get on very well."

"Ellery? As in Alistair's ex?" Could my day get any worse?

"That's the one, but of course that's long over. Alistair has moved on." She gives me a covert wink.

"I'm not sure he has," I tell her. "Have you seen the newspapers?"

"Not yet," she says. "But I'm sure there's a logical explanation for whatever you saw. Have you asked Alistair?"

"I haven't," I manage, even though my jaw is so tight it's practically locked.

"You should just ask him. I'm sure it's not whatever you think it is."

And suddenly I can't wait to go to tonight's dinner party. I'm sick of being treated like trash and dumped without consequence. No, sir, I'm going to attend this party and I'm going to out Alistair to his whole family. I'll probably have to find a new place to live when I'm through—I can't imagine the queen is going to want me around after I make such a scene—but whatever. I'll do whatever I have to do.

I'll go out in a blaze of glory and then I'll call my mom and tell her to put my house on the market. I can buy a cute little cottage for me and Beatrice. I don't need Alistair in my life to be happy. I don't need any man for that.

I spend the day alternately seething and getting ready for tonight. When it's time to go down, I give myself one last look in the mirror and admire my pink evening gown. The halter neckline not only accentuates my collar bones, but it makes me feel powerful. I lift my head high and straighten my shoulders, feeling like a warrior princess going into battle.

"Lutéce, dear," the queen greets me with open arms as I walk into the parlor. "You look beautiful."

"Thank you," I tell her. "You look quite lovely yourself." Much like my own mother, Queen Charlotte looks at least a decade younger than she really is.

She introduces me around the room, and I meet several people that I have never met before. Then I officially meet Ellery. Not only do I recognize her from the fountain, but also from recent photos in the newspaper.

Ellery smiles at me smugly and says, "Hello."

I don't bother returning the greeting. Instead, I ask the queen, "Where's Alistair?"

"I'm sure he'll be along shortly," she says. Ellery is eyeing me like I'm a particularly interesting-looking insect—half curious and half appalled.

"I see from the newspapers that you and Alistair are seeing one another," I tell her. I have to know. I have to hear it from her own lips. I cannot have one more man lie to me without losing my ever-loving mind.

She smiles impishly and leans in. "Promise you won't tell a soul," she says. "But Alistair and I are expecting."

"Expecting?" Even as I say the word, I can't fully process it. What are they expecting? A nice weekend away? A nice supper? A delivery of matching tennis sweaters?

"A baby," Ellery gushes. "We're so happy about it, but we want to wait a bit to share the news with his family."

"Yet you somehow felt this was appropriate news to share

with me? A total stranger?" I blurt out. My mouth goes dry. It's very possible my heart has stopped beating because my head starts to spin. It goes in one direction and the room takes off in the other.

The periphery of my vision is closing. As the floor rushes up to meet me, one last thought rushes into my brain. "Dammit, Alistair, why couldn't you have just been gay?"

When I open my eyes, I'm lying on a couch and the queen is fanning me. "Lutéce, dear, are you okay?"

"Yes. No. Maybe. What happened?" My eyes move past hers and connect with Alistair's. He's arrived and he looks concerned.

"You fainted," she tells me.

I have never fainted before, so it's a new experience for me— as opposed to my frequent experiences with cheating louses. I can't say I care for either.

Ellery says, "One minute you were standing and talking to me, and the next you were on the floor."

"What were you saying to her, Ellery?" Alistair's tone moves closer to rage.

"Darling, I was just making small talk," she says sweetly.

The king joins his wife at my side and suggests, "Maybe we should take you up to your room to rest. I'll call the doctor to come check on you."

This is my chance to escape, but one look at Alistair and I decide to see this night through to its fateful conclusion. "I'm fine." I push myself up to a sitting position. "In fact, I'm starving. Maybe if I just sit here for a few minutes." I force a brave smile to my face.

As the queen and her husband walk away, Alistair sits down

next to me and asks, "Are you okay? Really?"

"Right as rain," I tell him.

"If that's true, and I'm sort of doubting it, what's going on with you today?"

"Whatever do you mean?" I ask while going for a blank expression.

"I texted you all day and you never got back to me. When I got home, Bree said that you moved out. Hence my question. What is going on?"

"Why don't you ask Ellery, *Daddy*?" I say before pushing him aside and walking out of the room.

Chapter Forty

Queen Charlotte

"Once we leave the dining room, you just have to pull this lever and the door will pop open," Charlotte tells Sharon.

"You gave a phone to one of the servers so I can hear what's going on, right?" Sharon asks.

The queen nods. "I did. I gave her your number and she'll call as soon as the dinner guests are seated. Then she'll walk around so you can overhear snippets from various conversations."

"This is going to be fun!" Sharon squeals. "I'll make sure to let you know if anyone is plotting to overthrow the crown."

Charlotte laughs, "This isn't a scheming crowd for the most part. Most of them are family."

"You never know. Did you ever see that movie with Katherine Hepburn, *The Lion in Winter*?" Sharon arches her eyebrow in question.

"No, is it any good?"

"In the scariest possible way. I don't think there's ever been royal intrigue quite like it."

"Ah," the queen says, "I think I'll pass then."

"Good idea." Sharon kicks off her slippers and sits down to

wait until dinner starts.

"Do you have everything that you need?" When Sharon shakes her head affirmatively, Charlotte says, "I'd better back into the parlor then."

"Let's get this party started!"

Alistair

Apparently, Ellery has gone ahead and decided to announce that I'm the father of her child. That is the only explanation I can think of for Lu calling me Daddy. A sinking sense of dread crawls over me, causing my body temperature to drop. I don't imagine Lu will believe the truth easily, given her previous experience with infidelity.

Two thoughts are currently fighting for center stage in my brain. The first is that I need Lu to give me a chance to explain. She and I have already had a conversation about how I'm never going to lie to her, and that she can't believe what she reads in the newspapers. That needs to include anything my ex tells her.

The second thought is that Ellery had best watch her back because I will not be bullied into marrying her, and I sure as hell will not sit back and let her interfere in my love life. That is something she lost the right to participate in when she decided to date both me and Andrew at the same time.

I can't wait until dinner is over so I can take Lu into my arms and reassure her that I'm all hers. She needs to know that Ellery is a master manipulator, and that she means nothing to me. What Lu and I have is real, and I need to prove that to her.

Alas, royal duty calls, and I have no choice but to follow

behind my family and guests into the dining room. Tristan Ryan is trailing behind my sister Sophie like a bloodhound hot on the scent of a bone. Tristan has had a crush on Sophie for as long as he could walk. It can't be a coincidence that Mum invited him.

Speaking of my mum, I hurry to her side and whisper in her ear, "I'm going to need to talk to you later."

She shoots me her best, *who, me?* look, before saying, "Whatever for?"

"Don't play coy with me, Mother. It's not going to work." Irritation grates my nerves.

"You mean Ellery? Don't you worry about her, dear. I know you're through with her."

"And yet she's been invited to dine with us. Why?" I demand, not caring if my voice carries and others overhear us.

My mother shrugs. "She asked if she could come visit one night. I didn't see the harm."

"You didn't see the harm?" *What was she thinking?*

"Keep your voice down." My mother leans closer to me. "Just ignore her. Now that you and Lu are an item, we need never speak Ellery's name again."

"Except that Ellery has already told Lu something that has her angry with me," I say.

"All she had to do was look at today's papers for that, Alistair. You did see the papers, didn't you?"

A chill of dread rushes through me. I generally read the papers first thing in the morning, but I don't get them delivered on the boat. I can only imagine what those pictures looked like. Damn, I need to get Lu off by herself to explain before she decides to never speak to me again.

Hell, who am I kidding? She already saw the papers. That explains her reaction. And once again, another person I care about believing the gossip rags over me. I had hoped she knew me better than that.

I have more than a sinking feeling that I was wrong.

When I get to the dining room, I find that I'm seated to the left of my father, which is across the table from Lu, who is at his right. We're both at the other end of the table from Ellery, thank God.

Once everyone is seated and dinner service has started, I hear muted music coming from somewhere. It sounds like Tooty Jackson's "Pucker Up Romeo." *Where is that coming from?* I look around to see if anyone else hears it.

"Do you hear that?" my dad asks me.

I nod my head. "Where is it coming from?"

"I have no idea. How strange. I do love that song though."

One of the servers comes by with a silver tray full of stuffed figs. I take two before telling my father, "Mum is up to no good."

"You mean Ellery?" he asks. "That woman will not listen to reason. She's so sure she knows what's best for all of you kids that she's jumped right into the deep end with this one." He points at Andrew and says, "Look at your brother."

I peer down the length of the table at Andrew and find that he's staring daggers at the side of Ellery's head. "He looks furious." Then I look up at the server who has yet to move on. "I think we have all the figs we need, Mary, thank you."

"She must be under the weather tonight," my dad says. "She doesn't seem to be in any hurry to serve the food." We both watch as Mary moves to the end of the table where she proceeds to stand like cement has been poured over her feet.

My gaze moves to Lu. She's practically bending over backwards trying to pretend I don't exist. Her reaction to me does not bode well.

Tapping her wine glass to get everyone's attention, my mother announces, "Alfred and I are so pleased that you all could join us for supper this evening. It's not every day we have our nearest and dearest so close at hand."

Totally breaking character, Andrew grumbles, "*Please*, Mother. We all see this night for what it is."

"Which is?" The look she shoots him dares him to say more.

As the oldest, *and* the heir to the throne, my brother has been held to a higher level of decorum than the rest of us. As such, he reins in his temper and takes the hint that he's not to answer.

Sophie hurries to say, "I have to agree with you, Mum. It's very nice to be dining with our friends. We really need to do this more often." She casts a covert glance at Tristan. Would you look at that? Maybe the queen got it right for one of us, after all.

Mary has finally served all her figs, and she's moved to stand behind Ellery, who is whispering to her friend, Hailey. I'm guessing Mum invited the latter for Andrew. What she doesn't realize is that my brother is too smart to get involved with any friend of Ellery's.

This is a highly weird and uncomfortable dinner. Except for Sophie and Tristan, everyone appears to be trying too hard. Rigid posture and forced laughter seem to be the theme. Aside from Ellery's agenda, I wonder what other plots and schemes are being hatched.

I try to focus on my roast duck while plotting how to get Lu alone so I can explain about the "Daddy" comment and the pictures in the paper. If she doesn't believe me, then my hands are tied. Dating a royal has its downside, and nothing I can say or do will change that.

I'm starting to think this meal will never end when the side panel in the wall blows open and Lu's mum, Sharon—who appears to be wearing pajamas with pink bunnies eating tacos on them— bursts out wielding her cell phone. "You bitch!" she shouts. She looks around the table trying to find her quarry. Yet, she doesn't seem to know who it is.

Chapter Forty-One

Sharon

With the telephone pressed to her ear, Sharon listens to various dinner conversations. She hears King Alfred say, "Your mother truly only means to help."

Alistair responds, "Yet she seems to have welcomed Ellery back into the fold. Which as you know, is no help at all."

"She thought that maybe if you saw her, you'd realize you were over her and move on already."

"Which I have," Alistair says. "But now that Ellery is back, she seems intent on …"

The conversation abruptly ends when the server moves to a new location.

In hushed tones, a female voice says, "I told him about the baby."

"You did what?" another woman demands. She lowers her voice and asks, "Why? I thought the whole point was to get him into the sack so you could convince him that the baby was his?"

"Believe me, if Alistair showed the least bit of interest in me, I would have done just that. But he seems adamant that we're through."

"So why did you think telling him about the baby would make things different?" the other woman wants to know.

"Alistair and I are birds of a feather. We both like varied pursuits and yet both of our families are pressuring us to get married. I thought I could offer him a deal that would suit us both in the end. He'll marry someone his parents approve of, and then he can spend as much time as he wants with that American trollop."

Lutéce

My mouth falls open and a piece of duck falls out when my mother appears out of nowhere. Not only is she wearing her pajamas but she's calling someone out, big time. This is either really happening, or I'm drunk. I didn't think I drank that much, yet maybe it's time to remedy that. I down the rest of the wine in my glass in one dedicated gulp. Then I look back up and my mom is still there. Okay, this is really happening.

"Mom, what are you doing here?" I jump to my feet, nearly upsetting my wine glass.

She stares around the table looking for the person she just called a bitch—seriously, things have gotten surreal fast.

Mary points to Ellery, and from that moment on, all hell breaks loose. "You cannot pass your baby off as Alistair's!" my mom yells.

Ellery looks highly uncomfortable being the center of negative attention, although I'm guessing she's the kind of woman who otherwise relishes the spotlight. "I'm sorry, who are you and what baby are you talking about?"

She sounds convincing until my mom tells her, and everyone else at the table, "I heard it all!" She wields her cell phone in the air like she's the Statue of Liberty and her Android is her torch. *Are those bunny slippers on her feet?* "I heard how you contacted the press and were going to make sure that you and Alistair were front page news as often as possible …"

But Ellery doesn't let her finish. She turns to the queen and asks, "Ma'am, do you know who this crazy person is?"

"This is my dear friend, Sharon," Queen Charlotte says, with a sharp edge to her voice.

"No offense to your friend, but what is she talking about?" Ellery has stepped in it now.

"Sharon was helping me discover the truth behind a nasty rumor I'd heard." She takes what looks to be a fortifying sip of her wine. In other words, she slams back half the glass. *Go, Queen Charlotte!*

"Rumor?" Ellery's face turns beet red. "What rumor?"

The queen pins her with a death stare—seriously, it rivals my mom's—and says, "Duchess Pinkerton heard that you'd found yourself in the family way and were going to try to pawn off your baby as Alistair's. I told her that I couldn't imagine you would be so stupid. But then you called, wanting to get together, and I started to wonder. Especially after it's clear you've been trapping him in photo ops with the press lately."

Ellery looks between her friend—who is the same woman she was with at the fountain— and the queen, finally settling her gaze on her friend. She shouts, "You told your mother? Why would you do that?"

Looking uncomfortable, her friend answers, "I didn't think

she'd say anything. Mother is aware of the ways of court. I mean, my own brother isn't my father's …" Realizing she just confessed a family secret to the royal family, she jumps up and declares, "I have to go." Then she runs out of the room.

Holy. Hell.

The king starts laughing before asking his wife, "Why didn't you tell me what you were up to?"

She answers, "I didn't want to cast further aspersions on Ellery's character if it wasn't warranted." Ellery looks like she wants to run, too, but she doesn't move.

"So, you set up this whole dinner, going so far as having Sharon help spy, so you could find out the truth? What if nothing came to light?"

"Darling," the queen says, "something *always* comes to light."

"You've done this before?" He sounds as gobsmacked as everyone at the table looks.

"That's beside the point," the queen tells him.

"What's the point again?" he asks with shock etched on his face.

"The point is that we now know for certain that Ellery is up to no good. Which means"— she addresses Ellery—"it's time for you to go. And as much as it pains me to say, it's best if you keep your distance, indefinitely."

This is like a soap opera. Cheating, fainting, secret babies and false paternity. All we need now is a good slap and someone to toss the table. I volunteer to do the slapping.

"You're kicking me out without letting me explain?" She sounds panicked.

"Your actions are explanation enough. Please go." Queen

Charlotte turns to the server behind Ellery and says, "Mary, please show her the door."

I can barely bring myself to look at Alistair, but I know I must. He's staring right at me with a smug grin, yet he doesn't say anything. I'm guessing I'll be eating humble pie for dessert.

My mom sits down at Ellery's former place at the table and pours herself a fresh glass of wine. She raises it toward the queen and says, "To us."

The queen returns the gesture. "You've got that right."

The entire table seems to reanimate as if nothing happened. It's as though I never fainted, or Ellery wasn't trying to trap Alistair. It's as if my mother bursting out of the wall in her bunny attire before joining us for supper is perfectly normal behavior. The buzz of conversation ensues like none of that ever took place. Midway through dessert, I stand up and walk over to the vacant chair that once belonged to Ellery's friend, the one right next to Mom.

"When did you get back?" I ask her.

"I never left, hon," she confesses.

"What? Why?" Even while asking, I already know the answer. Some things never change. My mom will always meddle in my life.

"I couldn't leave you here alone. What if you needed me?"

"I'm thirty-six, Mom. I've been taking care of myself for a long time now." I roll my eyes.

"Yes, and you see where that's gotten you?" she asks cockily.

"I was doing quite a good job of it," I tell her, sounding annoyed.

"Hon, you were falling for a prince that was being maligned

in the press, all the while wanting to adopt my first grandchild. Forgive me, but that all sounded like you needed your mother on hand in case something went wrong. Which it did. So, you're welcome." She takes a triumphant sip of her wine.

She's got me there. Instead of holding onto my righteous indignation, I burst out laughing and tell her, "I can't wait to introduce you to Beatrice."

"I can't wait to meet her!" she says excitedly.

Chapter Forty-Two

Queen Charlotte

"I'm sorry," King Alfred says, pulling his wife into his arms.

"Whatever are you sorry for, dear?" she asks him.

"I'm sorry that I accused you of not minding your own business. Clearly, you knew exactly what you were doing." He nuzzles the side of her neck.

"Of course, I did. I've known Ellery her whole life and her flaws have never been a secret to me. There is no way I would have encouraged either of our sons' affections toward her again."

"You were just using her to make Lu jealous?"

"I was using her to help Lu realize how deeply she feels for Alistair," she tells him.

Taking her hand, he pulls her toward the stairs. "You scare me, woman. Let's call it a night, shall we?"

"First of all, you have no reason to fear me. You are the most loyal and loving man I could ever have hoped to marry. Also, I'd love to go to bed. I hope you didn't plan on going right to sleep."

King Alfred's eyes twinkle. "Perish the thought."

Alistair

Lu walks over to me after our party disperses, which is right after dessert has been cleared. "I think I owe you an apology."

"You think?"

"I definitely owe you an apology. But Alistair, before you get upset, you have to know that I've never dated someone in your position before." Her eyelashes flutter prettily.

"Yet you're from a famous family, so I'm sure you know the press's penchant for getting things wrong, and others' tendencies to lie when it suits them." I'm not going to let her off the hook that easily.

"I do, and yet, *I'm* not famous, so I've never been the topic of their lies before." She looks up at me and says, "I'm truly very sorry."

I clear my throat loudly, then in a very stern tone, say, "Lutéce, I cannot be with someone who takes everyone else's word over mine. I require real trust."

"I know. I reacted out of fear, and that's not okay. But in my defense, I'm scared to get involved with anyone again." She looks like a lost little girl, and it breaks my heart.

"Well, then, I think that's a question you need to ask and answer for yourself. Are you willing to put yourself out there one more time? Do you have the courage that will require? Because, Lu, anyone who dates me cannot lack courage." I take a deep breath and add, "There will always be people who try to take me down. You cannot trust them over me."

"I will do my very best," she says softly.

The sadness in her eyes has me saying, "Then, of course, I

forgive you. But if we are going to date each other, we have to always have an open line of communication."

"I agree," she says. "I have some things to overcome, but I promise while I do that, I will do my best not to try to make you pay for the misdeeds of others."

"In the end, that's all I can ask for." I open my arms to her and welcome her in.

"I'm a little terrified of your mother." Her words are muffled as I'm holding her closely.

"We all are," I assure her. "Your mother seems to be quite a force of nature herself."

I hear her giggle. "The good news is that now that we've found each other, they'll hopefully direct their attentions elsewhere."

"From your mouth to God's ear," I tell her. Then I take her hand and ask, "How about a nice walk in the garden?" Jokingly I add, "Unless you'd prefer my sisters' company." I'm referring to her first night in Malquar when she refused to let me show her the garden, but willingly went with my sisters.

Shaking her head, Lu shoots me a slow wink. "Claire mentioned that she and Geoffrey enjoyed their time in the orangery. Maybe we should go there instead?"

"Your wish is my command, madam." I pull her alongside me through the great hall toward the corridor that leads to our destination. As I open the greenhouse door, I lead her right to the orange trees. "You do know that visiting the orangery is code for making out, don't you?" I ask her.

"Um, yeah. I didn't actually want to come here to eat oranges."

"Before we get sidetracked," I tell her, "I wanted to discuss the competition at the orphanage."

"Oh, right, we're supposed to pick a winner soon." How in the world are we going to do that knowing that the children think the winner will be adopted?

"I was thinking that we might declare everyone a winner. I'll cater a peanut butter and bacon sandwich luncheon for everyone to celebrate."

"You're going to make over forty sandwiches by yourself?"

"Well, no, not personally," I tell her. "I figure I could show the kids how it's done so that they can make them anytime they want."

She nods her head. "It's a nice idea. But what about Curtis? He's got his hopes up."

"Sister Hennepin says that she has an idea that might work. Apparently, she's been talking to my mother," I tell her.

"Oh, boy. If your mom is involved, I'm willing to bet my mom is involved and this could turn into a real production."

"Yes. I have never known two more formidable women than our mothers. We've been asked to a meeting at the abbey the day after tomorrow."

"At least we don't have long to wait to find out what they're cooking up," she says.

"You could think of it like that, or you might consider that it gives us a full day to pack up and leave the country before our lives are turned upside down."

Lu playfully nudges my arm. "No way. I've already decided to turn my life upside down by adopting Beatrice. I'm not about to walk away from that."

"You're going to be a great mom," I tell her softly.

"I sure am going to do my best," she dreamily replies.

"Not only that, but you're going to live right here in Malquar." I give her my most seductive look.

"At least for part of the year…" she says playfully.

"Not if I have anything to say about it. I'm going to make it my top priority to entice you to stay forever."

"And yet we're in the orangery and all you've done is talk."

"Did you just drop the gauntlet? Because if you did," I pull her onto my lap, "I'm prepared to show you *all* the benefits of staying."

"Still talking …"

That's it. Wrapping my arms around the sweetest, sexiest, most beautiful woman I have ever known, I stop talking.

Chapter Forty-Three

Sharon

"Tooty, Toots, I'm so glad you got here this soon!" Sharon wraps her arms around her sister and does a little dance. She doesn't give her a chance to respond, she just declares, "You would not believe the dinner party last night!"

After dissecting the evening and sharing the good news that Ellery is out of the picture for good, Tooty says, "Hurry up and get dressed. Charlotte says we have a stop to make before meeting the kids at the orphanage."

"I'm so excited, how about you?"

"I really am," Tooty says. "Life never ceases to amaze me. Sometimes you spend years trying to attain something and you can never seem to get your hands on it. Then, other times, all you need to do is have a bare bones idea and bam! The universe gets busy and makes it happen."

"What in the world have you always wanted that you didn't get?" Sharon teases her sister. "You've got Country Music Awards, platinum records, a mansion in Tennessee, and a ski lodge in Aspen ... Should I go on?"

"I would give that all up to share my life with someone that I loved and who loved me without reservation. You can have stuff until it comes out of your ears, but love is the only thing that truly fills you up."

Sharon sighs. "You got me there. I think that maybe you're the next one we need to find love for."

"Yeah, because there are so many fantastic guys out there in their sixties looking for their soulmate." Sarcasm pours out of her.

"I'm going to say it right here and right now." Sharon prays, "Dear God, Tooty is doing a lot of good for the world, especially with her new project. What do you say you give her the reward she's looking for?"

Then she nudges her sister and says, "Buckle up, buttercup. I have a good feeling …"

Lutéce

Alistair picks me up at the palace carrying one red rose. "This is going to be our thing," he tells me.

"What?"

"I'm putting you on the red rose reward system."

"What is that, exactly?"

"One red rose for every day you make me smile," he says.

"That's very sweet, but what if you forget a day?"

"Then you'd better try harder to make me smile." He ducks before I successfully hit him with the first rose he's ever given me.

After we get into his car, I tell him, "When I came to Malquar, I was angry, bitter, and so full of despair over how my life was turning out that I couldn't imagine a happy ending for myself. I am so grateful that you didn't take my prickliness too seriously and kept trying to get to know me."

"I think your prickliness is part of your charm," he tells me with a sexy grin."

"You think, huh?"

"The truth is," he says, "I can't thank you enough for coming into my life when you did. It has not been easy carrying around the official title of 'the spare.' I keep hoping that Andrew will hurry up and get married and secure the future of the monarchy with a couple of kids, so I can get on with living my own life."

"Has it really been awful?" I ask.

"Not awful. More like I've been sitting on the bench for the whole game, waiting to see if I'm going to be needed. I'd like to know that I can move on and start my own game."

I reach over and take his hand. I don't say anything, I just give it a squeeze to let him know that I'm here.

We continue to drive quietly. I'm going to tell Beatrice my plans about adopting her today and I'm so excited I feel like I'm going to explode. I won't hurry her out of the abbey until she's ready, but I sure do hope she moves in with me soon. I don't want to miss a day with her.

As Alistair pulls up to the orphanage, Sister Hennepin is standing out front, talking to both of our moms. Tooty is there, too. I jump out of the car and ask, "Tooty, why didn't I know you were coming?"

She smiles at me slyly. "Because, hon, we've all been hard at work hatching a plan and we wanted to surprise you."

"What plan?" I ask.

The queen answers for her, "Get back into your car and follow us. We'll show you."

"But we came to talk about Beatrice…" Alistair says.

"This is partially about Beatrice," Sister Hennepin tells him. "Now go get in your car and don't make me have to tell you again."

I love how she treats Alistair like he's still a child. I unsuccessfully stifle a giggle at her bossiness.

As soon as we're back in the car, Alistair follows the Bentley that's carrying the rest of our party. "What do you suppose is going on?"

"You got me, but after the other night, I'm not going to argue with any of them."

When we drive through the gates of a large estate, I ask, "Are we visiting someone?"

Alistair shakes his head. "This is Holly Hope House. My grandmother moved here after my grandfather died. No one has lived here since she passed on."

"Your grandmother moved *here?* This place is huge!"

"You don't go from being queen to moving into a pensioner's apartment," he says. "In her eyes, she went from forty bedrooms to twenty, which was a real come down."

I can't tell if he's serious or not. But this house certainly looks big enough to have twenty bedrooms. "What do you suppose we're doing here?" I ask.

Alistair gets out of the car and opens the passenger door for me. "I think we're about to find out."

We join the rest of our party in front of the estate. Queen Charlotte says, "Alistair, being that Andrew will one day take up residence in the palace, your father and I thought we'd give you Holly Hope House." Holy. Crap.

"That's very nice, Mother, but what in the world am I going to do with a house this big?"

Tooty announces, "I thought you might like to rent it to me."

"You want to live here?" What in the world is going on?

Tooty shakes her head. "I want you to live here with Beatrice," she tells me.

"Why in the world do Beatrice and I need this kind of room?" I ask.

"You don't, dear. But you will if you agree to work for me," my aunt says.

"I have no idea what you're talking about, Tooty."

"I always wanted to open a camp for underprivileged children …" she starts to say.

"Here in Malquar?" I interrupt.

"Let her finish," my mom says. Then she motions for Tooty to keep talking.

"Your mother and the queen and I got to thinking that with a house of this size, we could move the orphanage here. The children will have much more room, and it would be the ideal location to house events to draw potential parents into their lives."

"Move the orphanage here? And I would be in charge?"

"Don't be ridiculous," Sister Hennepin scolds. "I will continue to be in charge of the orphans; you will be in charge of the camp."

"How will that work?" I am dying to know.

"Follow me," the queen says. And we do. We follow her along

a path to the back of Holly Hope House where there's a good-sized red brick Edwardian-style house. She says, "You and Beatrice would live here. The orphans and the sisters would use half of the main house, and the other half will be used for our camp attendees."

"I would live here," I repeat, sounding like I'm more than a few bricks short of a load.

"Lu, pay attention!" my mom practically yells. "You're being given a beautiful home for you and Beatrice to live in, and you'll have a job. There's nothing left for you to worry about."

Tooty announces, "Of course I'll pay a fair rent, Alistair. I don't want you to worry about that."

He just shakes his head, his smile so bright it's blinding. "Is five dollars a year too much?" he asks.

Tooty reaches into her purse and hands him a hundred-dollar bill. "Consider this payment for the first twenty years."

All of my dreams really are coming true. I am so thoroughly overwhelmed by gratitude, I think I'm about to cry.

Sister Hennepin announces, "All right, now that that's settled, let's go back to the abbey and tell the children that you've picked a prize for all of them."

She doesn't wait for us to respond; she merely turns around and strides back to the car.

"Thank you," I tell the remaining women. "Thank you so much."

"Psh," Tooty says. "No thanks are necessary. Now come on, your mama and I can't wait to meet your little girl."

Epilogue

Three Months Later...

"Christmastime is more special this year than ever before," I tell Alistair after letting him into Beatrice's and my new house. We've been here for two months and already it feels like ours. Toys are liberally sprinkled throughout, which is my favorite part about it.

"It's more special for me too." He pulls me into his arms for a searingly slow kiss. I lean into him and think that I would be happy staying like this forever... safe and secure in his arms.

He pulls away slowly. "Not to mention, today is your first party to introduce the kids to prospective parents. That's a red-letter day if there ever was one."

"I can't believe how many people are coming." I open the hall closet to pull out my coat. "I'm half-worried they're only coming to see you."

Alistair shakes his head. "Not a chance. Every one of them was vetted by Sister Hennepin herself. And you know she wouldn't allow any looky-loos."

"True," I say before turning and calling up the stairs, "Beatrice, come on! Prince Alistair is here, and we need to get up to Holly Hope House to make sure everyone is ready."

Beatrice practically skips down the stairs in her new, green velvet dress with the white lace Peter Pan collar, her curls bobbing up and down with each step. I tell myself fifty times a day that she's going to legally be my daughter soon, and fifty times a day, I need to pinch myself to know I'm not lost in a dream.

"You are as pretty as any princess I've ever seen," Alistair compliments her.

"I'm not prettier than my mum though." Beatrice's eyes sparkle when she looks at me. *I'm her mum.*

"You're a hundred times prettier," I tell her. "Now come on, let's shake our tail feathers. I have a feeling magic is going to happen today.

The three of us put on our coats and proceed to walk up to the main house, hand-in-hand.

I couldn't stop smiling if my life depended on it. I offer a prayer of thanks for all the goodness in my life. Then I say another prayer: Please let more than one child find their forever home today.

I squeeze Alistair's hand. If things go as well as they've been going between us, maybe one day we can adopt a few more children together. While I would still like a child or two of my own, I no longer feel the same drive I once did. I couldn't love Beatrice more than I do already, and if I can give that love to other children who are without parents, that would be an amazing gift for all of us.

As we walk into the house, we are besieged by the sounds of excitement and joy. This is truly the merriest of Christmases ever.

I cannot wait to see what the new year has in store.

About the Author

USA Today Bestseller Whitney Dineen is a rock star in her own head. While delusional about her singing abilities, there's been a plethora of validation that she's a fairly decent author (AMAZING!!!). After winning many writing awards and selling nearly a kabillion books (math may not be her forte, either), she's decided to let the voices in her head say whatever they want (sorry, Mom). She also won a fourth-place ribbon in a fifth-grade swim meet in backstroke. So, there's that.

Whitney loves to play with her kids (a.k.a. dazzle them with her amazing flossing abilities), bake stuff, eat stuff, and write books for people who "get" her. She thinks french fries are the perfect food and Mrs. Roper is her spirit animal.

Join her newsletter here for news of her latest releases, sales, and recommendations.

If you consider yourself a superfan, join her private reader group here, where you will be offered the chance to read her books before they're released.

Head Over Feet is coming in March 2022!

Princess Aubrey of Malquar has loved Grady Basset since they were kids. She followed him and her brother around wherever they went; she wrote his name in her diary repeatedly; and she even practiced saying her name with his last name—for years.

There's only one problem. Grady has never shown any romantic interest in her.

As the son of the king's secretary, Grady grew up playing with the royal children. His best friend is Prince Alistair, the second in line for the throne. While he's drawn to Princess Bree, he knows that there's no way they can be together. Bree's station is too far above his.

As the captain of the royal yacht, Grady sees Bree often, but in recent months the princess has been rude, belligerent, and an all-around pain in the butt. When unforeseen circumstances have Grady taking Bree on a cruise in the Mediterranean—alone—things really start to heat up.

Will Grady finally give Bree a chance? Will it be too late?

Find out in the deliciously fun fifth installment of the Seven Brides for Seven Mothers Series.

While you're waiting for Head Over Feet, check out my USA Today Bestselling novella, *Love for Sale*.

Chapter One

"I'm sorry, what did you say your name was?" I practically yell in the direction of my phone as I furiously type away on my laptop. I'm a multi-tasker extraordinaire, which is good because in my business, time is *always* of the essence.

I shift my computer so it's wedged up against the steering wheel of my three-year-old Audi. "April? Like the month?" I ask the caller.

"It is Abreeeeeel," the cultured Latina voice echoing through my car speakers tells me. "Abril Valencia. You were recommended to me by Sandrine Flowers?" She asks like it's a question I should already have the answer to.

"How is Sandrine?" It's been ages since I've seen my old client. I knew the minute she moved into her new place, that love was right around the corner. Sandrine hadn't wanted to look at the Coldwater Canyon property, claiming the commute to her office was a deal breaker.

When I told her I was positive that's where she would find her happy ending, she hemmed and hawed and still tried to fight for the house in Benedict Canyon. She finally gave in when I explained the Benedict house had sadness written all over it. Like seriously, I think there'd been some kind of gnarly death there or something.

It turns out Sandrine's future husband lived right next door to the Coldwater property. They were engaged within four months, and three months after that I attended their very fancy wedding at the Four Seasons Hotel. A week later, I listed both of their houses and found them the perfect marital love nest in Malibu. It was a real estate trifecta!

"Sandrine, she is as big as a house with los bebés inside her," Abril announces. "But she is so happy and she says she owes it all to you. She says you are her fairy godmother, her matchmaker."

"I'm not a matchmaker," I say as an image of Yente from *Fiddler on the Roof* pops into my head, full-on with a babushka and an all-knowing look in her squinty eyes.

"You find the house that brings the love, no?"

"No. I mean yes. But I am more of an intuitive realtor than a matchmaker. I don't know who the love interest will be, I just know where the love will happen." That sounds sketchier than I'd intended it to, but you get my drift.

"I am also ready for the love, so I call you to help me find it. Where should we start looking?"

"Let's meet," I tell her. "I won't start to get a feeling for the right area for you until I have a chance to get to know you better." I check my calendar. "I can meet you for coffee at eleven tomorrow morning at Perky Cups on Melrose, or Friday at two at The Farm in Beverly Hills."

"If tomorrow is the earliest, I will meet you then." She hangs up before I can tell her what I look like. *Guess I will look for a lovelorn Latina.*

I hurry and press send, and voilà, the offer for Xander Fellows is submitted. His perfect house is in Hancock Park even though he was sure he was destined to live in Venice. He was convinced Hancock Park was too family oriented and wouldn't have single men within miles of his doorstep. I assured him that single men live all over LA and that if it was a long-term relationship he was looking for, then the Hancock Park house was the right place for him.

After closing my laptop, I pull out onto the street in the direction of my office on Sunset Boulevard. I work at Pemberley Properties which is every bit as snooty as it sounds.

My office is full of women, and only women—other than my boss Frederic—who know how to play up their *assets* to their best advantage. Simply put, they have bleach blonde hair extensions, wear five-inch stilettos, and their boobs practically exist in another zip code. I'm nothing like them.

I, Emily Hargrove, am the epitome of the girl next door. I'm a Mary Ann in a world of Gingers. If you weren't a Nick at Nite fanatic like I was and the *Gilligan's Island* reference is lost on you, I'm a Betty, not a Veronica; a Monica, not a Rachel; a Reese, not an Angelina.

How in the world did I wind up working for a glamorous brokerage firm like Pemberley then? My best friend and queen bee of sales, Skylar Matisse, got me the job. At first, Frederic would only take me on a trial basis, as I clearly didn't look like his vision of success. But after selling three houses in a week, he no longer cared. I was a moneymaker, and he was willing to overlook my faults, aka normal physical attributes.

The unwritten rule at the office is that no broker can be under five foot nine. As if only giants can sell multi-million-dollar houses. That's why my fellow brokers stagger around like they're stilt-walkers in the circus.

While I did try to at least meet the height requirement, I fell off said shoes on three separate occasions. The first time, I accidentally pushed a client into the swimming pool of the house I was showing him. I fell in also. The second time, I tripped and landed on top of Frederic. He may have wound up with a hairline wrist fracture—the man needs a calcium supplement, if you ask me. The third time, I fell off a curb into oncoming traffic and nearly got run over by a gold-plated Hummer.

After the last occasion, my boss decided that if I were to live long enough to make him a huge amount of money, he would have to bend his rule and let me wear loafers, or Vans, depending on how I was dressed. It was the safest decision for all.

As if my style and height aren't enough to set me apart—I'm a solid five eight in flats—my hair is brown instead of blonde. I have never penciled my eyebrows into giant caterpillars with squared off edges in my life, and no one is allowed to superglue llama lashes to my eyelids. I don't even have cool tattoos. In fact, I don't have any tattoos. I'm just not that girl.

I'd rather eat burgers than sushi, pitch a tent on the beach than stay at a five-star resort, and horror of horrors—according to my coworkers anyway—I'd rather be a B-cup than go under the knife and have balloons stuffed inside my chest cavity.

According to Skylar, I'm refreshing and natural. According to Lucy, the one agent who hates me with a vigorous passion,

I'm boring and boyish. She thinks anything less than a D-cup lacks femininity.

I don't usually have any trouble with the other agents because I don't engage in office drama. Also, most of them aren't the least bit threatened by me. Hence, they barely give me the time of day.

They battle with each other all the time over who's going to secure the newest jaw-dropping listing. They fight dirty to win the business of the latest Hollywood star or the most recent tech refugee from the Silicon Valley. I just keep my head down and don't participate in their realtor *Hunger Games*.

I do, however, go to their open houses and support them. While they're competitive (like real estate is a blood sport), I need to see every house I can in order to find the perfect dwellings for my clients.

Not all my clients are single and looking for love. As a matter of fact, I have almost as many married couples as single ones. The married ones, who know about my extra talent, are looking for homes where their union will flourish.

As previously mentioned, those homes aren't always where my clients imagine they'll live. It can be hard to convince someone that Pasadena is where their happy ending is waiting when their heart is set on the Palisades.

While you might think my sixth sense would make me the most successful broker in the office, you'd be wrong. This is LA. It's the land where artifice is king or, as every casting director this side of Studio City will tell you, the place where you have to look the part you want to be cast as.

If you're in, or adjacent to, the entertainment industry in any way, that generally means going to the right parties, dating the right kind of people, and living in the right neighborhood.

I've had a lot of clients who don't take my advice, and a good number of them are perfectly happy. True love isn't as important to them as projecting the right image.

Most image-conscious clients choose to work with brokers like Skylar, Lucy, Crenshaw, or the other gals in my office. They want to buy their monolithic homes from somebody who looks like their idea of perfection. If that were my criteria, I'd have to move to the Midwest where people are inherently more real looking.

As soon as I park my car and walk into the office, I notice everyone huddled around my desk. They're staring at a giant vase of flowers that wasn't there earlier today. I hurry over, using my elbows to part the crowd when necessary, and pull the card out of Lucy's hands. It reads:

I'm ready to buy love. When can we meet? Jonathan Silver